Ascott R. H. Moncrieff

Black's Guide to the Isle of Wight

Including Sailing Directions for the Solent. Thirteenth Edition

Ascott R. H. Moncrieff

Black's Guide to the Isle of Wight
Including Sailing Directions for the Solent. Thirteenth Edition

ISBN/EAN: 9783337406356

Printed in Europe, USA, Canada, Australia, Japan

Cover: Foto ©Andreas Hilbeck / pixelio.de

More available books at **www.hansebooks.com**

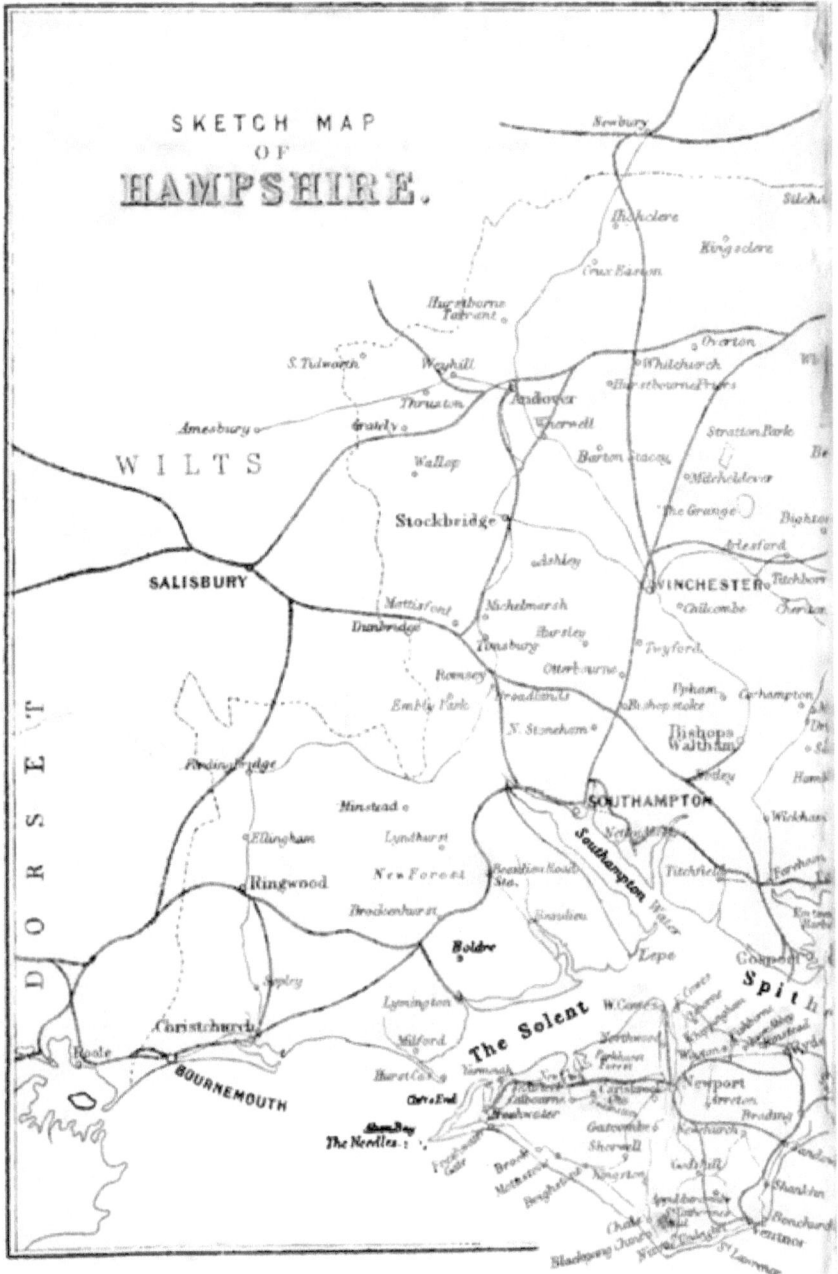

SKETCH MAP
OF
HAMPSHIRE.

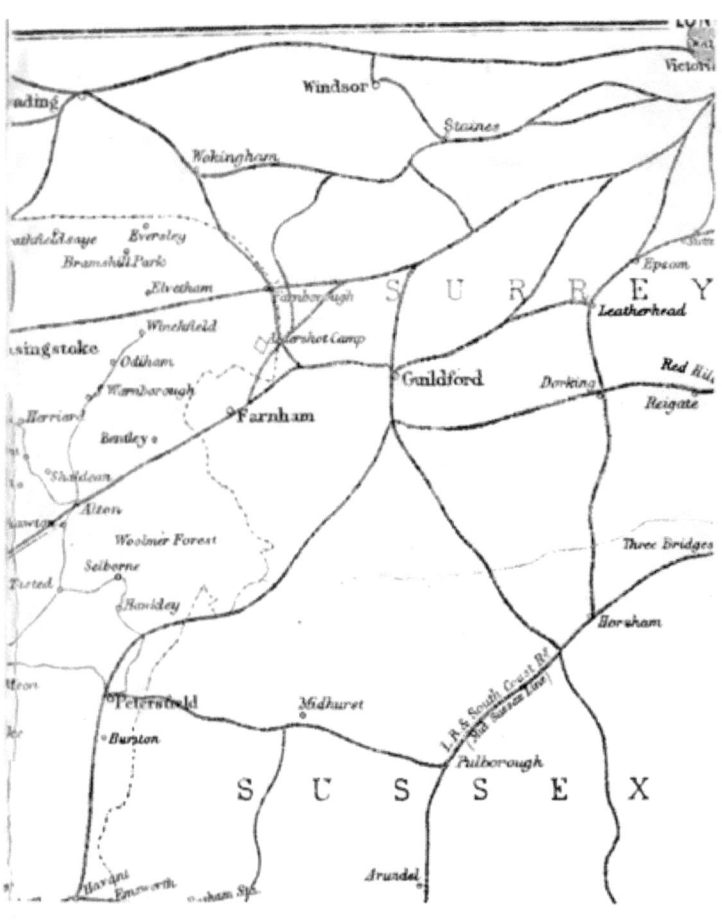

LONDON, BRIGHTON, & SOUTH COAST RAILWAY.

THE DIRECT MID-SUSSEX ROUTE
TO PORTSMOUTH, SOUTHSEA, AND TO THE ISLE OF WIGHT.

The Shortest and **Quickest** Main Line Route to or from the City and West End of London and the Isle of Wight

STEAMERS from RYDE and also from COWES, connecting with Fast Trains direct to London Bridge and Victoria.

Portsmouth Harbour, Station, and Pier. This Station enables Passengers to walk direct from Train to Steamer.

Ryde **Pier Railway.** Isle of Wight Trains now run to and from the Ryde Pier Head Station, connecting with the Through Service Steamers of this Route.

The BEST ROUTE to or from the Northern and Midland Districts is *via* Victoria.

The **Only Route** to and from PORTSMOUTH and the City and West End of London without change of carriage.

THROUGH TICKETS issued and LUGGAGE Registered, including all charges.

Week-end Cheap Return Tickets to PORTSMOUTH, Friday, Saturday, and Sunday to Monday, and to Portsmouth, Ryde, Cowes, and Isle of Wight Railway Stations, Friday, Saturday, and Sunday to Tuesday.

LONDON STATIONS.

London Bridge, Victoria, Kensington (Addison Road) West Brompton, Chelsea, Clapham Junction, New Cross, Old Kent Road, Peckham, Denmark Hill, Tulse Hill, Brixton, Streatham, &c.

Victoria Station connects with the London and North-Western, Great Western, Great Northern, Midland, North London, Chatham and Dover, Metropolitan, and District Railways.

Kensington (Addison Road) Station connects with the London and North-Western, Great Western, Metropolitan, and District Railways.

London Bridge Station connects with the Charing Cross, Cannon Street, and South-Eastern Railway.

BOOKING & ENQUIRY OFFICES.—**Ryde**: the Pier; Messrs. Curtis and Sons', Esplanade; Messrs. Pickford and Co.'s, 71 Union Street. **Ventnor**: the Railway Station; the Company's Offices, 32 and 55 High Street; Messrs. Pickford and Co.'s, High Street; Messrs. Curtis and Sons', Albert Street. **Newport**: Railway Station; the Company's Office, 116 High Street; Messrs. Pickford and Co.'s, 113 St. James Street. **Cowes**: the Railway Station; the Company's Office; Steamboat Quay; Messrs. Pickford and Co.'s, Town Quay. **Gosport**: Messrs. Pickford and Co.'s, 59 High Street. **Southsea**: General Booking and Enquiry Office, 18 Marmion Road; also at all the Stations on the **Isle of Wight Railways**.

☞ Ask for through Tickets by "South Coast Railway."

ALLEN SARLE, Secretary and General Manager.

LONDON BRIDGE STATION.

BLACK'S GUIDE

TO THE

ISLE OF WIGHT

BLACK'S GUIDE

TO THE

ISLE OF WIGHT

INCLUDING SAILING DIRECTIONS
FOR THE SOLENT

EDITED BY

A. R. HOPE MONCRIEFF

EDITOR OF 'WHERE SHALL WE GO,' 'WHERE TO GO ABROAD,' ETC.

THIRTEENTH EDITION

LONDON
ADAM AND CHARLES BLACK
1895

PREFACE

In preparing this edition, certain changes have been introduced which it is believed will be of advantage. Former guide-books have laid themselves out to conduct their readers along certain routes, stopping or turning aside to visit the various points of interest, a plan expressed in the French word *itinéraire*. But tourists now seem more in the way of taking up their quarters for a time at certain centres from which to make excursions into the surrounding country; and this is specially the case in the Isle of Wight, where, with abundant facilities for such expeditions, there is hardly any part which may not be visited in a single day from one or other of the chief resorts offering comfortable accommodation to strangers. These main resorts, then, in which the visitor is likely to spend most of his time, have here been thrown into more prominence, and the other places grouped around them on the scale of their relative importance.

It has been attempted to make the following directions and descriptions at once practical and readable, yet, as far as possible, without the use of such stereotyped phrases as Mr. Verdant Green's friend found so handy in filling up his home correspondence. Useful information of various kinds, welcomed by some and skipped by other readers, is given in separate articles where it seems most appropriate: thus the History of the island will be found summarised in connection with *Newport*, and an early opportunity has been taken to present an outline of its Geology, to many one of the most interesting features, in an article by Mr. Arthur Dendy, B.Sc., F.L.S.

An entirely new section is now added in the shape of practical directions for boat-sailing about the Solent, as it is believed that not a few amphibious tourists will appreciate some such guidance on sea as well as on land. This article has been written by Mr. C. F. Abdy Williams, M.A., a yachtsman familiar with these waters, and revised by Rear-Admiral Hamilton Earle.

These special articles form digressions from the course of our description, which, beginning with Ryde, as the place most likely to be visited, conduct the reader all round the island to leave him at Newport, its central point, whence he can easily reach any part that may have been neglected.

CONTENTS

LIST OF MAPS AND PLANS

INTRODUCTION

THE Isle of Wight is separated from Hampshire, to which county it belongs, by an arm of the sea, called the Solent, the breadth of which varies from one to six miles. In this channel are the great harbour of Portsmouth and other safe anchorage grounds. The form of the island is an irregular diamond, measuring 23 miles from east to west, and 13 miles from north to south. Its circumference is about 60 miles, and its superficial area 93,342 acres, in part highly productive. It was formerly covered with woods, but has been in a great measure denuded through its vicinity to Portsmouth, and the demand of that naval arsenal for timber.

The principal towns and villages are Ryde, Cowes, and Yarmouth upon the north coast; Newport, with the adjacent village of Carisbrooke, in the centre; Ventnor and Bonchurch on the south; Freshwater at the west end of the island; and on the eastern coast, Shanklin, Sandown, Brading, and Bembridge. Newport is the chief town, but Ryde of late years rather the largest, while Ryde, Newport, and East and West Cowes taken together, are all about the same size, with populations between 10,000 and 12,000. The population of the whole island, by the last census, was not far short of 80,000.

The "island," as it is fondly called by its natives, as if there were no other island worth considering, was formerly very clannish in its local patriotism ; and the "overner" did not then so readily find his way to the hearts of the people.   Modern facilities of travel, however, are fast breaking up this exclusiveness.   A great part of the upper class of the inhabitants, indeed, now consists of well-to-do strangers who have settled in the island, attracted by its various amenities, while the sons of the soil have too large experience of "overners" in the relation of profitable guests, to retain any suspicious dislike of their incursions. A certain insular independence, not to say rudeness, may still be observed occasionally in the manner of the local youth towards strangers.   Another old reproach against the Isle of Wight is that its women are not so beautiful as its gardens.   On that head, we may leave the reader to decide for himself.

It is divided into the two nearly equal hundreds of *East* and *West Medina* by the river of that name, the only considerable one, which rises near the south shore, to flow to the north, and is navigable up to Newport.   Two more small streams, both bearing the name of Yar, exhibit the same peculiarity of flowing almost right across the island. Other rivulets, drained from the Downs, have a very short course before reaching the sea.

Another division is formed by the great range of chalk downs which traverse the centre from east to west, on either side of which the scenery presents a somewhat different character.   On the north, the ground is undulating rather than hilly, richly wooded and, for the most part, sloping gently to the sea.   The southern half, especially on its coast-line known as the *Back of the Island*, is marked by sterner features and sharper outlines.   A striking peculiarity of the north shore is the low creeks which wind their way deep into the land, so that sometimes one is astonished to come upon the brown sail of a boat making its way apparently among trees and hedges. On the precipitous walls of the south coast this feature is replaced by the abrupt chasms known as *Chines*, which are so notable among its attractions.

These characteristics of luxuriant verdure and picturesque wildness are sometimes mingled, remarkably so in the tract called the *Undercliff*, which for some 10 miles forms the south-eastern corner. This singular district consists of a series of terraces, broken by rocky knolls and fragments of chalk and sandstone, which have, in the course of time, through well-known causes, been detached from the cliffs and hills above. The whole of the *Undercliff* is completely sheltered from cold winds by the range of lofty downs, which rise boldly from the upper termination of these terraces to a height varying from four to six and seven hundred feet, and rising about a hundred feet higher at each extremity. The protection afforded by this natural barrier is greatly increased by the very striking abruptness with which it terminates on its southern aspect. This, in many places, consists of the bare perpendicular rock of sandstone ; in others of chalk, assuming its characteristic rounded form, covered with a fine turf and underwood. Thus the *Undercliff* forms a sheltered winter resort, as well as one of the most famed beauty spots of England.

The south-western end, a peninsula of rarely bold and varied cliffs, terminating in the rugged Needles, which stand here as sentinels of English ground, is also a choice resort, none the less so in the eyes of some, as it lies a little more out of the way of ordinary excursionists, though indeed the railway to Freshwater seems likely to break in upon the comparative seclusion of this corner.

It is in summer that the north side of the island will be chiefly frequented, its exposure to cold winds making it less fit for a winter residence. Yachting may be said to be here the main interest, its centre being at Cowes ; and those who cannot afford so expensive an amusement have numerous opportunities of taking steamboat trips to many attractive points of the coast. The Undercliff, and especially Ventnor, has its chief season in winter and spring, yet is by no means deserted in the height of summer, when many foreign as well as English tourists are attracted by its renown. Perhaps the best time to visit the island is in its emptiest season, the early summer, for then, if strangers knew it, are at their richest its charms of umbrageous foliage, glowing meadows, blooming cottage gardens and windows, hedgerows and copses smelling with gay blossoms, and turfy slopes spangled with fresh wildflowers.

There are few manufactures here, none we can recall but the shipbuilding at Cowes, and the cement works on the Medina. Sea-fishing is carried on to some extent, lobsters and prawns being pretty plentiful on the south coast, and an attempt at oyster culture having been made in the creeks of the north. Many of the farms look prosperous, though the quantity of marguerites and other "weeds of glorious feature," which almost whiten some of the pastures, must make a more pleasing view for the picturesque-hunting stranger than for the cultivator of the soil. Perhaps the chief harvest of the people lies in profiting by the many visitors whom most seasons bring among them, and who, as at other such resorts, are apt to complain of prices that do not seem higher than is usual in districts with the same attractions.

There is a plentiful supply of hotels on the island, some of which are good and many dear. Generally speaking, there seems rather a want of good second-class hotel accommodation, that is at moderate prices, for inferiority in other respects will often be found united to high enough charges, even at hostelries which are little better than village taverns. It is not uncommon, as in the Highlands, for such a house to face the stranger with the name, style, and prices of an hotel, while, not to scare away the thirsty but frugal inhabitant, it presents itself under another aspect as an unpresuming inn. Boarding-houses flourish at Ventnor and in its neighbourhood, which receive more visitors for a stay of some length ; but this enterprise seems to do badly on the other side. Two old-established boarding-houses at Ryde have of late been closed, while, indeed, two new ones have been opened on the coast of the corner beyond, at Seaview and Whitecliff Bay, to which we wish the success they deserve. Except perhaps at the most expensive, and in the high season, boarding terms would commonly be given by the hotels, in many of them, out of the season, at very moderate rates.

Everywhere we have endeavoured to name all the leading hotels and boarding-houses. While we have shrunk from the responsibility of recommendation, it has been our design to arrange the hotels, as far as possible, in order of reputation and expensiveness. We should be particularly glad to be corrected here in any particular, the character of houses being so apt to change with their management, or through other causes.

The charge for carriages here is the usual one of 1s. 3d. per mile for one horse ; 3s. per hour, or 20s. by the day ; for two horses, 1s. 8d. per mile, 5s. per hour, 30s. per day. But out of the season, when so many horses must be eating their heads off, arrangements could probably be made for cheaper terms. In the season, at the chief resorts, there will be numerous sociable coach or brake excursions to all parts of the island, which are very popular with most visitors.

Cyclists are frequently found spinning over the island, where the roads are good as a rule, though with not a few break-neck descents to be looked out for. For the benefit of this independent class of travellers, we have sought to indicate by the letter (C.) those hotels recognised as head-quarters by the Cyclists' Touring Club.

Pedestrians are at great advantage within these narrow bounds, since they can make their headquarters at some central spot, and visit every side of the island at ease, coming home to a dry shirt and a comfortable meal, so as not to be so much dependent on the cold meat and chops, which at irregular, or even regular, meal hours often prove the only refreshment procurable in wayside inns. For their caution, we will only remind them, when off beaten tracks, to beware of a particularly tenacious and treacherous mud that here and there forms the bottom of some inviting wildernesses. Waterproofs and thick boots often come in handy for tramps across the Isle of Wight.

Almost every part of the island is now opened up by railways, running from *Ryde* and *Cowes* to *Freshwater* through *Newport*, and from *Ryde* to *Ventnor*, with a branch to *Bem-bridge*, and a connecting line from *Sandown* to *Newport*. A new line is in construction from Ventnor, which will make the Back of the Island still more accessible. There is no deficiency of trains on these lines ; but the dearness of their charges is a frequent cause of complaint. They have no third-class carriages ; yet by certain trains, one may travel second at parliamentary fare ; and the economical visitor will do well to study their announcements of cheaper return tickets, and of weekly season tickets available all over the island railways. Cheap through excursions are also frequent in summer from various parts of the mainland.

We conclude with the routes of approach from London to the Isle of Wight. These, it will be seen, offer a choice of some half-dozen routes, the fares being much the same, and the return tickets of either company available over the other line, when taken to a station reached by both.

1. By London, Brighton, and South Coast Railway from London Bridge or Victoria, *viâ Portsmouth* for Ryde or Cowes.
2. By London and South-Western Railway from Waterloo, *viâ Southampton* for Cowes ; *viâ Portsmouth* or *Stokes Bay* for Ryde ; and *viâ Lymington* for Yarmouth.
3. By steamer from Southsea to Sea View ; and by other steamers running in summer from different piers on the mainland.

wherry as far as it could go, then carried ashore in a cart or on a man's back. This bed of mud has now been covered by or given place to sand, over which the tide recedes a long way ; but all the difficulties of access are met by the pier, which successive additions have carried out over 2000 feet. It is provided with a pavilion and other shelters ; and the railway runs to the Pier-head, where is the station of that name. The Esplanade station is at the gate of the pier, close to the chief hotels. St. John's station, at the back of the town, is more convenient for some of the residential quarters. But economical minds, in considering to which station they shall book, are apt to be influenced by the fact that the journey between them is perhaps the dearest railway ride in England. The fare from one end of the pier to the other is fivepence for a third of a mile, including of course the pier dues. Beside the railway runs an electric tram, by which this short trip may be taken at a much cheaper rate. Close to the large pier is another known as the Victoria Pier, which has come to an end before getting far enough out to sea, and now serves only as a bathing and fishing place.

Eastward from the piers, stretch the esplanade and sea-wall, forming a very pleasant promenade, with its view of Spithead, where occasionally is presented the grand spectacle of a British fleet. About twenty acres have been reclaimed from the sea, and laid out as gardens ending in an ornamental lake, on the shallow waters of which boats and canoes voyage safely. In winter it would be a capital place for skaters, but this water seldom takes on more than a slight coating of ice. Round it runs a track used for bicycle races. The gardens are a highly popular rendezvous when the band plays in the pavilion on fine evenings.

The most striking public buildings are the churches, of which the most notable is the parish church, *All Saints'*, in the upper part of the town, where its spire makes a far-seen landmark. It is in the decorated style, after designs by the late Sir Gilbert Scott. The reredos, pulpit, and font are elaborate works of art, of variously-coloured

marbles ; and there is much good painted glass, the west
window of the nave being particularly fine.   At the east
end of the north aisle is a magnificent tower and spire
nearly 200 feet high, visible for many miles in every
direction.   Visitors should ascend the tower, for which a
small charge is made.

St. Thomas', thickly covered with ivy, has at first sight
more the look of a venerable parish church, but does not
so well repay examination.   It will be remembered that
none of these Isle of Wight watering-places can show much
ancient church architecture, having usually, as they sprang
up, been separated from older parishes, sometimes stretching
across the island.   Both Ryde and Ventnor, for instance,
were once dependent on Newchurch.   Of the other chapels-
of-ease here, we need only say that *St. James* has the reputation of being "low," while *St. Michael and All Angels*
outdoes the others in ritual.   There are a Roman Catholic
and several other Dissenting chapels, more than one of them
by no means Puritan in its architectural pretensions.

Among other public buildings may be mentioned the
Town Hall and Market House in Lind Street, which contains
some paintings that have given rise to difference of opinion.
A little way west from the pier is the *Royal Victoria Yacht
Club* with its saluting battery.   In Union Street we find
the *Royal Victoria Arcade*, a covered bazaar of what may be
called "Margate ware," and such like.   In the same broad
thoroughfare, the Regent Street of Ryde, stands the *Post
Office*, on the left-hand going up, and at the top of it,
where the High Street begins, is the *Theatre*.

There are excellent shops in Ryde, which has a considerable suburban population of retired officers and other more
or less moneyed idlers.   Of late years, however, it is said that
the better class of residents are inclined to desert it, while
the town seems to have been overbuilt, judging from the
number of houses to let.   Unlike the other chief towns in
the island, its population had slightly decreased at the last
census.   Its gay times are in early summer, when the
Yeomanry assemble here ; then in August during the
regattas.   All through the summer it is largely visited by

tourists and excursionists, for whose benefit we will now deal with its resources in the way of amusement.

The bathing at Ryde is naturally bad, the shore being so low and the tide running so far out. This difficulty has been partly met by adapting the unfinished *Victoria Pier* as a bathing place, where (besides other baths) for a few pence a swim may be had in graduated enclosures, for both ladies and gentlemen, with the choice of launching out into the deep, if there is any deep, for during part of the day even the end of this pier will be left high and dry. Still more limited are the hours during which become available the town bathing sheds under the sea-wall, beyond the lake, the charge at which is only a halfpenny. The class of the community most like to enjoy and profit by a dip cannot always command even so little as a halfpenny; and it seems a pity that the perspiring but impecunious youth of Ryde should be thus restricted in the interest of genteel watering-place amenities, especially considering that their aquatic gambols are after all very visible from the favourite promenade. In the morning, indeed, one may bathe on the sands before the esplanade, when the tide serves. The shallowness of the shore may seem a merciful provision of nature to keep enterprising swimmers from venturing out too far, as there is a strong current here to be reckoned with, which should be borne in mind by boating amateurs also. Boats and boatmen for hire abound off the pier.

The best point of Ryde is the many walks about it, which we will here indicate; and first, the short stroll to Quarr Abbey, which no one should miss, yet many do miss for want of knowing the way.

To BINSTEAD, QUARR ABBEY, WOOTTON, Etc.

On the west side of the pier, the sloppy shore, with its prospect of hospital hulks, is not available as a promenade, the banks being monopolised by private grounds. But if the stranger be inclined to grudge this exclusion, he will find the proprietors by no means churlish in sharing their

RYDE

Hotels: *Pier, Esplanade, Sivier's, Eagle, Albany, Waverley Temperance,*
etc. (facing the sea). *Yelf's, York* (C.) *Crown, etc.* (in the town).

Banks: National Provincial Bank of England, and the Capital and Counties
Bank, the latter of which has branches at most towns in the island.

RYDE, with its population of 11,000, is practically the
chief town in the island, and the most used entrance into
it. The crossing from Portsmouth is only four miles;
then the traveller is met by train at the end of the pier, a
convenience offered by no other landing-place.

The first view of the town from the water is very
attractive, displayed as it is on a hill-side, with its steeply
sloping streets, its prominent spires, its fringe of handsome
villas, embowered in trees, and the rich woods that border
it on either side, running down almost to the shore. The
author of *Tom Jones*, who stayed here on his way to Lisbon,
was struck by the pleasant situation of what at that day
seems to have been little more than a few fishermen's
huts on the beach, and a straggling line of cottages peeping
out upon the wooded crest. The main events of Ryde's
history are having been burnt by the French in the reign
of Richard II., and in 1782 the famous wreck of the *Royal
George*, the bodies from which came ashore in great numbers
to be buried where now runs the Esplanade. It is only
in our century that Ryde became the flourishing and frequented resort we now see it.

The main obstacle to its progress was long the awkward-
ness of landing. Both Fielding and Marryat mention the
wide mud banks over which visitors had to be taken in a

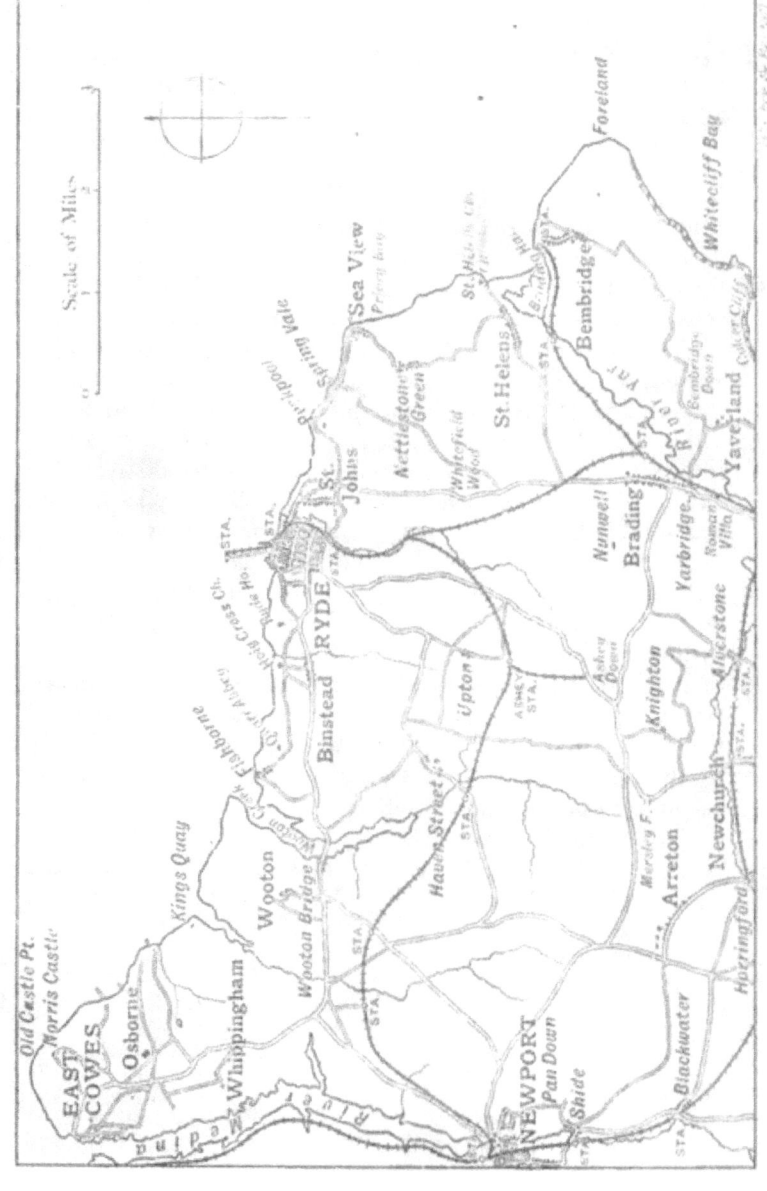

wherry as far as it could go, then carried ashore in a cart
or on a man's back. This bed of mud has now been
covered by or given place to sand, over which the tide
recedes a long way; but all the difficulties of access are
met by the pier, which successive additions have carried
out over 2000 feet. It is provided with a pavilion and
other shelters; and the railway runs to the Pier-head,
where is the station of that name. The Esplanade station
is at the gate of the pier, close to the chief hotels.
St. John's station, at the back of the town, is more convenient for some of the residential quarters. But economical minds, in considering to which station they shall
book, are apt to be influenced by the fact that the journey
between them is perhaps the dearest railway ride in
England. The fare from one end of the pier to the other
is fivepence for a third of a mile, including of course the
pier dues. Beside the railway runs an electric tram, by
which this short trip may be taken at a much cheaper rate.
Close to the large pier is another known as the Victoria
Pier, which has come to an end before getting far enough
out to sea, and now serves only as a bathing and fishing
place.

Eastward from the piers, stretch the esplanade and sea-
wall, forming a very pleasant promenade, with its view
of Spithead, where occasionally is presented the grand
spectacle of a British fleet. About twenty acres have been
reclaimed from the sea, and laid out as gardens ending in
an ornamental lake, on the shallow waters of which boats
and canoes voyage safely. In winter it would be a capital
place for skaters, but this water seldom takes on more than
a slight coating of ice. Round it runs a track used for
bicycle races. The gardens are a highly popular rendezvous
when the band plays in the pavilion on fine evenings.

The most striking public buildings are the churches, of
which the most notable is the parish church, *All Saints'*,
in the upper part of the town, where its spire makes a far-
seen landmark. It is in the decorated style, after designs
by the late Sir Gilbert Scott. The reredos, pulpit, and
font are elaborate works of art, of variously-coloured

marbles ; and there is much good painted glass, the west window of the nave being particularly fine. At the east end of the north aisle is a magnificent tower and spire nearly 200 feet high, visible for many miles in every direction. Visitors should ascend the tower, for which a small charge is made.

St. Thomas', thickly covered with ivy, has at first sight more the look of a venerable parish church, but does not so well repay examination. It will be remembered that none of these Isle of Wight watering-places can show much ancient church architecture, having usually, as they sprang up, been separated from older parishes, sometimes stretching across the island. Both Ryde and Ventnor, for instance, were once dependent on Newchurch. Of the other chapels-of-ease here, we need only say that *St. James* has the reputation of being "low," while *St. Michael and All Angels* outdoes the others in ritual. There are a Roman Catholic and several other Dissenting chapels, more than one of them by no means Puritan in its architectural pretensions.

Among other public buildings may be mentioned the *Town Hall and Market House* in Lind Street, which contains some paintings that have given rise to difference of opinion. A little way west from the pier is the *Royal Victoria Yacht Club* with its saluting battery. In Union Street we find the *Royal Victoria Arcade*, a covered bazaar of what may be called "Margate ware," and such like. In the same broad thoroughfare, the Regent Street of Ryde, stands the *Post Office*, on the left-hand going up, and at the top of it, where the High Street begins, is the *Theatre*.

There are excellent shops in Ryde, which has a considerable suburban population of retired officers and other more or less moneyed idlers. Of late years, however, it is said that the better class of residents are inclined to desert it, while the town seems to have been overbuilt, judging from the number of houses to let. Unlike the other chief towns in the island, its population had slightly decreased at the last census. Its gay times are in early summer, when the Yeomanry assemble here ; then in August during the regattas. All through the summer it is largely visited by

tourists and excursionists, for whose benefit we will now
deal with its resources in the way of amusement.

The bathing at Ryde is naturally bad, the shore being
so low and the tide running so far out.   This difficulty has
been partly met by adapting the unfinished *Victoria Pier*
as a bathing place, where (besides other baths) for a few
pence a swim may be had in graduated enclosures, for both
ladies and gentlemen, with the choice of launching out into
the deep, if there is any deep, for during part of the day
even the end of this pier will be left high and dry.   Still
more limited are the hours during which become available
the town bathing sheds under the sea-wall, beyond the lake,
the charge at which is only a halfpenny.   The class of the
community most like to enjoy and profit by a dip cannot
always command even so little as a halfpenny ; and it
seems a pity that the perspiring but impecunious youth of
Ryde should be thus restricted in the interest of genteel
watering-place amenities, especially considering that their
aquatic gambols are after all very visible from the favourite
promenade.   In the morning, indeed, one may bathe on the
sands before the esplanade, when the tide serves.   The
shallowness of the shore may seem a merciful provision of
nature to keep enterprising swimmers from venturing out
too far, as there is a strong current here to be reckoned
with, which should be borne in mind by boating amateurs
also.   Boats and boatmen for hire abound off the pier.

The best point of Ryde is the many walks about it,
which we will here indicate ; and first, the short stroll to
Quarr Abbey, which no one should miss, yet many do miss
for want of knowing the way.

To BINSTEAD, QUARR ABBEY, WOOTTON, Etc.

On the west side of the pier, the sloppy shore, with its
prospect of hospital hulks, is not available as a promenade,
the banks being monopolised by private grounds.   But if
the stranger be inclined to grudge this exclusion, he will
find the proprietors by no means churlish in sharing their

advantages. One of the very prettiest rambles here takes
him by the coast-line, a little way back from the sea indeed,
among magnificent trees and park scenery that recall the
richest inland country. The *Spencer Road* must be followed
past the Yacht Club, till, keeping to the right, he enters a
private avenue of fine elms. At the end of this, passing
through posts and crossing a road, he will see a broad
gravelled path between trim hedgerows, that, winding up
and down along the grounds of Ryde House, leads over
a tiny brook separating the parish of Ryde from that of
BINSTEAD, and up a steep but short ascent to *Holy Cross
Church* of the latter village (1¼ mile). This church was
rebuilt in 1842, from the designs of Mr. T. Hellyer. What
was once the old Norman north door of the church has
been set up as a gateway into the churchyard. Over the
door is a curious figure, which some hold to be an ancient
idol. In the interior are noticeable the font, the reading-
desk, and some fine carving.

Close at hand are interesting quarries of the Upper
Eocene freshwater limestone, which is composed of com-
minuted shells, held together by sparry calcareous cement.
This stone was largely employed in the erection of Winchester Cathedral. A few fossils may still be obtained
from the *débris* of the disused quarries, such as freshwater
shells (*Limneus longiscatus, Bulimus ellipticus*), the fruits of
freshwater plants (*Chara*), and mammalian remains (teeth of
Palæotherium, etc.).

Beyond the church, the lane bears always to the right,
through a long stretch of oak copses, giving glimpses of
Spithead and the Hampshire coast-line, till it merges in a
broad road, at the foot of which stands Quarr Abbey (2 m.),
its ivied walls forming a contrast to the roses blooming
in front.

QUARR ABBEY, anciently Quarraria, was so named from
the quarries in its neighbourhood. Its ruins have in part
been turned into commonplace farm buildings. The large
barn is said to have been the monastic refectory. Remark
a small building (to the east) with a perpendicular door,
and three arches in tolerable preservation ; remains of a

fine decorated doorway ; a moulded segmental arch, and a few other remains of old work may also be seen. The abbey, founded in 1132 by Baldwin de Redvers, afterwards Lord of the Island and Earl of Devon, was the second Cistercian house established in England, and so well endowed that the Abbot became one of the leading magnates of the island. By license from Edward III., the abbey, which was often exposed to the attacks of sea-rovers, was fortified with a stone wall enclosing an area of 40 acres. The sea-gate and portions of the wall may still be traced, and the foundations of the old abbey have recently been uncovered.

Many distinguished personages were buried at Quarr :— the founder, and his wife Adeliza ; William de Vernon, lord of the island ; and the Lady Cicely, second daughter of Edward IV. Among the numerous traditions attached to the abbey there is one that connects a wood now consisting of brushwood and a few decayed oaks, Eleanor's Grove, with the queen of Henry II., said to have been imprisoned here.

From Quarr the walk may be continued for half a mile, through the grounds of Quarr House (by gate at porter's lodge) to FISHBOURNE at the mouth of Fishbourne Creek, or, as it is more commonly called, *Wootton River*. At high water, for the river is tidal up to *Wootton Bridge*, this inlet makes a pretty sight, its sloping banks fringed with oak copses reflected in the waves beneath. From Fishbourne, turning our backs to the sea, we soon gain the high road between Ryde and Newport. The return may be thus made over Binstead Hill, at the top of which is a choice of following the high road through the village, or keeping to the left to regain the lane at the church.

If in no hurry to get home, we might go on a mile or so to *Wootton Bridge*, either by road or path along the creek ; then a further round would be to take the road going off to the left short of Wootton Bridge, or to follow for a couple of miles the wooded bottom of the creek, up to HAVEN STREET (*White Hart Inn*), a neat village, looking over finely-diversified country. It is distinguished by a quite palatial public club, the *Longford Institute*, built by private generosity, the reading-room and other accommodation of which are open to residents for a trifling monthly subscription. From Haven Street a walk of 3 miles soon brings one into the far-stretching suburbs of Ryde.

The high road both to Newport and Cowes respectively, 7 and 8 miles distant, runs through Binstead to WOOTTON, through an agreeable wooded country, crossing the Wootton Creek by a bridge (*Sloop Inn*). Wootton Church has some points of interest—a Norman doorway, with chevron mouldings, on the south ; an Early English arch, which formerly opened into the chantry of St. Edmund the King ; and the Early Decorated windows on the east and west. A little way past Wootton, the land is indented by another creek called *King's Quay*, beyond which we approach the grounds of *Osborne*.

The excursionist is sure to make acquaintance with this road on his coach trips ; and the points beyond Wootton will come in for notice farther on. We may leave this side for the present, by quoting a paragraph of useful hints from the *Isle of Wight Advertiser*.

"Another favourite walk is, starting from the Parish Church along the Queen's Road, turning to the left, following the Pellhurst Road until the farm is reached, then turning to the right into a pretty lane, from which a very pretty view is obtained of Osborne Palace and the domain, also the opposite coast and Southampton Water. Descending the steep bit of continuation of this lane, Dame Anthony's Common is reached, leading on to a number of nice rambles by and through farm lands, to the right out into the Binstead Road, and to the left to Ningwood, Haven Street, Upton, etc. Another walk is up West Street and direct to Haylands and Upton, where, nearly opposite the windmill, a pretty road runs down to the railway, which may be crossed at Smallbrooke, where Whitefield Woods are soon entered, with rambles into the Brading Road, and across the fields to St. Helen's, etc. Or, from the top of West Street, the main turning to the left is the Ashey Road, which may be followed to the Green Lanes, there turning to the left on to Nunwell Park and Mansion, and so on to Brading ; or, following the direct main road, Ashey Down and Obelisk is crossed, and beyond is the road on to Knighton and Newchurch. Each of these rambles— either within a reasonable walk—will discover many pleasant detours *en route*, but these across and around Dame Anthony's Common, Firestone Copse, Ningwood, etc., are specially worthy the regard of visitors, who, as a rule, hug the seashore too closely, and thus miss a great deal of the beauty and luxuriance of the district so near to it. To the lovers of wild-flowers and ferns we commend especially these somewhat inland rambles."

It may be added that the view from *Ashey Down*, to which we shall return later, is particularly fine, and well worth the walk of about 4 miles.

To BEMBRIDGE AND BRADING

We now take the coast eastwards. A walk at all times of the year dry and agreeable is that by the sea-wall, continuing the esplanade and keeping a good view over the Solent, with its circular forts and stir of shipping, beyond which at night the lights of Portsmouth and Southsea make a bright show. On the other hand, this road is shut in by enclosed woods and castellated villas ; but the stranger has a choice of turning inland by a path opposite the private pier of the Hutt family, and making his way through rich country, with occasional glimpses of the sea, to very agreeable neighbours of Ryde, notably *Sea View* at the eastern corner of the island, which stands in much the same relation to Ryde as Broadstairs to Ramsgate.

By road Sea View is a short 3 miles ; but it may be reached rather more directly on foot along the sea-wall, which only once breaks into a sandy road at *Spring Vale*, a row of seaside lodgings with a cosy-looking inn (*Battery Hotel*), nestling under the wing of a formidable but unobtrusive battery that makes part of the defences of Portsmouth. *Puckpool* is another name for this point.

SEA VIEW (*Pier Hotel, Sea View Hotel, Bungalow Boarding*

House) is a flourishing little watering-place of the family order, with a long chain pier of its own, from which boats run regularly to Southsea. It has many picturesque or smart houses, and the somewhat uncommon feature of wood coming down to the edge of the water, only to tantalise the visitor, however, by notices that trespassing is prohibited. Boating and fishing are favourite pastimes in the bay, where tents give accommodation for bathing. The sands of Priory Bay round the corner are used for the same purpose by the less modest sex. Sea View comes into history by an unsuccessful attempt at invasion made here, in 1545, when a French force was easily driven back.

St. Helen's lies rather more than a mile beyond Sea View, by road through the hamlet of *Nettlestone Green*, or by a rough walk round the sands of Priory Bay. It has also a station, some way from the village, on the branch line to Bembridge, with which place it is connected by a ferry, across the mouth of *Brading Harbour*. The golf-links that have done so much to make Bembridge's reputation are on the St. Helen's side, covering a sandy spit, at the neck of which may be seen the ivied fragment of the old church, disfigured by whitewash on the sea face, the better to serve for a landmark, as does the more conspicuous obelisk on the downs beyond. The village of St. Helen's itself stands some half a mile back on elevated ground, looking over the windings of Brading Harbour, a tidal creek that at high water goes far to dignify the landscape. This place, with its spacious green and the leafy lanes into which it straggles, has an air of rural charm, enhanced by the view of the wooded point on which stands its seaside neighbour Bembridge. With a railway so close at hand, St. Helen's wants only a good hotel to make—or spoil— it as a most agreeable resort; at present it has two inns, but appears rather a place of snug homes than of temporary quarters.

Bembridge (Hotels: *Royal Spithead*, with special terms to golfers, *Bembridge*—Inns: *Prince of Wales*, *Pilot Boat*,

Marine) is a place risen of late years into considerable note as a resort of golfers and headquarters of the Isle of Wight Golf Club, though the links and Club House are on the other side of Brading Harbour, reached by the ferry-boat. The only fault of these links is their being too small ; their great advantage is the mildness of the climate, which favours their use in winter. The village stands prettily on a wooded point, from among the trees of which its church may be seen rising. A very pleasant path runs straight across (1 m.) to the hamlet of *Lane End*, a little way beyond which is the *Foreland*, the north-eastern corner of the island. The path round the beach offers more prospects, but is tryingly rough and at one point too well fortified by *chevaux de frise* of nettles. There are tents, a shed, and other conveniences for bathing ; and the rather shingly shore has some stretches of sand. But perhaps Bembridge's chief patrons think only of the sea as casting up golf-links for their absorbing pastime, while this stretch of sandy ground is also noted by botanists for the richness and variety of its flora. The air here is said to be particularly healthy, and the climate milder than in opener parts of the north coast.

We have reached Bembridge along the coast ; but cut off as it is by Brading Harbour, the road to it runs inland ; and it has a small railway with a station below St. Helen's. This branch joins the line to Ventnor at BRADING (Inns : *Bugle*, *Wheatsheaf*, etc.), which is little more than an hour's walk from Ryde by the road through *St. John's*, *Elmfield*, and *Whitefield Wood*, and if not on foot, by rail or coach makes one of the favourite excursions from almost all the Isle of Wight resorts. Brading, unimportant as it looks now, is one of the oldest towns in the island, formerly returning two members to Parliament. It has curiosities to show as relics of its ancient dignity, the old Bull Ring, the parish stocks, once a terror to evildoers, and a restored church, boasting to be the oldest in the island. It is mainly Transition-Norman in character, with a few fragments of an earlier building. In the interior are a fine incised slab of Flemish work, adorned with figures of our Lord, the Blessed Virgin,

and the Twelve Apostles, and an effigy in full armour of
Sir John Cherowin, d. 1441, constable of Portchester Castle.
In the Oglander Chapel (at the east end of the south aisle)
may be seen tombs and effigies of the Oglanders, one a
knight in armour, another that loyal cavalier, Sir John
Oglander, whose diary has often been drawn on by historians
as giving an account of the island at the time of the Civil
Wars. *Nunwell*, the seat of this good old family since the
Conquest, stands on Brading Down, in a park distinguished
by some fine old oaks.

In the churchyard some epitaphs of unusual merit will be
found, especially the well-known lines " Forgive, blest shade,
the tributary tear," set to music by Dr. Calcott ; and the Rev.
Legh Richmond's tribute to " Jane the Young Cottager."
Legh Richmond was curate of Brading and Yaverland
from 1797 to 1805. The house of the " Cottager " is
situated at the foot of the hill. Whitecliff Bay in this
vicinity is associated with another of the same author's
once popular tracts " The Negro Servant."

But the pride of Brading is the Roman Villa, discovered
at *Morton Farm*, a mile or so S.W., where it had long lain
buried out of sight and memory. This miniature Pompeii
is said to be the finest collection of Roman remains in
England. For antiquarians it is of very great interest, while
the general public are more likely to be deterred by the
charge of 1s. for admission. The way is easily found by
direction posts, the high road being left at Yarbridge.

THE ROMAN VILLA

At the entrance (marked No. 6 on the plan) is a very fine
piece of pavement, the central design of which is Orpheus
playing on the lyre, surrounded by animals attracted by his
music. Near the left shoulder of Orpheus is the figure of a
monkey wearing a red cap ; the other animals are a coot, a
fox, and a peacock. The whole composition is surrounded
with an elaborate guilloche border.

To the right of the entrance is a large chamber (No. 12
on the plan), 40 feet long by 19 feet wide. This has a

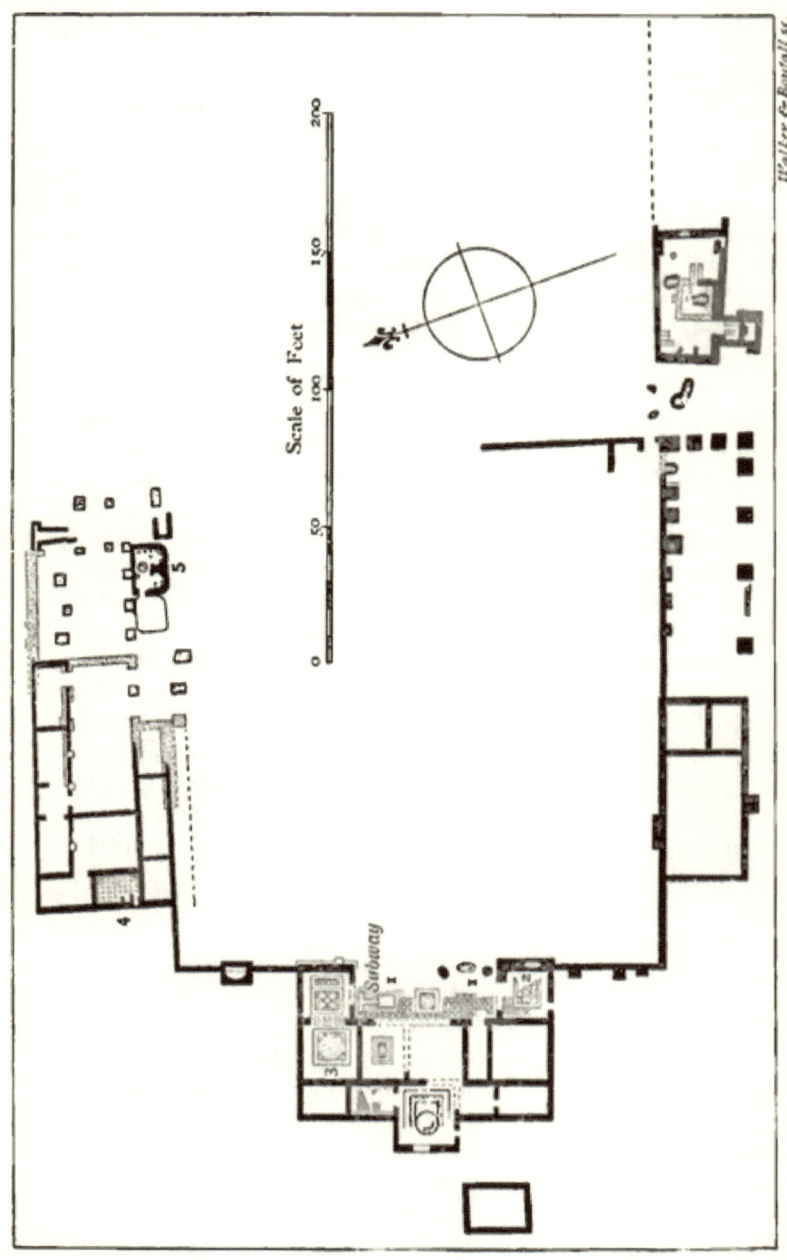

Scale of Feet

0   50   100   150   200

Subway

PLAN OF ROMAN VILLA NEAR BRADING, ISLE OF WIGHT.

Walker & Boutall sc.

remarkable pavement. This room, known as the Medusa
Room, has been divided into two portions; the eastern
division contains the largest and most important of the
mosaics yet found. In the centre is a large medallion containing the head of Medusa. Springing from this centre
are four compartments arranged crosswise; each of these
is bordered by the guilloche pattern; at the angles, north,
south, east, and west, are triangular compartments which
contain bucolic figures blowing horns. The designs which
make up the four large panels are of great interest, each containing two figures of a male and a female; the subjects
appear to be of a pastoral character, as evidenced both by the
costume and the objects borne by each figure. The inter-
pretation of the subjects is uncertain. All the panels have
elaborate guilloche borders, and the whole is surrounded
with red inch-tesseræ. The western portion of the pavement was of most elaborate design, but is much injured.
Originally there were nine compartments surrounded with
the same guilloche border as the pavement in the eastern
part of the room. The centre panel contained a circular
medallion, but the subject is destroyed. Upon each side
are oblong panels containing mythological subjects, and at
the four corners semicircles enclosed in compartments;
these are occupied, with the exception of one which has
perished, by busts in illustration of the Four Seasons, the
missing one, from the north-west corner, having probably
represented Spring. Summer appears at the south-west
corner, and is tolerably well preserved; the head is that of
a female, her hair decked with poppies. Above a semicircle
of guilloche pattern there is in the angle of this compartment a figure of a peacock with flowing tail, represented
pecking at a vase of flowers. There are also traces of a
bird in the injured composition supposed to contain Spring.
It is therefore probable that there were figures of birds
in each compartment suitable to the season of the year.
Autumn is a female figure, treated in a similar manner
to the former, her hair ornamented with ears of corn in
illustration of Ceres. The last, Winter, is the most perfect
of all; this is also a female figure closely wrapped, her

garment being fastened across her left shoulder by a brooch, and attached to the dress is a hood, similar to that worn by ecclesiastics. In her left hand she carries a leafless bough from which is suspended a dead bird. Between the four angle compartments of the Seasons are four oblong panels. These probably represented mythological subjects, because in the one which is tolerably well preserved appear figures which may be recognised as Perseus and Andromeda. Between the eastern and the western pavements is a subject of considerable interest : in the centre a square panel containing a male figure wearing a black beard, seated in what appears to be a chair ; he is semi-nude, there being but little drapery except at the lower portion of the figure. At his left side stands a pillar, surmounted by a gnomon or sun-dial. Beneath the pillar is a globe or sphere, which appears to be supported on three legs. The tesseræ are so arranged as to define the four quarters of the world, and to this globe the figure is pointing with a wand, as though casting a horoscope ; at his right hand is a cup or vase in which is apparently a pen. This illustration of an astronomer in the exercise of his profession is one of the most interesting of the novelties yet revealed ; the figure is probably intended for Hipparchus, whose observations were made between the years 160 and 125 B.C. At the west end of the chamber is a figure of the Svastika or Vedic cross.

To the left of the entrance, and of the Orpheus pavement, is a chamber measuring 15 feet 6 inches by 17 feet 6 inches (marked No. 3 on the plan). This also has an elaborate pavement. It is arranged in nine compartments. In the centre is a circular medallion with the head of a Bacchante, and a similar figure appears at the only remaining angle of the pavement. Four larger panels occupy the centre of each of the sides ; one, however, is entirely destroyed, and two are partially so. The panel in the best state of preservation contains the representation of a small house with steps leading up to it ; the figure of a man, with the head and legs of a cock ; and two winged gryphons. The panel on the west side contains two gladiators ; and that on the north side, a fox under a tree and a building with a cupola.

At the back of these rooms are other chambers, some paved with rough tesseræ of chalk and others unpaved.

To the north of the entrance are more chambers ; one particularly interesting (marked No. 15 on the plan). It measures 15 feet 2 inches by 10 feet 7 inches, and contains fifty-four pillars of tiles arranged upon a floor of rough stones. These pillars, 2 feet 6 inches in height, originally supported the floor of the apartment, forming a hypocaust under it. On the west side is a neatly-turned arch of large flat tiles with wide mortar joints ; at the mouth of this arch a large and massive stone was placed across it. Here was the furnace used for supplying hot air to the hypocaust. The actual floor of the chamber has perished.

Eastward of this hypocaust are several other rooms ; one in particular may be mentioned (No. 28 on plan), containing a deep well, the rim of which has been restored. The diameter of this well is 4 feet 3 inches, its depth 78 feet.

Opposite, to the south, another line of buildings has been more recently unearthed, showing how the villa consisted of a central block of apartments (those containing the tesselated pavements), and a large wing of buildings on either side. The central portion was doubtless occupied by the owner of the villa, and the two wings by his slaves and by his soldiers. There are traces of two distinct periods of occupation, and indications that the villa was ultimately destroyed by fire. In the course of the excavations quantities of tiles, broken pottery, coins, bronze implements, and other things were discovered, besides the bones of animals, and shells.

We have thus gone through all the chief places of interest in this corner of the island, and those most likely to be visited from Ryde, lying within an hour or so's walk as they do. But Ryde is a capital centre for excursions to every part. From it a good walker could get to any point in a day's tramp. The railways put it in communication with all the chief resorts. Daily in summer there is a choice of coach excursions to goals near and far, at a fare of four or five shillings, that to Carisbrooke being perhaps the favourite one, especially when it includes Osborne as well as Newport, or when the return, in good weather, is made over the Downs. The touts for rival coaches are so active and insinuating that the difficulty is to avoid going on these pleasant trips. Unless in the height of the season, the visitor will do prudently to resist all invitations to book his seat beforehand, as, waiting to see how the weather goes, he will generally find room on one or other coach at the time of starting, which is often delayed for a full complement of passengers or till the arrival of the boats from Portsmouth. Then there are the steamer trips in all directions, and especially the sail round the island, done in about six hours, so as to allow of Londoners making this voyage and getting home the same day. The places visited by coach will better be described farther on. Here the tourist may find useful a short chart of the whole coast, which is all some of us have time to see of the Isle of Wight.

THE TRIP ROUND THE ISLAND

The steamers making this voyage of pleasure, usually from Portsmouth and Southsea, but calling at Ryde, take it sometimes in one, sometimes in the other direction, according to the tide. Let us suppose that we leave Ryde Pier for the westward.

The first thing that strikes us is the picturesque appearance of the town as seen from the water, the lofty tower and spire of All Saints' Church standing up prominently above the other buildings. The detached villas and houses straggle out among the trees for nearly a mile until we come to *Binstead*, where the woods run close down to the water's edge. We pass the three hulks placed here to receive the crews and passengers of such homeward-bound ships as are sent into Quarantine. The easternmost ship is the *Edgar*, an old two-decker. She was one of the ships of the Baltic fleet in the Russian War. The westernmost vessel is the *Eölus*, a French prize taken in 1815; and the middle one an old English frigate, the *Meneläus*. Beyond the Quarantine Ground, we arrive off *Quarr*; but the ruins can scarcely be made out from the steamer. We next pass the mouth of the *Wootton river*, and then *King's Quay*, and speedily come in sight of *Osborne*, Her Majesty's marine palace. From the deck of the steamer a very good view—the only view open to the public—is to be had of the grounds and Castle. *Norris Castle*, the seat of the Duke of Bedford, comes next. The Castle, partially covered with ivy, standing on a fine lawn amidst magnificent trees, is extremely picturesque. Rounding *Old Castle Point* we immediately come into view of *Cowes*. The river *Medina*, which here falls into the sea, opens out into a fine harbour, usually crowded with yachts. Cowes being the headquarters of the Royal Yacht Squadron, the finest yachts afloat are to be seen in the Roads. The town is prettily situated on the western side of the harbour, the Club House standing at the point, and immediately behind it Trinity Church. To the westward of the Club House lies the district known as "*Egypt*." The houses continue, dotted along among the trees, nearly as far as *Gurnard Bay*, a small hamlet about a mile from Cowes. We next cut across *Thorness Bay*, but the shore is low and uninteresting until we pass *Hempstead Ledge* and come within sight of *Yarmouth*, at the mouth of the river Yar, a quiet little town with a short wooden pier, whence small steamers run across to Lymington, on the Hampshire coast. After leaving Yarmouth we round *Sconce Point* and see the two very ugly red-brick forts, *Victoria Fort* and *Albert Fort*, on the Isle of Wight shore, and *Hurst Castle* with its lighthouses on the mainland. These fortifications are mounted with heavy guns to defend the western entrance of the Solent. Hurst Castle is a telegraph station for reporting the passage of mail steamers. We now run across *Colwell Bay* and *Totland Bay*, and beyond the picturesque headland of *Headon Hill* enter *Alum Bay* with its wonderful vertically-striped cliffs of coloured sand. A small pier has been constructed at Alum Bay, and sometimes the steamers call here for a short time. We round the *Needles*, upon the outermost rock of which is the lighthouse. The light itself is 80 feet above high-water mark, and shows a white light to the westward, visible for 14 miles; and a red light to the south, visible for 9 miles.

Immediately after passing the Needles we see *Scratchell's Bay*, and may observe the wonderful alcove carved out of the high chalk cliffs. Rounding *Sun Corner* we come upon the high cliffs known as the *Mainbench*, and from this point the chalk cliffs run on without interruption to *Watcombe Bay*. Upon the highest point is a beacon, the *Nodes Beacon*, about to be replaced by a cross to the memory of the late Poet Laureate, where the cliff is 490 feet in height. From here the steamers usually steer a straight course for *St. Catherine's Point*, leaving the land at a considerable distance on the left hand, so that the shore is very indistinctly seen. We may, however, make out *Freshwater Gate* at the eastern end of the chalk cliffs. The land now becomes low until we approach *St. Catherine's Point*; but we can distinguish *Compton Bay*, where the chalk cliffs give place to the dark strata of the greensand, succeeded by *Brook Bay* with its mottled muddy cliffs of Wealden age. Next comes the long expanse of *Brixton Bay*, reaching as far as *Atherfield Point*, surmounted by its white coastguard station, where the Wealden formation again gives place to the greensand. *Chale Bay* follows next, and stretches on to near St. Catherine's Point Just before we reach it we see *Chale*, and the low square tower of its church, then *Blackgang Chine;* and then we enter the *Race* at *Rocken End*, where, during bad weather in winter a tremendous sea runs, and come in sight of *St. Catherine's Lighthouse*. We are now at the extreme south point of the Isle of Wight, and from here to Dunnose we keep tolerably near the shore. From St. Catherine's Light to Ventnor is the *Undercliff*, a strip of land varying from a quarter of a mile to half a mile in width, lying between the beach and the cliff, and clad in the richest verdure. Near *St. Lawrence* is the National Consumption Hospital—a long row of detached houses with the chapel in the centre. *Steephill Castle* is passed, and then the town of Ventnor and the heights of *St. Boniface Down* come into view. We approach *Bonchurch*, and pass under *Dunnose*, catching a glimpse of the landslip, and of *Luccombe Chine*. It was off Dunnose Point that the hapless training frigate *Eurydice* foundered in a squall on Sunday, March 24, 1878.

The steamer, once round this south-eastern corner, stands across *Sandown Bay*. The towns of *Shanklin* and *Sandown* may be seen at the bottom of the bay, and soon we near the magnificent cliffs of *Culvers*. Here, as at the opposite extremity of the island, the strata forming the chalk cliffs, well marked by the lines of flints, have been tilted up into a nearly vertical position. We now enter *White Cliff Bay*, and make for the *Foreland Point*. This is the extreme east end of the island. About 2 miles away on our right is the *Nab Lightship* with its two masts with balls on the top, and right ahead the *Warner Lightship* with one mast only. Here we come in sight of *Spithead* with its circular granite forts, and *Portsmouth* in the distance. We next come upon *Brading Haven*, at the upper end of which stands the town of *Brading*; while on the left and at the mouth of the harbour lies the village of *Bembridge*. On the right bank is seen the old tower of *St. Helen's*, now used as a landmark, and then passing *Watchhouse Point* we come upon *Priory Bay*. The fine pier of *Sea View* is touched at, and we are soon once more in sight of Ryde.

NEWPORT AND COWES

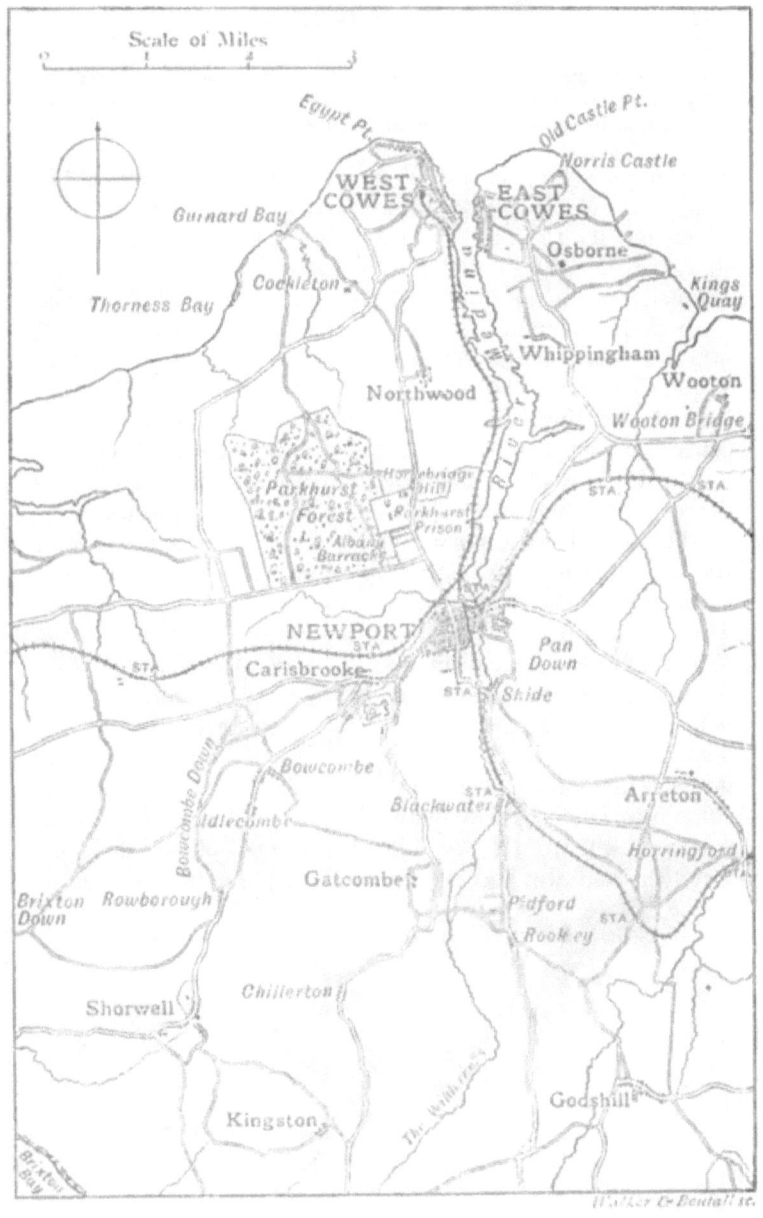

COWES

Hotels: West Cowes--*Gloster*, *Marine* (C.), *Globe*, on the parade. *Fountain*, at the pier. *George Inn*, etc.—East Cowes—*Medina*, near the shore; *Prince of Wales Inn*, on the hill at Osborne.

THE other chief entrance to the island is Cowes, the passage to which from Southampton is a matter of an hour or so, but for the most part sheltered between the wooded shores of Southampton Water, and itself a trip to be recommended in fine weather. Passengers are landed on the short pier, a pier of business, from which it is two or three minutes' walk across the main street to the station. From Ryde, Cowes may be reached, in a rather roundabout way, by rail, the line taking a sweep by Brading to follow the central downs, and near Wootton coming back to the course of the high road to Newport, whence the train carries us down the farther bank of the Medina to West Cowes.

The two Cowes, separated by their river harbour and its stir of shipping and shipbuilding, have a look and character of their own unique among the island resorts. The well-known yacht-building yards of the Messrs. White were originated in 1815. The Medina Dock, 330 feet long by 62 feet wide, was built in 1845. Long before this firm's time indeed, Cowes was celebrated for its dockyards. Nelson's ship the *Vanguard* and many other famous men-of-war were built at Cowes, but it did not come into much general note till the founding of the Royal Yacht Club in 1812. The advantages of its harbour, however, had always been appreciated ; Sir John Oglander tells us that in 1620 he saw as many as 300 craft there at anchor.

EAST COWES, though distinguished as the birthplace of Dr. Arnold, may be shortly dismissed as a suburb of ambitious roads mounting the wooded background from a rather mean frontage, so as to bring into curious juxta-position some characteristics of Norwood and Rotherhithe. At the seaward end it has a short esplanade of its own, from which is to be had a fine sunset view over the Solent. The new building behind the esplande is the Coastguard barracks. Beyond, unfortunately, the point is enclosed by private grounds.

The two towns are united by a floating bridge, on which, coach, horses, and all, if our journey be in this manner, we cross to WEST COWES. There has been some talk of a tunnel here, which as yet remains in the air. Leaving the roomy but commonplace river suburb of *Mill Hill*, we follow the long narrow main street, with its crooked turns and drops, that makes the backbone of West Cowes proper. In the heart of the town, close together are the pier and the station, both designed rather for use than ornament. Before coming to any other features of interest, we must press on to where the street becomes parade, past the chief hotels and lodging-houses with their embowered frontages, to the projecting structure which was the nucleus of the place, and may now be called its Acropolis. This is the old *Castle*, in 1856 turned into the Club House of the Royal Yacht Squadron. Originally it was one of the circular forts built by Henry VIII., but ceased to be of use after the entrances east and west of the island were guarded by the new fortifications. During the Commonwealth it was chiefly made use of as a state prison, and here Sir William Davenant, during his incarceration, wrote a portion of his epic of *Gondibert*.

Everybody knows how the "Squadron" is the leading yacht club of the world, and it has here a house not unworthy of it, snug-looking, and standing out prominently on the sea-front, with its glass gallery that may be called the Grand Stand of yacht racing, its flagstaff, battery, and the jetty at which no one may land but members of the club and officers of the Navy. Admission to this select body is a much-coveted privilege, every member being entitled to fly St. George's white ensign on his yacht, if of more than 30 tons.

Here, then, is the headquarters of yachting, and the finest yachts afloat are often to be seen at anchor off this amphibious club house. The height of the yachting season is in August, when Cowes becomes a very fashionable place indeed, especially during the Regatta week, wound up by a display of fireworks and illumination of the hundreds of smart vessels lying crowded together, decked out in their rainbow bunting. These gaieties have of late years been somewhat damped by the omission of the annual ball given by the club, whose senior members, it is understood, did not relish their snug sanctum being turned upside down for the amusement of frivolous youth. There are no Assembly Rooms at Cowes, which has only its Foresters' Hall as an apology for a theatre. The town does not seem to lay itself out for the entertainment of any but its special patrons; and those who would find quarters here in August, during the gay regatta week, must be well prepared to pay for them.

Beyond the club, Trinity Church, and a few gardened villas of much amenity, the parade, making a bend, becomes fringed by *Prince's Green*, a strip of grass well provided with sunny and shady seats from which to watch the yachting that goes on almost daily in the season. The end of this is the point called *Egypt*, where stands Egypt House, a yellow brick building, ivy-clad, very effective against its background of dark foliage. "Egypt" occurs in other parts of Britain as a place-name, and may sometimes be traced to gipsy occupation; we do not know whether it be so in this case. The esplanade and sea-wall have recently been extended some way farther. If, just before reaching Egypt House, we turn up the hill, the way back may be made by a shorter road above the parade, from which a lane turns upwards to the parish church of *St. Mary*, dating from the Commonwealth time and partly rebuilt in our own day. Above this stand the somewhat gloomy grounds of the manorial mansion, with its funereally classical gates. Now we have seen all Cowes worth seeing, including the yachts, of all sorts and sizes, often so thickly anchored along this cheery shore.

Originally Cowes put forward another pretension to favour. A rhymester named Jones, in a poem dedicated to the glorification of the Isle of Wight, exclaims in 1760—

> "No more to foreign baths shall Britain roam,
>   But plunge at Cowes, and find rich health at home!"

This poet must either have had a strong Celtic imagination or a business-like interest in the town's prosperity. The bathing at Cowes is bad. At Egypt, in a somewhat too public situation, stand a row of bathing machines, supplied with long ropes, by no means superfluous, for the high-water level deepens suddenly, and the tide runs very strong here. Bathing from boats is rather to be recommended for good swimmers; but strangers must be cautious about the currents.

GURNARD BAY

The extended promenade brings us to a high and wide bank of wild shrubbery, a miniature Undercliff, which seems too pretty in its way to be rooted out, as must be its fate some day. This "Copse," as it is called, affords many delights to the boys of Cowes, while indeed the imaginative and adventurous spirit of youth is needed to adventure oneself in the often impassable jungle, a rank wilderness such as few now existing on English soil. On the low sandy shore, along which runs a small path, at morn and dusky eve may often be seen flesh-and-blood replicas of Frederick Walker's "Bathers." We are now some half an hour's stroll out of Cowes, and soon come round into *Gurnard Bay*, where there are good sands and children's playing-ground. Bathing here is quite *al fresco*. On the cliffs above, a little way back from the sea, appear the beginnings of the family watering-place Cowes may once

have been. The low cliffs of Gurnard Bay are of Upper
Eocene formation, and farther to the west abundant fossils
may be obtained (see *Geological Article*). The tourist may
here ascend from the shore by Whippance Farm on to the
road and return to West Cowes by Tinker's Lane through
Lower Cockleton.

All the way along the shore we have had a fine view of
the Hampshire woods opposite. The walk might be
pushed on for another half-hour to the crumbling promontory which gives a look round into THORNESS BAY,
and down that part of the island coast which seems least
interesting to strangers.

OSBORNE, WHIPPINGHAM, Etc.

Cowes is not so well off for walks as Ryde. The east side
is naturally finer than the west, but it has too many great
personages for neighbours, and, as Mrs. Gamp says, "must
take the consequences of living in such a situation." The
point is occupied by *Norris Castle*, now in possession of the
Bedford family, where many royal and noble guests have been
entertained, who must have enjoyed the prospects it commands of Southampton Water and the New Forest. It is a
modern building, but its ivied front gives it quite a venerable
aspect. Above East Cowes stands Lord Gort's Castle, possess-
ing an unusually spacious conservatory. Close to its gate is
seen another blazoned simply with the initials *V.A.*, as if here
its owner desired to be thought a wife rather than a queen.

Osborne Manor was anciently called Austerbourne or
Oysterbourne, and derives its name, it is said, from the
"oyster-beds of the Medina." From the Bowermans, an
old island-family not yet extinct, the estate passed into the
hands of one Eustace Mann, who, during the troubles of
the Civil War, buried a mass of gold and silver coins in a
coppice still known as *Money Coppice*, and having forgotten
to mark the spot, was never afterwards able to recover his
treasure. A Mr. Blachford married his grand-daughter, and
transmitted the estate to his heirs. From Lady Isabella
Blachford it was purchased by Queen Victoria in 1840, and

it has since been enlarged by the addition of Barton and other demesnes, until it includes an area of upwards of 5000 acres,—bounded north by the Solent, south by the Ryde and Newport road, east by the inlet of King's Quay, and west by the Medina. The stone mansion, built by Mr. Blachford, was pulled down when the Queen became its possessor, and the present Palace of Osborne erected, in the Italian style, under the direction of Mr. T. Cubitt. The campanile is 90 feet high, the flag-tower 112. The royal apartments are adorned by a large and choice collection of statuary and paintings, and look out upon terraced gardens, and a breadth of lawn which stretches to the shore of the Solent. The surrounding grounds are of considerable beauty, and the Model Farm established by the Prince Consort exhibits every modern improvement. The head steward of the royal estates resides in *Barton Court House*, recently rebuilt, but still retaining its characteristic Tudor front.

The fine grounds of Osborne are somewhat meanly bordered by a high close paling, that does not protect their privacy from the coach tops on which most visitors approach them. From the hedgerows of the Ryde Road, before it joins that from Newport, the towers of the house may be seen peeping out above the trees. The place is not open to the public ; and a full and fine view of it can be had only from the Solent.

The coaches usually turn aside to WHIPPINGHAM, to give their passengers a view of the church, looking over the Medina side of this wooded promontory. The situation is fine, and the building singular. It is understood to have been designed by the late Prince Albert, on which account Her Majesty's loyal subjects would fain admire the cruciform structure, a kind of German Romanesque in style, with an aisled chancel, and large central tower surmounted by a spire. But to tell the plain truth, it is hard to admire either the general effect or the internal decorations. One feature which will excite no critical feeling is a white marble monument, by Theed, to the late Prince. Two angels are represented holding an *immortelle* wreath, and crowning a medallion bust of the Prince. The monument records that it "is placed in the Church, erected under his directions, by his broken-hearted and devoted widow, Queen Victoria, 1864." There is also a memorial to the father of Dr. Arnold of Rugby. This is the parish church of the Royal Family, who, when they attend, occupy the south chancel aisle, where they can see the clergyman at the reading-desk and the altar without themselves being seen by the general public in the nave, so that ill-placed curiosity will be baffled, such as is said to have driven Her Majesty from the services of Crathie Church.

From Whippingham Church, it is as near two miles as one to the station of that name on the line from Ryde. The Medina is not far off, and the pedestrian might descend to that very humble hostelry the *Folly Inn*, where at high water he may find an opportunity of crossing. Else he must take his choice of going back to Cowes much as he came (varying the route by a pretty lane running from Whippingham parallel with the main road for some three-quarters of a mile), or walking up the river to Newport, (about 3 m.), there being no regular ferry. About half way on the opposite bank the cement works of Messrs. Francis and Co. form a more prominent than pleasing feature in the landscape. This round by Newport bridge would make at least 10 miles, that might be extended by taking in Parkhurst Forest and Gurnard Bay. The high road on the left side of the Medina, passing Parkhurst Barracks and Prison, is the shortest route from Newport to W. Cowes (5 m.). Before reaching the large military establishment, we may take the high road to the left, and strike through Parkhurst Forest by the first lane, which brings us back to the Cowes Road at *Horsebridge Hill*, where it takes an ascent so long and dusty that we are little surprised to find three public-houses not far from each other. At the midmost, the *Horse Shoe Inn*, a road to Gurnard Bay branches off leftwards. A little before, to the right would be seen the spire of NORTHWOOD Church, of which Cowes is ecclesiastically a dependant, but which has not much other interest. For its last 2 miles the high road winds down by the Waterworks, the Cemetery, and Mill Hill, with a pleasant look-out over the Solent.

The resources of Cowes, landwards, it will be seen, are somewhat easily exhausted. By rail and road, this town lies as near as Ryde to the chief points of interest on the island; but here it is more the way to take trips by water. Plenty of coaches come to Cowes, while few start from it; and the visitor will be refreshingly surprised by the absence of those touts for excursions who may have plagued him at Ryde or Ventnor. The frequenters of Cowes, indeed, are apt to hold themselves above such sociable diversions, and would have us know that their joy is on the briny deep.

For yachting is to Cowes what golf is to St. Andrews, or racing to Newmarket. Not all the gentlemen who swagger about in blue jackets here, and sometimes on coming ashore appear suspiciously ready to order champagne or other restoratives, are really much at home on the ocean wave, if for the nonce they would fain be thought so. Not all those big and smart schooners so much admired in the roads of Cowes are very familiar with the breeze or the billow of the open sea, though now and then they may make a holiday trip as far as the Needles. We remember Jack Brag and his skipper Bung. The sailing masters and crews of some of these sumptuous yachts must have a fine easy time of it; and one suspects they prefer being in the service of a fine-weather amateur, whose purse is his main qualification for seamanship, to taking orders from some old salt who knows the ropes as well as they do, or from one of those real yachtsmen who may have gone the length of earning a master's certificate. At Cowes it may be seen how yachting tends to two different forms— on the one hand, steam vessels, models of elegance and comfort, for use in pleasure cruises—on the other, the graceful craft which are little but racing machines. In any case, rich patrons of this sport have their skippers to depend on, who are not likely to err on the side of rash enterprise. But there are yachtsmen of another school, whose blood has the salt in it that goes so far to make England what it is,

men who, without having the means to own idle vessels,
dearly love playing the sailor in good earnest, and can
spend no happier holiday than in working some small craft
with their own hands, taking rough and smooth as it comes,
getting health and pleasure cheap by return for a month or
so to something like the independence of the old Viking
life and all its tingling charm of a struggle with the forces
of nature. To would-be sailors of this class, we may
modestly offer useful suggestions as to how they can best
enjoy their favourite pastime in the waters of the Solent
and about the Isle of Wight.

SAILING DIRECTIONS FOR THE SOLENT

NOTE.—The following abbreviations are used in this chapter: B., black;
G., green; R., red; W., white; Cheq., chequered; H.S., horizontal
stripes; V.S., vertical stripes; H.W., high water; L.W., low water.

All bearings are magnetic. The compass courses are given in every
case to assist the stranger in picking out particular buoys, etc., from
among the number he will see. Moreover, the atmosphere is often thick,
in which case the compass is the best guide. The depths of water given
are at low tide ordinary springs, unless otherwise stated. The large
Admiralty Chart, "Owers to Christchurch," No. 2045, 4s. 6d., includes
the whole of the ground we shall describe. If larger-scale charts are pre-
ferred, Nos. 2050 "Spithead" and 2040 "Solent" will answer all requirements. They are published by J. D. Potter, 31 Poultry.

Lights.—The buoys at *East Lepe*, *West Bramble*, and *East Bramble* in the
Solent, and *Netley Shoal* in Southampton Water, were in October 1894 replaced by *gas buoys*, each showing a white occulting light. All other
lights are fully described on the charts.

The Solent is one of the best cruising grounds in England,
some say in the world, for small yachts such as can be handled
by amateurs. It combines the safety of an inland lake with the
excitement of occasional rough seas: and in case of bad weather
coming on there is always a safe port within a few miles. Moreover, its many creeks and inlets afford opportunities for dinghy
explorations in the midst of pleasant scenery, while the yacht
is left safely anchored in harbour. But this cruising ground
has certain difficulties also to be reckoned with; the shore
lines are so broken, the tides so peculiar, and the beacons
so confusingly numerous, that the nautical stranger may well

thank us for a few hints that will assist him in spending a fortnight here.

First, as to the yacht. We imagine that the reader is capable
of managing, with the assistance of an amateur companion, a
yacht of from 5 to 8 tons. Such a yacht should have accommodation for two in the cabin and one in the forecastle, who
may either be a friend, or a paid hand, man or boy.

It is of course much the pleasantest if one possesses one's own
yacht, or can at any rate do without professional assistance; fail-
ing this, it is possible to hire a yacht by engaging one early in
the season; later on it is difficult to find a suitable craft. As
a rule, the owners of small yachts do not care to let them to
strangers without a man: and rightly so, for although the
Solent is a safe cruising ground, yet accidents are quite possible,
especially in the crowded harbours, owing to the strength of the
tides. The cost of hiring a 5 or 6 ton yacht, with one hand,
should be from £4 to £6 a week. The price varies according to the
place she is hired from, the length of time, the arrangements
about food for the "hand," the time of year, etc. For early or
late in the season, the terms will be less than at its height. The
best plan is to advertise in the yachting or local papers, stating
the kind of craft required. And if a suitable yacht cannot be
found at Cowes or Southampton, it may be as well to try
Lymington or Poole, at which places, especially the latter, the
price will probably be considerably less. Excellent centre-board
boats of 3 to 4 tons, with large open cockpits, easily handled by
one amateur, can be had at about 10s. a day from the boat-owners
on the West Quay at Southampton. These, of course, have no
sleeping accommodation, but they are very handy for cruising
among mud-banks, as the drop keel "acts as a pilot," and can be
lifted if one gets caught. When hiring one of these boats see
that there is an anchor and a warp on board.

Assuming then that the stranger, if he have no craft of his
own, has arranged to hire one, with or without a paid hand,
we shall give brief sailing directions for various ports and
rivers, taking Cowes as our starting-point, with approximate
distances in nautical miles. (One nautical mile=6075½ feet, or
about 1⅓ statute miles.)

Cowes Harbour.—This is the headquarters of the Royal Yacht
Squadron, and during the season is crowded with yachts of every
size and description. Large yachts anchor in Cowes Roads,

small ones inside the harbour, on the east side of the red and white chequered buoys which mark the fairway. It is forbidden to anchor in the fairway. Be careful not to anchor too near the "Shrape Mud," a large spit running out from the eastern shore, or you will ground at low tide. If this part of the harbour be too crowded, you can run up above the floating bridge between East and West Cowes, into the Medina river, remembering, however, that the tide runs very strongly in and out of the harbour, causing danger in light winds. If you decide to take up a berth in the Medina, drop your anchor in the channel, and then warp in near the bank, making fast to some of the yachts lying on the mud. This will get you out of the way of the barge traffic, which is considerable.

From here an expedition can be made in the dinghy to Newport, 4 miles. Start about half flood ; give the mud-banks a fair berth ; avoid a hard patch on the starboard hand after passing Newport Rowing Club House, about 2½ miles up. Leave the dinghy in charge of the proprietor of "Noah's Ark" Boatyard on the right bank just before reaching Newport. You can walk, rail, or coach to Carisbrooke Castle from here, and be back in time to catch the ebb.

Cowes to Wootton Creek, 4 *miles.*—Leave about two hours before high-water if possible. After passing Old Castle buoy (R.) steer for the spire of All Saints' Church, Ryde (the highest spire) S.E. ½ S., passing between the two buoys belonging to the royal yacht off Osborne, until you see the beacons leading into Wootton river, the outermost of which bears from the inner royal yacht's buoy S.E. ¾ S., 2 miles distant. If beating, give the shore a good berth, to avoid several rocky patches, especially Wootton rocks, which run out from the western shore of the Creek. Do not attempt to enter unless these rocks are covered, or you will find less than 5 feet in the channel. The entrance will be recognised by a row of posts, the outermost having a triangle on the top, the second having a crosspiece, and the third a notice-board. A single post on the Ryde side of the chaunel marks the outermost point of the eastern mud. To enter, leave the *triangle,* the *cross,* and the *notice-board* on your *starboard* hand. Leave the next post *to port.* The channel now becomes very narrow. The western mud is marked by small sticks. After passing the Coast-guard boathouse (the Coastguard on duty will usually sing out directions to you if asked) port your helm, and sail close past a crowd of small yachts and boats, leaving them on your right. The left-hand mud, opposite the boats, is marked by diminutive sticks. Anchor in a pool above the boats, close to a boathouse in a wood, keeping well off the eastern shore to avoid a mud-bank. From here you can sail in the dinghy about a mile up the river at high tide, to Wootton Bridge, through a very charming bit of scenery. Do not stay long on shore at Wootton Bridge, as the river dries completely out at low tide.

Cowes to Ryde, 5 *miles.*—After passing Old Castle buoy (R.), steer for the head of Ryde pier, S.E. ½ E., 4¾ miles, and anchor (in fine weather) among the other yachts near the end of the pier, taking care to keep clear of the prohibited anchorage off the pier-head, which is marked by three red and three red and white buoys, No. 5 being a bell buoy. The best place is rather inside the pier-head on the W. side.

At Cowes, Ryde, Southsea, and similar places, small yachts frequently either lose their anchors, or are seriously delayed, through getting foul of old moorings. This is avoided by the simple expedient of always bending a buoy rope to the anchor before letting go in these places. Ryde is not a place for a small yacht to anchor for the night, except in very settled weather.

Cowes to Bembridge, 10 *miles.*—After passing Old Castle buoy (R.) steer for Sand Head, B. and W. Cheq. buoy S.E. by E., 6 miles. This will keep you clear of Ryde Sand, which stretches nearly a mile and a half from the shore, and dries at low tide. If beating, it will be best for a stranger not to approach the shore nearer than a line joining Ryde pier-head with Sand Head buoy; but at certain states of the tide, and after consultation with local seafarers, you can sail over Ryde Sand, and thus save a considerable distance.

Leave the Sand Head buoy on your starboard, and steer for the Warner Light-vessel S.E. ½ E., distant 2¼ miles, until you are between No Man's Fort, and the first of four torpedo G. and W. buoys. You can then port your helm, and steer for Bembridge Fort, S. ¼ W., 2 miles. If you are able to go over the sand, you can steer from Ryde pier-head direct to Nettlestone Point, on rounding which you will see Bembridge Fort ahead of you, distant 1½ mile. This saves a distance of about a mile, but should only be attempted after due consideration of the state of the tide, as before mentioned.

Entering Bembridge requires care, as the bar is very shoal and the bottom rocky. Leave the fort on the *port* hand, and make the fairway buoy (B. with staff and head), leaving it on your *starboard* hand. Leave the B. and W. Cheq. buoys on your *port* hand, the black ones to *starboard*. The third buoy, an open frame, must be left to *starboard*. The bar dries at L.W. springs. The depth on the bar can be found by observing the rocks on St. Helen's Point, to the right of the sea mark. If these are just covered, there will be not less than 6 feet over the bar; or if the rocks round the base of Bembridge Fort are covered, there will be 9 feet. Heave to or anchor if there is not water enough to enter.

Bembridge to Sandown Bay, about 8 miles.—Consult the local fishermen as to whether there is water enough to take a short cut across the sand. If so, bring St. Helen's sea mark at least two degrees south of St. Helen's Church N.W. ½ N. in order to clear the Cole Rock, off Bembridge Point, which uncovers at L.W. (The rock lies due east 700 yards distant from the Lifeboat House on Bembridge Point.)

Steer S.E. ½ S. until Bembridge buoy (B. and W. Cheq.) bears S.S.E. ¼ E., distant 6 cables, or rather over half a mile. This will bring you clear of Cole Rock, and you can steer S. by W. ½ W., ¾ of a mile, until Culver Cliff bears W. by S. distant 1¾ mile. Now steer for Culver Cliff, giving it a berth of ¼ mile to avoid the rocks at its base: and you will see the town of Sandown, due west of Culver Cliff, 2¼ miles. Anchor for a few hours, a quarter of a mile off the pier in about 6 feet. This expedition should only be undertaken in settled weather. When the weather is unsettled, strong squalls are apt to come off the shore, such as proved fatal to H.M.S. *Eurydice* in 1878.

In case the tide does not suit for going over Bembridge Sands, all danger from Cole Rock will be avoided by keeping outside an imaginary line joining Bembridge Fort with Bembridge buoy (B. and W. Cheq.) S.E. by S. ½ S.

Cowes to Langston Harbour, 12 miles.—After passing Old Castle buoy (R.) steer for the buoy off Gilkicker Point, E. by S. ¾ S., 5 miles. This buoy is white, with a red staff and ball, and is the eastern of two similar buoys marking the course of the measured mile. Pass it on the north side, between it and the G. and W. torpedo buoys. The tide runs very strong here. After passing the buoy steer for the Langston Harbour fairway buoy,

(B. and W. H.S.) E. ¾ S., distant 4⅞ miles, sailing just north of the Spit Fort.

On reaching the fairway buoy, the entrance will be seen between the two points, N. by E. Steer straight in, remembering, however, to allow for the tide, which sets very strongly *across* the channel, outside the entrance. The channel lies between the E. and W. Winner banks, which both dry at L.W. The best time to run in is one hour before H.W. if possible. There are places on the bar of only 1 foot at L.W., and the water is very shallow off the coast from Southsea Castle eastwards: the stranger should therefore not approach the fort on Eastney Point (on the W. side of the entrance to Langston Harbour) within a mile and a half in any direction at L.W. This will ensure him at least 6 feet of water, in which, if the sea is calm, he can anchor and wait for the tide, feeling his way in with the lead.

After passing between the points, as far as the ferry, a snug anchorage will be found in Sinah Lake, in 2½ fathoms, amongst other small craft, on the east side of the entrance. Langston Harbour affords plenty of opportunity for explorations in the dinghy. One can go through to Chichester Harbour, on the east (lowering the mast to pass under two bridges) or Portsmouth Harbour on the W. The mud flats are very extensive, but the principal channels are buoyed. Sinah Lake is a blind.

From Bembridge to Langston.—After crossing the bar, steer for Langston fairway buoy (B. and W. H.S.) N.W., 5½ miles, passing close to on the western side of the Warner Light-vessel, 1½ mile from Bembridge Fort; and on making the buoy, proceed as above.

Cowes to Portsmouth, 8 *miles.*—Steer as for Langston, as far as the white buoy with red staff and globe off Gilkicker Point. Then, if the tide is at half flood or later, leave the G. and W. torpedo buoys to port, and steer for the narrow entrance of the harbour N.E. ½ E. between Blockhouse Fort on the west side, and the town of Portsmouth on the east. Run in and anchor on the Gosport (W.) side, near H.M.S. *Victory,* amongst other yachts, or run higher up past the crowd of shipping before anchoring. There is also good anchorage between H.M.S. *St. Vincent* and the floating bridge. Be careful not to anchor in the line of the floating bridge, which runs across the harbour about ¾ of a mile above the entrance. The tides run very strongly in and out of Portsmouth Harbour, and the wind is baffling, so that it is advisable to have the anchor ready to let go at a moment's notice.

If the tide is lower than half flood, after passing Gilkicker buoy you must steer for the Swashway off Southsea. The leading marks are St. Jude's Spire, Yacht Club House, and Lifeboat House in line E.N.E. St. Jude's Church bears E. by N. ¼ N., distant 2½ miles from the staff and ball buoy off Gilkicker. On passing the B. and W. Cheq. buoy No. 2 you will be in the channel, when you should starboard your helm, and enter Portsmouth harbour as described above. In fine weather, or with the wind off shore, yachts can anchor in Southsea Pool off the bathing machines on Southsea beach (very crowded in summer), but the holding ground is bad, and it is best to pick up a mooring if possible. Beware of getting your anchor foul of old moorings here (see p. 38). The depth is four to seven fathoms.

Cowes to Hamble River, 5 miles.—Leaving Cowes Harbour at any time on the flood, steer for the W. Bramble gas buoy (R. and W. H.S.), which will easily be recognised, about 1 mile from the anchorage. Thence to Calshot Spit Light-vessel (2 masts) N.E. ¼ N., 1¼ mile. Leaving this on your starboard, steer for Castle buoy, also called "Black Jack" (B. and W. Cheq.), N. ¾ mile from the lightship, taking care not to go W. of a line joining it with the lightship. The above course is intended for the guidance of strangers at low or half tide. Near H.W. one can steer direct from Cowes to "Black Jack" (B. and W. Cheq.) N. by E. ¼ E. easterly, 3 miles, and sail over Bramble Bank. This bank uncovers at L.W. springs, and small vessels have been wrecked on it in bad weather.

Leaving Black Jack on the port hand, steer for Hamble Spit buoy (R.) N. ½ W., 1¼ mile. Leave this to *port*, and look for two posts on the eastern mud with *solid* black balls on the top. Leave these on the *starboard* hand. Opposite the second is a third post with a *hollow* ball, which marks the western mud and must be left to *port*. Then steer for red-roofed houses on the Warsash (eastern) shore till abreast Hamble Point, on which is Luke's shipbuilding yard. The channel between Hamble and Warsash will now be open before you. Anchor off Hamble or Warsash in 2 or 3 fathoms, or go higher up, above the training-ship *Mercury*, where a comfortable berth will be found in a bend of the river. The ebb runs very strong here. An expedition up the river Hamble can be made in the dinghy.

Cowes to Southampton, 9 *miles.*—The course is the same as for Hamble as far as "Black Jack," after passing which you simply sail up the middle of Southampton Water, the channel of which is half a mile wide, and is well marked by B. and W. Cheq. buoys on the west, and R. buoys on the east side. Fawley beacon, a post with a triangle, marks the outermost point of the western mud, about 2 miles above Calshot Castle.

After passing Netley Hospital, a magnificent building on the eastern shore, you will see Hythe Pier on the western shore. Leave the Itchen Spit Light-vessel and all red buoys on your *starboard* hand, H.M.S. *Trincomalee* (shortly to be replaced by another man-of-war) on your *port,* and continue your course between the yachts and the Royal Pier, leaving three small B. and W. Cheq. buoys to *port.* The channel is very narrow opposite the Royal Pier, and the tide runs strongly. When past the pier you will see some coal hulks on the west of the channel ; anchor on the town side of the channel opposite these, amongst other small yachts, of which you will see plenty ; or go inside the end of the pier and anchor in 1 fathom well out of the traffic, where you will be sheltered from southerly and easterly winds by the pier. This part is, however, usually very much crowded with small yachts and boats.

In strong N.W. winds you should run up the Itchen River, leaving the light-ship to *port.*

The "Gymp" is a bank of mud and gravel which nearly dries at L.W., stretching from H.M.S. *Trincomalee* to a little above the coal hulks. It is marked on its eastern side by the three small B. and W. buoys mentioned above ; but there is a channel on its western side, known to those familiar with the place. At any high tide a yacht drawing 6 feet can freely sail over it.

The double tides at Southampton (see p. 47) cause the estuary to stand practically at high water for 4 hours ; and excellent sailing can be done on this splendid piece of water. The Royal Southampton Yacht Club, and the Castle Club, organise races for small craft nearly every week in the summer. Dinghy expeditions can be made up the Test and Itchen.

Hamble River to Southampton, 4 *miles.*—On leaving Hamble, do not on any account be tempted to take a short cut over Hamble Spit as the bank is very high, and reaches nearly out to the buoy. Sail out as far as the Hamble buoy, and leaving it on your *star-*

board with a good berth, proceed up Southampton Water, as in the course from Cowes.

Cowes to Newtown River, 5 miles.—After passing Egypt Point, follow the line of coast, keeping outside Gurnard Ledge buoy (R.) and Saltmead buoy (R.). On passing the former, steer for the Newtown River fairway buoy (B.) W. by S. ¼ S., distant 1¼ mile. Pass this buoy close to on either side, and sail in through the middle of the entrance between the two points, using the lead to see that you do not approach either shore too near. Anchor in mid-channel, abreast the second of two notice-boards on the eastern shore. You will probably be at once visited by the coastguard, who is only too glad to converse with a stranger in this lonely part of the coast : and in case you are becalmed outside he will tow you in for a trifle.

If the fairway buoy is not there, or is invisible for want of paint (no buoy could be seen when we visited the place for the purposes of this chapter), you must, after passing the Saltmead buoy (R.), steer for Hamstead Ledge buoy (R.) W. ½ S. until the Newtown coastguard station is over the western shore of the entrance, when you can steer in as above. This will bring you clear of a spit running out from the eastern side of the entrance. The fairway dries to 1 foot at L. W., so it will be best to wait for at least half flood before entering. Approaching from the west, after passing Hamstead Ledge buoy (R.), give the shore a good berth until the C. G. Station shows as above, and then steer in.

Expeditions can be made up the Clamerkin Lake, 4 miles (to the left), and Western Haven, 4 miles (to the right), in the dinghy at high tide.

Cowes to Yarmouth, 9 miles.—Steer as for Newtown River, after passing which, leave Hamstead buoy close to on either side. From here Yarmouth Pier-head bears W. ¾ S., 2¾ miles. Anchor on the east side of the pier at sufficient distance to be out of the track of the Lymington steamers. There is a small harbour on the west side of the pier, with depths of 1 to 2 fathoms, which, however, the stranger should not attempt to enter without local guidance. It is advisable to get a berth in this harbour should the wind come easterly. If a visit to Lymington is contemplated it might be as well to take the steamer across from Yarmouth and back in order to get an idea of the entrance to Lymington River, which is somewhat difficult to make.

Yarmouth is the headquarters of the Solent Yacht Club.

Cowes to Totland Bay 12 *miles, Alum Bay* 13½ *miles, and the Needles* 15 *miles.*—After passing Yarmouth, keep outside the Black Rock buoy (R.), which marks a dangerous rock (N.W. by W. ½ W., ⅓ mile from Yarmouth Pier-head). During springs there is a race in strong winds from Black Rock buoy towards Hurst Castle, about a mile in length, called locally the "Fiddler's race." To avoid it, keep well off shore. After passing two forts, Fort Victoria and Cliff End, giving the latter a good berth, look out for the Warden Ledge buoy (R.), ¾ mile W. by S. ¼ S. from Cliff End Fort. Leave this buoy on the *port* hand, and steer for Totland Pier, ¾ mile S. ¼ W. from it. Anchor in fine weather off the pier in 2 fathoms amongst other yachts. To go from here to Alum Bay, steer for Hatherwood Point, after rounding which, steer for Alum Bay Pier, giving the shore a berth of ¼ of a mile to avoid "Five Rocks," distant 1½ cable N.W. ¾ N. from the pier-head. You can also avoid these rocks by keeping close inshore, but we should prefer to keep outside them. Anchor off the pier in fine weather in 2 fathoms. The Needles Lighthouse is 1 mile from Alum Bay Pier. You can sail down to it from here, taking care to avoid Goose Rock ½ a cable N.W. by N. from the lighthouse. Do not round the Needles, unless you have a fair amount of wind for getting back, as the tides run very strong in all this part. To visit Freshwater Bay, it would be best to round the Needles at about half ebb, and then sail against the tide to Freshwater: anchor there for an hour or so, and start back before the western stream has finished running. This will bring you to the Needles at slack water, and you will have the eastern tide to take you back into the Solent. This expedition is, however, not to be recommended; for if you failed to get back to the Needles before the strength of the flood commenced (if the wind were westerly), your only course would be to run round the whole of the south coast of the Isle of Wight, and make for Bembridge or Portsmouth, a distance of some 25 to 30 miles, as there are no harbours on this coast. There is a race off St. Catherine's Point. In fine weather, and with a westerly wind, by leaving Yarmouth or Lymington about 2 hours before low tide, one can easily make the expedition round the south coast of the Wight by daylight, but it should not be attempted in unsettled weather.

Note that outside Hurst there is a dangerous bank called the *Shingles*, over which the sea constantly breaks, even in fine weather. It stretches from about ¾ of a mile off Hurst Castle, in a south-westerly direction to abreast the Needles. It is marked by three buoys, the one nearest Hurst being B. and W. H.S., the middle R. and W. V.S., and the outer R. and W. Cheq. staff and cage. The ebb sets obliquely across this bank in a westerly direction, and it is advisable therefore not to approach too near in light winds.[1]

Cowes to Beaulieu River, 2½ *miles.*—On leaving Cowes Harbour, the white coastguard boat-house of Lepe will be seen as a prominent mark on the north shore of the Solent, bearing N.W. ½ W., 2½ miles distant. Steer for this till within about a a mile of it, when you must alter your course westerly to avoid the shoal off Stone Point. The best guide for the stranger to avoid this danger is not to go nearer the shore than to bring the two lightships Calshot Spit and Calshot into line, bearing E. by N. ¾ N., and to steer for the red-roofed houses on Need's Oar Point, when they bear W. by N., 2¼ miles distant, until the two white landmarks on the left of the Lepe boat-house are in line. These lead over the deepest part of the bar (3 feet at L.W.). Steer in for the landmarks until you come to some booms with boughs on the top marking the edge of Beaulieu Spit. Give them a fair berth, leaving them to *port.* They are apt to get knocked down by vessels, so that it is as well to use the lead for getting round the end of the spit. Close in to the leading marks the channel takes a sharp turn to the west, and becomes very narrow opposite some black boat-houses about 200 yards above the coastguard boat-house. The shore mud is here marked by a boom. Keep close to this, leaving it to *starboard.* After this, the channel, which widens a good deal, is boomed fairly well the whole way up to Gilbury Hard, some 4 miles from the entrance. Here you can anchor at a sharp bend in the river in 2½ fathoms, and take the dinghy with the rising tide up the river to Beaulieu, some 2 miles above Gilbury. Beaulieu lies in the New Forest, and its river is perhaps the most beautiful of all the Solent inlets.

Beaulieu River should not be attempted by a stranger on the ebb, even with a fair wind, unless he is prepared to run the risk of spending several hours on the mud. If, however, there

---

1 "Use *great caution* in approaching either side, for the strong tides and the heavy breaking sea in bad weather would entail certain destruction on any vessel that might be driven on them."—King's *Channel Pilot.*

is any reason for entering against the ebb, such as night coming on, one might anchor or lie to, and send the dinghy ashore to get the assistance of a coastguard to pilot one in.

Cowes to Lymington River, 8½ *miles.*—After passing Egypt Point steer W. ¼ N. At 3 miles you will pass about 2 cables south of West Lepe, R. and W. Cheq. buoy. With a good glass, and on a clear day, you ought to be able to see "Jack in the basket" from here, a large post with a barrel at the top, which marks the entrance to Lymington River, bearing as above.

When within a mile of "Jack in the basket," steer a little south of the above course, to avoid the large mud-flats on the east side of Lymington River, and in case of doubt use the lead. The channel is not much over 100 yards wide at the entrance. If the banks are covered give "Jack" a berth of 20 to 30 yards, leaving it to *port.* Leave all other beacons to *port* (with a good berth) save two small ones, just inside the entrance, which leave to *starboard,* and anchor in 2 fathoms about ½ a mile above the entrance. You can sail farther up, but as the channel is complicated it would be best to wait for low tide before doing so. You can land either at the coastguard station, and walk to the town, about ½ a mile, or row up to the ferry above the shipbuilding yard, about 1¼ mile from the anchorage.

In approaching Lymington from Beaulieu or Southampton Water, give the shore a berth of at least ½ a mile to avoid the mud-flats. For clearing Stone Point, see p. 45.

In approaching Lymington from the west, keep well outside a beacon situated half a mile S.W. by W. from "Jack in the basket," marking the end of a sewer-pipe, and give "Jack in the basket" a good berth in rounding.

We have now described some of the principal expeditions to be made from Cowes. We have not given directions for night work, as the distances are so short that, with the exception of the one round the island, they can all be easily accomplished by daylight and on a single tide. In case it is ever necessary to anchor in a fog, or for the night, in the Solent it will be best to get close to one of the shores, in order to avoid the steamer traffic ; and a riding light must always be shown at night, however secluded you may imagine your anchorage to be.

Longer expeditions can of course be made to Chichester, Littlehampton, Shoreham, etc., on the east, and Poole, Swanage, or Weymouth, on the west. But directions for these are outside the scope of this work, and must be sought in the ordinary pilot books.

Tides.—The tides in the Solent are very strong, and must be carefully studied. It will be useless to attempt any long expedition, as say from Cowes to Lymington or back, against a spring tide, unless a strongish fair wind is blowing. But, on the other hand, it does not matter which way the wind is blowing, if you have the tide with you; the only drawback to a head-wind in this case being that if it has any strength you will certainly get very wet. At Hurst the tide runs at the rate of 5 knots during springs, and rates of 3 to 4 knots are met with in other portions of the Solent.

A remarkable feature here is the occurrence of double high tides. That is to say, after ordinary high water the tide falls for about an hour (the time varies according to the place), and then rises again for about an hour, till it reaches a somewhat higher level than before. It then falls rapidly for 4 hours, when low tide is reached. It will be seen therefore that the fall, which elsewhere takes 6 hours, in the Solent has to be done in 4 hours; and this is one cause of the strong currents. This phenomenon is supposed by some to be caused by the main channel tidal wave meeting the portion which runs inside the Wight, at Spithead, and causing a reflex wave in the Solent.

At Cowes the double high water occurs only at spring tides; while at Southampton, Beaulieu, Lymington, etc., it occurs at neaps as well.

The second high tide occurs at Cowes 1 hour after the first, at Southampton 2¼ hours, Lymington 1 hour 50 minutes, Yarmouth and Hurst 2 hours after. Hence, if a stranger gets aground on any of the numerous mud-banks (as he is bound to do occasionally) within a short time after high tide, he has the comfort of knowing that the second tide will come to his rescue. But if, on the other hand, he gets aground after the second tide has commenced to fall, he will find himself high and dry in an astonishingly short space of time; and if he does not wish to remain in one place with no possibility of moving or getting ashore for many hours, his best course is to drop his anchor, lower his sails, and take to the dinghy as quickly as possible.

The times of first high water in the Solent vary considerably at different places. Thus, it is high water at the Needles 1 hour earlier than at Cowes; at Hurst and Yarmouth ¾ of an hour earlier, Lymington 20 minutes earlier, Calshot ¾ of an hour *later*, Southampton 15 minutes earlier (so that, strange as it may appear, it is high water at Southampton Docks 1 hour earlier than at Calshot). Ryde high water is 45 minutes later, and Portsmouth about 1 hour later, than at Cowes.

The set of the current is affected by the meeting near Spithead of the two tidal streams, as well as by the various inlets. In the Solent the west stream commences at H.W., and the east at L.W. During springs the rate is 3½ to 4 knots. Off Cowes the west stream commences about an hour before H.W. and the east about 1¼ hour before L.W.—rate, 3 to 3½ knots.

At Calshot Light-vessel the western stream begins ¼ of an hour before H.W. at Cowes, and the eastern stream 5 hours after.

At Spithead the west stream makes 1¾ hour before H.W. at Cowes, and the east stream 3¼ hours after.

Off Bembridge the ebb makes N.W. 1½ hour before H.W. at Cowes.

Off Hill Head the west stream makes at 1½ hour before H.W. at Cowes, and the east stream at 3¾ after.

At certain states of the tide, the current opposite Calshot will be found to flow into Southampton Water on one side of the channel, while it flows out on the other. The lightships and the fishing boats at anchor (if any) will show which way the tide is setting.

A useful card, called the "Solent Tide Calculator," is published by Norie and Wilson, 156 Minories, E.C. (price 1s.). The tides are calculated from H.W. at Portsmouth, the time of which can of course be found from any nautical almanac. Messrs. Norie and Wilson also publish a series of Solent tide charts at 7s. 6d., which would be very useful to the stranger.

In the above remarks we do not pretend to treat the Solent tides exhaustively, but merely to give the reader a general idea of what to expect. The coastguards and the local fishermen are usually very obliging in imparting information regarding tides and currents and other local matters; while, on the other hand, the amateur yachtsman will sometimes find himself consulted by the captain of a passing coaster on questions of local pilotage. He must remember that some of the marks in the smaller inlets, being little better than sticks set up in the mud, are liable to be washed away, or knocked over by boats. They are usually replaced within a reasonable time; but it is as well always to have the lead and kedge ready for use in entering unknown creeks.

FRESHWATER AND YARMOUTH

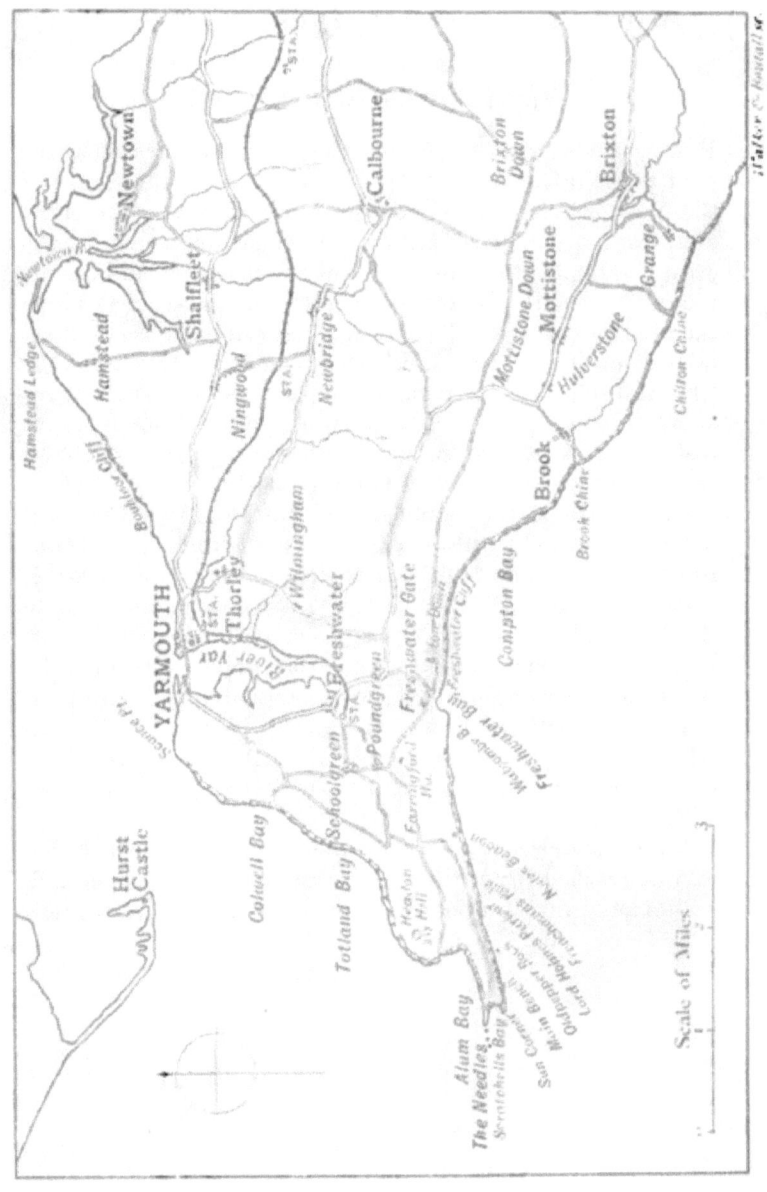

Scale of Miles

YARMOUTH

FROM COWES TO YARMOUTH

FEW tourists care to follow the coast to *Yarmouth*, the
next point of much note, broken as it is by the creeks of
the Newtown River. NEWTOWN itself (*The Newtown Arms
Inn*) was once a parliamentary borough, for which sat the
great Churchill, afterwards Duke of Marlborough, and George
Canning ; but it is now only a scattering of cottages along
the shore of a navigable creek, preserving in the school-
house, once the Town Hall, a silver mace of Edward IV.'s
time as a relic of its bygone municipal dignity. The scenery
about this creek is often attractive ; fair fishing is to be
had in at least one branch, and the botanist will find
several notable aquatic plants on its banks.

Yarmouth is more likely to be reached from Cowes, if
not by steamer, by rail through Newport, from which trains
run to it in half an hour. The first station is Carisbrooke,
where the castle may be seen on its wooded eminence to
the left, and on the right the edge of Parkhurst Forest.
The country then becomes somewhat tame, enlivened by
glimpses of the Solent over a stretch of green. But the
next station serves for two villages, *Shalfleet* and *Calbourne*,
lying a mile or so respectively to each side of the line.
which may be judged worth a visit.

SHALFLEET (*New Inn*) is on the way to Newtown, which
may be reached hence through a pleasant lane. The church
will at once arrest attention with its large square western

4

tower. This tower is Norman, the work of the eleventh
century, and there is other work of the same date in the
church. The north doorway is Norman, and the tympanum
is filled up with a curious sculpture of a figure resting his
hands on two animals, though some antiquaries will have
it that the allegory so rudely carved represents *David
contending with the Lion and the Bear.* The remainder of
the building is of various dates, but chiefly of the fourteenth century, and its most interesting features are the
windows in the south aisle, the chancel-arch, and the
arcades which separate the nave from the aisles. There
are some rudely-sculptured shields, dated 1630, in the
south aisle, and a monumental slab on the chancel-floor;
the latter, measuring 5 feet 10 inches, is adorned. with
shield and spear, and evidently dates from the early part
of the thirteenth century.

CALBOURNE (*Sun Inn*) lies to the left under the Downs,
with its green and pond, making a very pleasant bit of
village scenery. Around it are quarries of freshwater limestone, where excellent specimens of the fossils peculiar to
these strata may readily be obtained; and the botanist
should be on the look-out for the *Orchis ustulata, Inula
Helenium, Verbena officinalis, Neottia Nidusaris,* and *Bup-
leurum rotundifolium,* of which some fine plants are often
procurable.

The old Church, dedicated to All Saints, one of the most
interesting in the island, consists of a nave and south aisle,
chancel and south aisle, a north transept, and a tower at the
west end of the aisle. There is a good deal of fair Early
English work. The east window of the chancel consists of
two lancets with a trefoiled circle above; the east window of
the aisle also of two lancets with a quatrefoil above. The
tower, which was rebuilt in 1752, bears the inscription:
"I am risen from the ruins of near 70 years, A.D. 1752,
T. Hollis, J. Casford, Churchwardens." In a slab inserted
in the pavement of the south aisle is a well-preserved and
beautifully-executed brass effigy of an armed knight, his
feet resting upon a dog, of the time of Edward III. (1340),

supposed to commemorate one of the Montacutes, Lords of Swainston. A quaint brass plate, bearing two figures of Time and Death, affixed to the north wall of the chancel, is inscribed to the memory of the "reverend, religious, and learned precher, Daniel Evance" (died 1652), with an anagram on his name, " I can deal even."

The chancel was renovated and a reredos erected some years ago.

Near Calbourne are the *Stone Steps* pleasure gardens, frequented for concerts, holiday fêtes, etc., by the people of Newport, from which this village is 5½ miles by road. Some agreeable walks may be taken hence, by way of *Newbridge* to *Yarmouth* (6 m.), through Lynch Lane and Calbourne Bottom over the downs to *Brixton* (3½ m.), or from Calbourne to *Freshwater Gate* (6 m.). The railway carries us on by *Ningwood* and *Thorley*, till at Yarmouth we again touch the sea, and two miles more brings us to the terminus at Freshwater.

YARMOUTH

(George Hotel, Bugle Inn).

This little town or big village is of no great interest to the strangers except as one of the entrances into the island. Steamers cross from the L. & S.W. trains at Lymington, communicating with those between Newport and Freshwater. The passage in open water is so short as hardly to give time for being sick ; but an inconvenience of this route is that at Yarmouth one has to walk some little way to reach its most unpretending station. Coaches run also, in summer at least, to Totland Bay, and Freshwater Gate. The passage to Lymington puts us there on the edge of the New Forest scenery.

Yarmouth—not to be confused with its great namesake in Norfolk, as this Yar is a different river from that of the same name on the other side of the island—is a sleepy old place of less than a thousand inhabitants that can boast to have seen better days. In the thirteenth century it was a port of some importance ; and up to 1832 returned two members to parliament, though the number of electors seldom exceeded nine. Its most renowned worthy was Sir Robert Holmes, governor of the island, 1667-1692, and one of the stoutest seamen of his day. His mansion is now the *George Hotel.*

The church, the original one having been burned by the French, was built 1611-1614, and repaired in 1873. On the south side of the chancel stands a fine white marble statue of Sir Robert Holmes, beneath an arched canopy with Ionic columns of solid porphyry. A Latin epitaph records the chief events of his stirring career. The body of the statue—an exquisite work of art—as well as the sculptor engaged upon it, were captured, it is said, by Holmes on board a French ship. It was intended to be completed with a head of Louis XIV., but Holmes "compelled the sculptor to receive him as a sitter," instead of *le Grand Monarque.* This rough old seaman conferred many benefits upon Yarmouth; and the embankment of its marshes was carried out under his direction.

Some remains of the old castle have been incorporated in the battery defending the Yar, to be seen on application, but there is not much to see. The collection of curiosities including a Clepsydra, a black-letter Bible (1613), formerly kept at the *Bugle Inn,* is now shown at Butler's refreshment rooms opposite the church.

About a mile to the east of the town, the *Bouldnor* estate is being developed as a watering-place, for which its wooded shore and sandy beach seem to recommend it. A sea-wall and road among the building plots have already been made. There are pleasant walks along the Bouldnor cliffs to *Hamstead,* which we have heard described, on high scientific authority, as the most interesting place, geologically, in the island; then inland to Shalfleet (2½ miles) and the other villages of this too much neglected district. Our next edition will probably have to make more of Bouldnor.

The town of Yarmouth gives itself no watering-place airs, unless a feeble claim to be not so much exposed to cold winds as Ryde, and to hot suns as Ventnor, yet we have seen watering-places with less to build on. There is a stretch of sand for children, and at low tide a smell from the Yar estuary that should be medicinal. The mouth of this estuary is crossed by a wooden bridge, beyond which a rather pleasant walk runs along the shore, soon blocked by *Fort Victoria*. But the stranger may turn up through the woods by a military road, formally barred once a year, thence reaching *Cliff End Fort* in an easy half-hour, from which he may turn inland for *Freshwater*, or with a little license of harmless trespassing get down into *Colwell Bay*. The high road makes it about 2 miles to *Freshwater* village. On the other side of the Yar, a road through *Morley*, *Wilmingham* and *Easton*, leads below Afton Down to *Freshwater Bay*, where the Yar rises close to one shore of the island to run its course of a few miles to the other. So close indeed to the beach is its source that the salt water will be washed into the stream by rough weather.

The peninsular promontory on which we now enter is strongly fortified, commanding as it does the entrance to the Solent. The eccentric and dissipated painter George Morland spent some time in this neighbourhood at the end of last century, when, flying to Yarmouth from bailiffs, he was taken up as a spy, his sketching no doubt having brought him into suspicion. Our authorities are not given to over-jealousy on this head; but the pleasure-seeking public must not complain if they find their movements here a little restrained by the frequent fortifications.

Before leaving Yarmouth, as we have found so little to say about a part of the island least visited by ordinary tourists, we will take the opportunity of inserting a general account of its geology for those to whom the section of the coast thus cursorily treated will have a special interest through its Eocene formations and fossil beds.

GEOLOGICAL STRUCTURE OF THE ISLE OF WIGHT

Among geologists the Isle of Wight has acquired a well-deserved reputation as a locality of exceptional interest, and the geology of the district has been the subject of much careful and painstaking research. This is mainly due to the fact that a large number of highly fossiliferous strata, ranging from the Wealden

at the base to the Upper Eocene at the top, are favourably exposed
for study within its limited area. But not only is the interest
attaching to the locality exceptionally great from the strati-
graphical and palæontological points of view, but also from the
point of view of the physical geographer, for there are few places
in the British Islands where the effects of the geological structure
of a district upon its scenery are better exemplified. Indeed,
some acquaintance with the geological structure of the island is
necessary in order to appreciate fully the great diversity and
wonderful beauty of its scenery, and therefore a few remarks on
the subject are offered in this place.

The following list of the different geological formations found
in the Isle of Wight is taken from Mr. H. W. Bristow's excellent
memoir on the subject, explanatory of the Geological Survey Map
(sheet 10) :—

KAINOZOIC OR TERTIARY STRATA.

Fluvio-Marine.

Hamstead Beds } Upper Eocene.
Bembridge Beds }

Osborne or St. Helen's Beds
Headon Beds

Bagshot Beds.

Upper Bagshot Sands
Barton Clay }
Bracklesham Beds } Middle Bagshot
Lower Bagshot Beds

Middle Eocene.

Lower Eocene.

London Clay.
Plastic Clay, or Woolwich and Reading Series.

UPPER MESOZOIC OR SECONDARY STRATA.

Cretaceous.

Chalk
Upper Greensand } Upper.
Gault

Lower Greensand
Hasting's Sand and Weald Clay } Lower.

The surface distribution of these strata is shown in the accompanying map. It will be seen that the northern half of the
island is composed of Tertiary strata, and the southern half of
secondary (Cretaceous) strata.

A range of high chalk downs, forming the uppermost portion of the cretaceous system, runs from west to east along the middle of the island, and breaking off abruptly at either extremity, forms the precipitous chalk cliffs of Freshwater on the one hand, and Culver on the other.

This range of chalk downs (comprising High Down, Afton Down, Shalcomb Down, Mottistone Down, Brixton Down, Apes Down, Bowcombe Down, Gallibury Down, Rowborough Down, Lemerston Down, Gansons Down, Gatcomb Down, Chillerton Down, Mount Joy, St. George's Down, Arreton Down, Messley Down, Ashey Down, Brading Down, and Bembridge Down) may be regarded as the backbone of the island. It varies considerably in width, being narrow at the two extremities, and widest in the neighbourhood of Gallibury and Rowborough Downs, where it attains a width of over 3 miles. It is traversed in its centre by a fault running in a north and south direction, which has given rise to the valley of the Medina. The same thing appears also to have occurred at Freshwater, where the River Yar, rising within a few yards of the beach at Freshwater Bay, runs in a northerly direction through a gap in the chalk range, to empty itself into the Solent at Yarmouth.

The chalk downs are not entirely confined to the central range, but, owing to the manner in which the strata are folded, occur again in the south of the island as Shanklin Down, Boniface Down, Rew Down, Week Down, and St. Catherine's Down. In fact, the enormous pressure to which they have at some remote period been subjected has caused the cretaceous strata in the Isle of Wight to become bulged upwards, so that each bed appears, when seen in north and south section, to have the form of an arch. The uppermost portion of this arch was originally formed by a continuous layer of chalk of enormous thickness, with the Greensand lying beneath it. The northern slope of the chalk arch is covered up and entirely concealed by the later Tertiary beds. In the centre of the island, however, it appears as the great central range of chalk downs. South of this range the chalk, which originally formed the uppermost part of the arch, has been entirely denuded by atmospheric agencies, so as to expose the underlying Greensand ; while south of the broad track of Greensand it appears again in St. Catherine's Boniface, and Shanklin Downs, etc. This will be better understood by reference to the accompanying section.

The uppermost portion of the chalk, or white chalk, is
characterised by the presence in it of enormous quantities of
flints. These may be well seen in the cliffs in the neighbourhood
of Freshwater, where they appear in long lines following the
almost vertical planes of stratification. The lower, or grey
chalk is distinguished from the white chalk by the absence of
flints.

The chalk formation may be studied to the best advantage in
Scratchell's Bay, near Freshwater, and at Culver Cliff, at both
of which localities good series of fossils may be collected. Fossils
may also be collected, but not nearly so abundantly, from the
numerous chalk pits which occur at various localities inland. The
commonest fossils found in the chalk are molluscs (*Belemnites,
Inoceramus, Terebratula*), Echinoderms (*Ananchytes ovatus,
Galerites albogalerus, Micraster coranguinum*), and fragments
of vitreous sponges. Belemnites and Echinoderms may be
abundantly collected from a recent fall of the cliff in Scratchell's
Bay, the former being known to the inhabitants of the island as
"Fairy's fingers." Here also may be obtained quantities of a
curious little fossil hydrozoon (*Porosphæra*), called by the inhabitants "seeds."

The strata below the chalk may be studied to great advantage
in the cliffs between Freshwater Bay and Rocken End. In
Compton Bay is seen the junction between the chalk and the
underlying Greensand, and farther south, in the neighbourhood
of Brook Point, the Wealden, the lowermost of all the strata
represented in the island, makes its appearance in the form of
red and green variegated marls, constituting the earthy cliffs.

From the Wealden cliffs in the neighbourhood of Brook and
Cowlease Chines abundant remains of great extinct reptiles
(*Iguanodon*) have been obtained, but it is not easy to find any
fossils of value without prolonged and systematic search. At
Brook Point also are the remains of a fossil forest of Wealden
age. "The ledge at the base of the cliff, which formed so
prominent a feature of this part of the coast when seen from a
distance, consists of indurated sandstone enclosing trunks and
branches of large trees completely petrified, many of which are
strewn along the strand, and half buried in the sand and shingle.
The projecting masses at the foot of the cliff are the broken edges
of the strata, and the trunks of fossil trees ; the upper and less
coherent deposits having been washed away. . . . The trees are

all lying prostrate and confusedly intermingled. There are no erect trunks, nor any other indications that the forest was submerged with its native soil, like that of the Isle of Portland. On the contrary, this accumulation of fossil trees resembles the rafts, as they are termed, that are annually brought down from the interior of the country by the tributary streams of the great rivers of North America, and which, hurried along by those vast floods, entangle in their course the remains of animals and plants that may happen to lie in the beds of the rivers, or be floating in the water. These rafts are at length drifted out of the course of the currents, and becoming loaded with mud, sand, and other extraneous matter, sink down, and are engulfed in the bed of the delta " (Mantell).

The Wealden strata are also exposed over a small area in Sandown Bay, but not nearly so advantageously for the purposes of study as on the opposite coast, between Brook and Atherfield.

Pursuing our journey from Brook along the shore in the direction of Rocken End, at Atherfield Point we again come upon the Greensand formation. The high sandstone cliffs to the south-east of Atherfield are abundantly fossiliferous, and many interesting specimens may be obtained from the fragments of rock which lie scattered at the foot of the cliff. One of the commonest and most perfectly preserved of the fossils here found is the *Terebratula sella*, which may often be obtained in handfuls. Here also are found the so-called "fossil lobsters" (*Meyeria vectensis*), in reality a species of cray-fish, of which the present writer has obtained remains of as many as ten specimens from a single block of sandstone lying on the beach.

At Blackgang, a little farther to the south-west, may be seen perhaps the best example of those remarkable chines, or ravines, excavated in the cliffs by the action of running water, for which the island is so famous. "These chines owe their origin, in the first instance, to springs of water, which, in their short and rapid course from the higher grounds, wear away the land and the face of the cliff, where they find an outlet to the sea, into the steep and precipitous escarpments which bound the sides of the narrow gully through which the water runs " (Bristow).

Between the upper and lower divisions of the Greensand occurs a layer of blue clay, known to the inhabitants under the expressive name of "Blue Slipper," and to geologists as the Gault. To the presence of this layer of clay is mainly due the very characteristic, wild, and romantic scenery of the Undercliff.

The Undercliff is a narrow tract of country lying along the south coast of the island between St. Catherine's and Boniface Downs. This strip of land is shut in and protected on the north by a high range of perpendicular chalk and sandstone cliffs. The lower portion of these cliffs is formed of Upper Greensand rocks, which rest upon the above-mentioned layer of blue Gault clay. This clay, when saturated with water, yields under the pressure of the superincumbent rocks, and allows them to slide off. Repeated falls of the cliff have been brought about in this manner, so that the land between the foot of the cliffs and the sea is now a tumbled mass of huge fallen rocks.

"Most of the old churches on the south side of the island have been built of Upper Greensand stone, which, though soft and easily worked when first taken from the quarry, becomes excessively hard and tough after it has been exposed to the atmosphere for a short time" (Bristow).

Having now traced the strata from the top of the chalk to the Wealden, which it will be remembered is the oldest of the formations exposed in the island, it remains to speak of the more recent, Tertiary (Eocene) beds which constitute the northern half of the island.

The junction of the chalk with the Eocene formation is admirably shown in Alum Bay. "In this remarkable section the whole of the strata from the chalk to the Fluvio-marine formation are displayed in unbroken succession, and that too in a manner the most favourable for close examination, in consequence of their being thrown into a vertical position by the action of the same elevating force which has caused the chalk to assume its present high inclination.

"When the face of the cliffs has been laid more than usually bare, and the colours of the various beds have been heightened by heavy rains, the aspect of the bay, always beautiful, is rendered still more striking. Every bed is then revealed to the eye from the base of the cliff to where it crops out at its summit, and while some of the beds attract the attention by their contrast in colour, others, like the coals in the Bracklesham series, the conglomerate bed dividing that series from the overlying Barton Clay, and the bed of white pipeclay in the lower Bagshot series, which is so crowded with vegetable remains, are not only rendered conspicuous by their different colours, but, standing out from the rest of the strata, they become useful by enabling the observer more readily to perceive from a distance the positions and limits of the various formations " (Bristow).

Leaving Alum Bay and continuing our journey around the base of Headon Hill, we come upon the well-known Headon Beds, which constitute the lowest portion of the Fluvio-marine series. The strata are here no longer inclined at a high angle as in Alum Bay, but lie almost horizontally. The broken crumbling cliffs which form the northern side of Headon Hill abound with well-preserved fossils, the most beautiful and at the same time perhaps the commonest of which is the *Planorbis evomphalus*.

From this point onwards to Cowes the shore is formed of low, earthy crumbling cliffs, with occasional bands of freshwater limestone. Almost everywhere they are highly fossiliferous, and in Thorness Bay the fossil shells may be picked out from amongst the decaying clays in any quantities. Farther on, on the south side of Gurnard Bay, an interesting Insect bed has been discovered. It consists of a single thin stratum of very hard, fine-grained grayish rock, with a conchoidal fracture, and many exquisitely preserved fossil insects and spiders have been obtained from it.

In the neighbourhood of Binstead, near Ryde, extensive quarries have been excavated in the freshwater limestone, from which formerly numerous fossils were obtainable. The quarries are now, however, deserted, and but few fossils are to be found.

The visitor who is desirous of making a more thorough examination of the Tertiary formations of the island should on no account omit to pay a visit to Whitecliff Bay, where the Eocene beds may again be studied to great advantage in a section somewhat similar to that exposed in Alum Bay, and where abundant fossils may be obtained.

The influence of geological structure upon scenery is, as has been already indicated, very strikingly illustrated in the case of the Isle of Wight. If we contrast the gently-undulating barren chalk downs in the centre of the island with the well-wooded country to the north, and the high, precipitous chalk cliffs of Freshwater and Culver with the low, crumbling muddy cliffs of the north coast, and with the Greensand and Wealden cliffs of the south-west coast, we have sufficient evidence of the truth of this statement.

We ought not to dismiss this portion of our subject without

at least a passing reference to the excellent collection of local fossils in the Isle of Wight Museum at Newport. This collection has recently been rearranged, and affords great facilities for the identification of specimens. It ought certainly to be inspected by all visitors who are interested in the subject.

FRESHWATER AND YARMOUTH

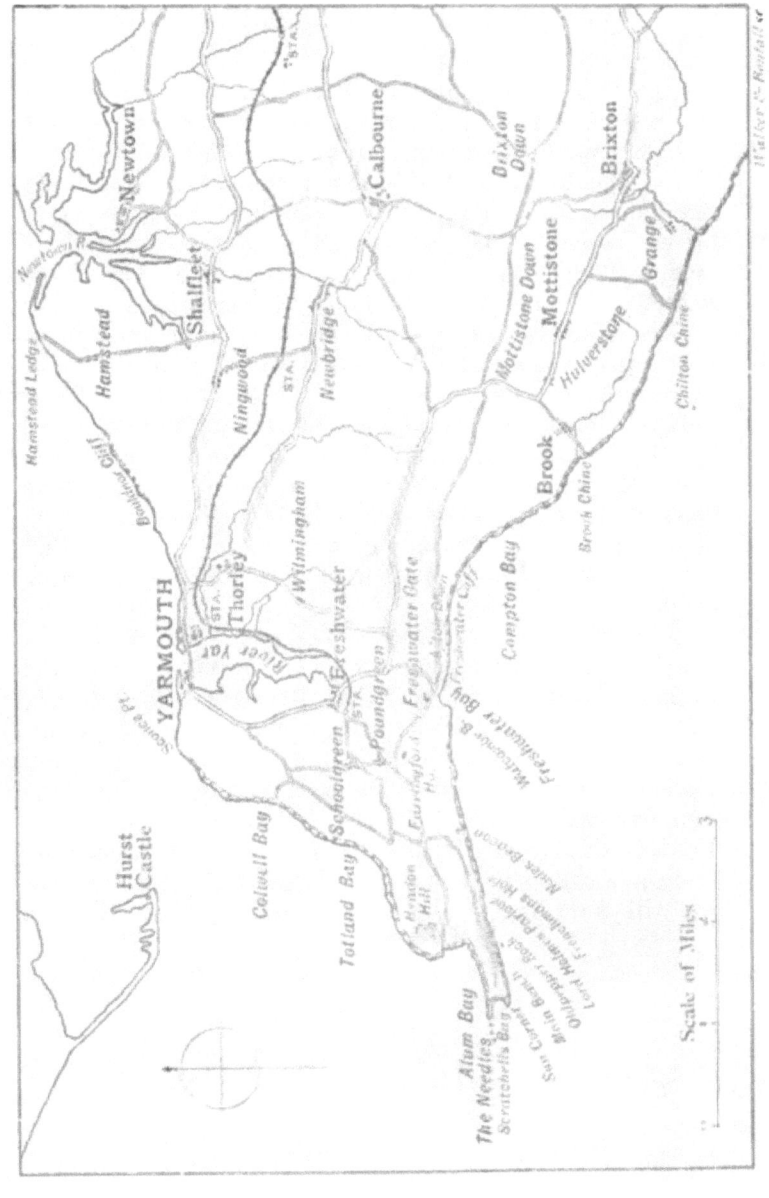

FRESHWATER

UNDER this name, probably derived from the peculiarity of a stream of fresh water rising so near the sea, we must include a whole district forming the south-western corner of the island, which is of singular attraction, as within a space to be walked round in a couple of hours or so, it presents some of the finest specimens of the two kinds of Isle of Wight scenery. Between the grand downs of the south side and the pleasant cliffs of the north, lie two miles of very pretty rurality, with lanes, shady hedgerows, stiles, field-paths, and scattered hamlets that recall the most characteristic beauties of the English Midlands. The village of Freshwater itself, near the station, is surrounded by others sociably straggling into each other, *School Green*, *Pound Green*, *Sheepwash Green*, whose very names almost describe them ; then the coast is dotted with an alternation of young watering-places, and forts or military posts that help to swell the population of this prosperous-looking neighbourhood.

The village of FRESHWATER (*Red Lion Inn*) consists of a few houses clustered round the old church, close to the station. In the larger adjacent village of School Green, and elsewhere, are various inns, which in more than one case take the style of hotels ; but we fancy their main custom comes from Mr. Thomas Atkins, or his non-commissioned officers. All the best accommodation is at Freshwater Bay, or Freshwater Gate, as it is called from lying in a *gap* in the Downs ; and this very agreeable place we will accordingly take for our headquarters. It is a small place as yet, the late Poet Laureate, who was the chief proprietor, having disfavoured its development ; and we cannot expect cheapness at such a choice retreat.   In winter, indeed, when the climate is by no means severe, one might have board in the hotels at very reasonable prices ; in August it is otherwise.

FRESHWATER BAY

Hotels : *Freshwater, Albion, Temperance ;* by the sea ;—*Stark's* (C.), a little way back, near the Post Office.

All the Freshwater coaches make this their goal, putting up at the chief hotel, which from the slope of the Downs overlooks the little bay.   The Albion stands at the very edge, so that one has only a few yards to go to the half-dozen machines which exploit this convenient shore, with all the half-dozen idlers of the place as rather too close spectators. There is a little esplanade that has much ado to hold its own against winds and waves ; and behind it a group of genteel cottages and gardened lodging-houses displays itself effectively in the hollow.   The main body of the village stands rather farther back, throwing out outposts indeed all the way to the station, which is little more than a mile off.   The church here is represented by an iron room, where services are held in the season.   One or two dissenting chapels are located near the bay ; and Mr. Ward's private chapel near Totland Bay is open to his Catholic co-religionists.

At the eastern horn of the little bay stand two prominent masses of chalk, separated from the cliff, and resembling the Needles on a smaller scale.   One of these is the celebrated *Freshwater Arch,* the arched formation of which is not apparent from the other end.   At low tide it can be inspected, with its companion the *Stag Rock,* as can the *Freshwater Cave* on the other side of the bay, but only at very low water.   A swim may be had towards the arch with the morning tide ; but better, at high water, in *Watcombe Bay* round the opposite corner, reached by a steep path from beyond the fort.   The safest bathing for nonswimmers is on the smooth and spacious sands of *Compton Bay*, reached by half-an-hour's walk along the Downs eastwards. Those who can fully trust themselves on such enterprises may by boat or canoe gain plenty of secluded spots along this precipitous coast, where—

> "The hoary channel
> Tumbles a breaker on chalk and sand."

We all know something of the beauties of Freshwater from its illustrious squire, the late Poet Laureate, who shrank in almost morbid horror from sight of the strangers he helped to bring here, and finally built himself another residence on the wilds of Blackdown, near Haslemere, henceforth spending only part of the year at Farringford House. This mansion lies hidden among thick trees, a little way back from the bay, "close to the ridge of a noble Down." Behind the "carelessly ordered garden," a bridge across the lane is said to have made a favourite observatory for the poet, who would stand there by night looking down towards the sea in the moonshine.

There are various amusing anecdotes going to show how those who came here to hunt a lion were apt to find a bear. The first Lord Tennyson's dislike to intruders has proved infectious among some of his neighbours; or it may be said that for their exclusion from certain of the pretty spots on the island, the public are themselves to blame by abuse of a privilege they might have continued to enjoy had vulgar mischief been always duly restrained. Still, however, there is no lack of charming bye-ways open hereabouts. For instance, in going across to *Totland Bay* the shady lane round Farringford House may be taken, through a gate on the left just before reaching the Post Office from the sea. By the first turn to the left, this also gives access to the *Freshwater Down*. Holding on to the end of this lane, one can find one's way across the peninsula by permitted paths; but we shrink from the intricacy of direction, and must refer the reader to local guidance, while the Beacon on the height of the Downs will always serve as a landmark, Totland Bay lying opposite this point. The

walker by the road takes most of its turns to the left ; but
the last steep rise, indicated by a bend of the telegraph
wires, bends abruptly to the right.　Near the top of this,
at the left, a gate gives entrance to a hedgerow path, by
which one descends behind a farm to the west end of the
turf walk that serves Totland Bay as an esplanade, and the
base of Headon Hill.　Almost any of the parting roads,
however, if we keep the general direction, will bring us
eventually to the Totland Bay Hotel, through one or other
of the inland villages ; and it may be said that there
is here, as in most parts of the island, a commendable
abundance of guide-posts.

But most visitors will prefer to pass all round the coast
of this grand promontory ; and thus we propose to conduct
them first on foot, then, if they have stomach for such an
adventure, by boat.　The way on to the Down leads behind the stables of the Freshwater Hotel, and past a fort
that takes up the first point on which one would like to
linger.　A steady ascent brings us to the *Nodes Beacon*,
where from the height of 500 feet we have a splendid view
of the whole peninsula and the sea on either side—on
the left the Channel, on the right Alum Bay, Headon Hill,
Totland Bay, and the stretch of the Solent.　The present
commonplace landmark is being replaced by an Iona Cross
in memory of Tennyson.

On we go along the crest of the Downs, so smooth that
bicycles find a track here.　Another sport forces itself on
our attention.　The Downs above Alum Bay are now laid
out for golf ; and the same game has lately been started on
Afton Down, so that Freshwater enjoys the distinction of
lying between two golf-links, both of them, we fancy, more
favoured in the air than in the ground, which seems too
unbroken in its character.

After half-an-hour or more steady walking, we gradually descend towards the *Needles*, the three outmost masses
of which are soon visible at the foot of the promontory,
where the Downs drop precipitously from a height of 440
feet into *Scratchell's Bay*.　But we may no longer approach
the point thus, as a new fort is being built here, to replace

the old one, the site of which became insecure; and the
end of the projecting height is at present cut off by a
formidable fence of barbed wire, where threatening notices
drive us to the right down the path into *Alum Bay*, backed
by a broken heathy hollow known as the *Warren*, that rises
up to *Headon Hill.*

ALUM BAY is one of the lions of the island, its
coloured cliffs forming a spectacle that will appeal to
the least scientific mind; while here also may be noted
the junction which takes place between the chalk and
the Eocene strata, referred to in the Geological article.
The strata are vertically arranged, and their tints are
wonderfully bright and varied: "Deep purplish-red, dusky
blue, bright ochreous-yellow, gray approaching nearly to
white, and absolute black, succeed each other, as sharply
defined as the stripes in silk; and after rain the sun, which,
from about noon till his setting in summer, illuminates
them more and more, gives a brilliancy to some of these
nearly as resplendent as the high lights on real silk"
(Englefield).

Septaria (cement-stones) occur here on the shore, and
fossils are also numerous. The *alum* which gives name to
the bay is no longer gathered for commercial purposes, but
considerable quantities of the white sands found at the foot
of Headon Hill are exported for use in glass factories; and
the coloured sands, as every visitor to the island knows, are
arranged in fantastic forms as pictures or ornaments for sale
to curious strangers. A small spring issuing from the chalk
cliff is known as *Mother Large's Well*; the same old lady's
Kitchen is a cavern at a slight distance farther, which a
constant percolation of water renders, we fear, unpleasantly
damp.

There is almost no accommodation here except the *Royal
Hotel*, with its tap, and other humbler refreshment rooms.
Lodgings may be had at the old *Needles Hotel*, which stands
a good way behind at the back of the hollow. The place is
chiefly visited by excursionists, who come by steamer from
Ryde, Bournemouth, etc. In summer there is a daily boat
from Lymington, and one twice a week to Southampton and

Portsmouth. We are here an hour's walk from Freshwater Station.

If no steamer have disembarked its crew of pleasure-seekers, one may be thankful to find this bay and chine almost deserted, and to spend a quiet hour in examining the remarkable contrast between those gray chalk cliffs on one side, ending in the dazzling masses of the Needles, and the bright tints of the other. The Down we have just left, also, appears smooth as if shaved by a razor ; *Headon Hill*, which we are about to ascend, is all broken edges and banks of heather, its ragged sides brightly clothed with yellow flowerets and scanty tufts of grass. Before long we come upon another sharp contrast between the works of man and those of nature, for the face of Headon Hill is disfigured by one of three hideous brick forts that dot the Solent coast, along which we are now taking a rough track over the hill and down into Totland Bay. Nothing, however, can destroy the wild charms of this moorland height which gives us such fine views both landward and seaward.

TOTLAND BAY is a rising watering-place, all new and smart, with its big hotel standing out over the pier like captain of a company of red brick villas. There is riding for yachts here, as we see, and good bathing on the sands, where stands a refreshment and reading-room, with a very fair show of books and papers at the service of visitors for a small weekly subscription. The next corner is occupied by a fort, behind which, or on the sea-wall below, we pass into COLWELL BAY, lying under low cliffs, broken by two small chines, a mile or so of good sands, with plenty of room for the watering-place which will spring up here some day. By the first road we can now return across the peninsula, passing the *Nelson Inn*, alias *Colwell Bay Hotel*, or by a perhaps directer turn to the right of this ; but we might as well push on by the shore to the farther horn of the bay, where *Albert Fort* commands the narrowest part of the Solent, and we look across to *Hurst Castle*. To this point the reader has been already conducted from Yarmouth ; and the road hence to *Freshwater Station* will have taken him all round the peninsula formed by the Yar.

On the eastern side of Freshwater Bay rises *Afton Down* (500 feet), its chalk side scarred by the military road, the end of which has tumbled into the sea close to the esplanade. A new loop road makes it still available for travellers who would enjoy the fine sea views. The steeply-sloping verge of the cliff beside it is by no means a safe play place for children, as shown by a little monument commemorating the death of a poor boy who fell over here in 1846. When the turf is slippery from long drought, caution is especially desirable in peering over the broken edge. The Down is crested by numerous barrows of British inhabitants, over whose remains their descendants now play golf.

A SAIL ROUND THE NEEDLES

Before leaving Freshwater let us make this trip under care of an experienced boatman. The usual charge for taking a party to Alum Bay and back is ten shillings.

Rounding the point protected by the New Fort, we immediately enter *Watcombe Bay*, whose wall of cliff is burrowed by four cavernous recesses, and its farther extremity denoted by a pyramidal mass of rock. The cliffs beneath which we glide along gradually rise to a height of 490 feet—this eastern portion being known as the *Nodes*, the western portion (as far as Sun Corner) as the *Main Bench*. There are numerous cavities in the face of the cliff, from one of which percolates a spring of fresh water. The larger and more important recesses, which we pass in the following order, are named :—

1. *Neptune's Caves*, one of which is 200 feet deep ; the other 90 feet.

2. *Bar Cave*, 90 feet deep.

3. *Frenchman's Hole*, 90 feet deep, so called from an escaped prisoner said to have been starved to death here.

4. *Lord Holme's Parlour*, where that noble governor of the island was wont to entertain his friends. His *Kitchen* and *Cellar* are close at hand.

5. *Roe's Hall.*

6. *Preston's Bower.*

The *Wedge Rock*, a triangular mass 12 feet by 8, wedged in between the cliff and an isolated pyramidal rock some 50 feet high, and the *Old Pepper Rock*, will serve to indicate the commencement of the *Main Bench*. This line of cliffs is a great nesting-place of marine birds, which may be startled by firing a gun from the boat.

Rounding the bold abrupt headland of *Sun Corner*, we sail into *Scratchell's Bay*, where the cliffs are about 400 feet in height, and the sea has hollowed out a stupendous *Arched Cavern*, 300 feet high, which the voyager should assuredly land and explore. "Its edges are worn to an astonishing thinness by the action of wind and rain ; a segment, as it were, of a dome, from beneath which he looks out on the ocean, with all its breadth and sparkling points rolling away, till it seems piled up against the sky" (Sterling).

The *Needles Cave* is a recess, about 195 feet in depth, in the cliff on the south side of *Scratchell's Bay*, into which small boats can enter. On the north side of the bay a mass of fallen chalk contains some good fossils.

Here the Needles are seen to much greater advantage than from above ; though the tallest pinnacle, known as "Lot's Wife" (120 feet), was broken off by the waves more than a century ago, and many other sharp projections have probably shared the same fate, one can still perceive how these fantastically-pointed rocks may have come by their name, which some, however, connect with the German *Nieder Fels*.

We have already spoken of *Alum Bay*, whose glowing walls now welcome us. Rounding *Hatherwood Point* (beneath Headon Hill), we lose sight of the chalk, and come upon the darker cliffs of the Eocene formation. We now enter *Totland Bay* ; pass *Warden Point* ; shoot into *Colwell Bay* ; observe the *Albert and Victoria Forts*, which, with those of *Hurst Castle*, completely command the entrance of the Solent ; and, rounding *Sconce Point*, glide into the sheltered harbour afforded by the estuary of the Yar.

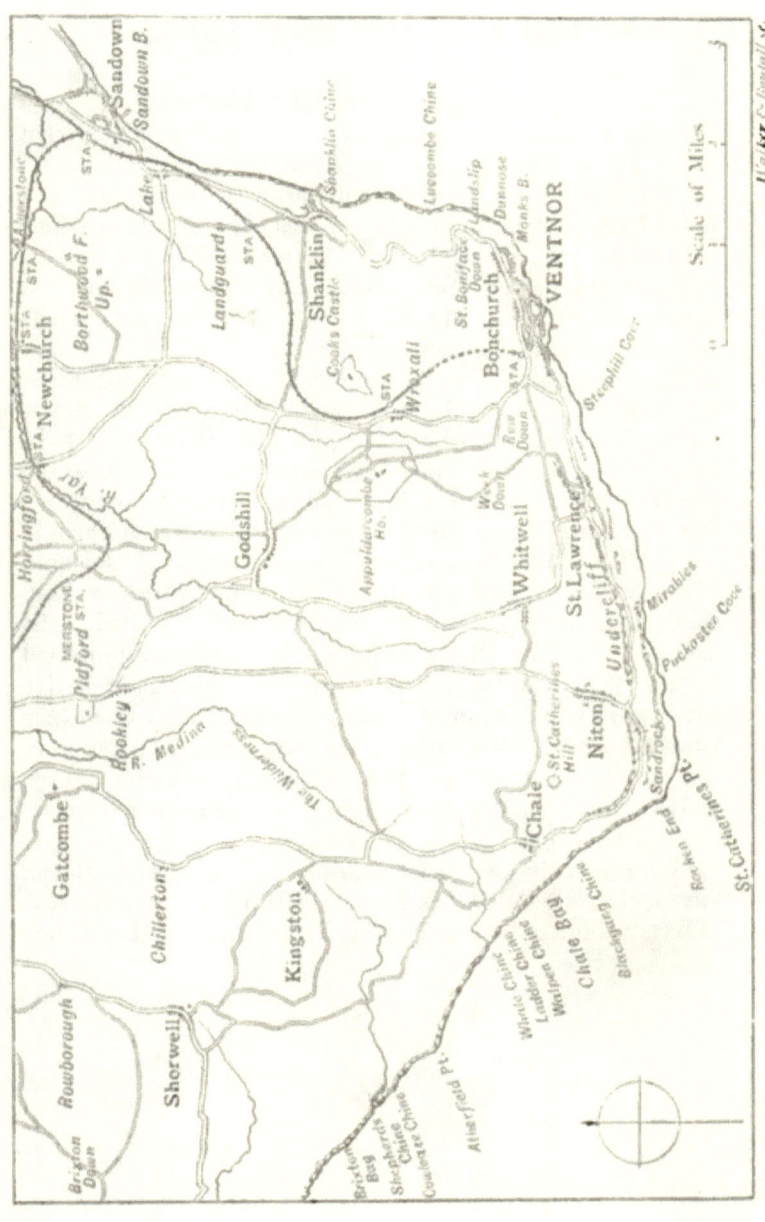

VENTNOR AND BACK OF ISLAND

THE BACK OF THE ISLAND

THE route from Freshwater to the Undercliff, a coach drive of some twenty miles to Ventnor, leads us along what is known as "the Back of the Island."

The coach road turns inland at first, taking a sweep behind the Downs, to regain the sea, by the ravine which debouches upon *Brook Chine*. The road to the left runs to *Calbourne* by *Chessel Down*, where several *tumuli* have been excavated. These high lands seem to have been a favourite burial-place of the ancient inhabitants.

BROOK is noted for its chine, and for the fossil forest at *Brook Point*, a little way westward along the beach. These petrified branches, boughs, and trunks of trees evidently originated "in a raft composed of a prostrate pine-forest, transported from a distance by the river which flowed through the country whence the Wealden deposits were derived, and became submerged in the sand and mud of the delta, burying with it the bones of reptiles, mussel-shells, and other extraneous bodies it had gathered in its course. . . . Many of the stems are concealed and protected by the fuci, corallines, and zoophytes which here thrive luxuriantly, and occupy the place of the lichens and other parasitical plants with which the now petrified trees were doubtlessly invested when flourishing in their native forests, and affording shelter to the Iguanodon and other gigantic reptiles" (Mantell).

We rejoin the high road at *Hulverston*, lying beneath the lofty crest of *Mottistone Down*, nearly 700 feet above the sea. MOTTISTONE itself is soon gained, and the tourist will not fail to admire its ancient Church, its Jacobean Manor-House (built in 1567, by one of the Cheke family), and its little cluster of gray cottages. The Church, restored in 1863, shows interesting traces of mediæval work. From the church a steep narrow lane leads up the hillside to the *Long Stone* or *Mote Stone* (*môt*, Saxon, a public assembly), which gives the name, it is said, to the neighbouring village. The Long Stone is a rudely-shaped block of ferruginous sandstone, 13 feet high, 6½ feet wide, and 20 feet in circuit ; and near it lies a similar pile, 9¼ feet long and 4 feet wide—the remains, perhaps, of an ancient cromlech or sepulchral chamber.

Two miles more bring us to BRIXTON (*Five Bells, New Inn*). This place, commonly pronounced and more correctly spelled *Brightstone*, has been well called "a cheerful little village, on the sunny side of the Isle of Wight, sheltered from cold winds by overhanging hills, with a goodly church, and a near prospect of the sea." It is associated with recollections of Bishop Ken, who was rector here from 1667 to 1669 ; and of William Wilberforce, who spent at the rectory, then occupied by his son, afterwards Bishop of Oxford, the summer of 1832. Brixton Church was restored in 1852. The chancel is of the thirteenth century, but the east window a century later. The nave is Transition-Norman work, and the tower apparently of the fourteenth century. The stained-glass window in the tower was the gift of the Bishop of Oxford.

The active pedestrian would now do well to follow the cliff path to Blackgang, lingering on a strip of this coast, which, though comparatively deserted, deserves to be as well known as it would be if nearer to any of the chief resorts. In that case he will first direct his steps seaward to *Grange Chine*, sometimes called *Jackman's*, a rough, gaping, gorse-grown cleft in the Wealden cliffs, which is not without a certain savage grandeur of its own. Or he may commence his journey at *Chilton Chine*, about a mile to the west, and nearly opposite the dangerous mass of sandstone called the *Bull-faced Rock*. Continuing our eastward route along the shore, if the tide permits,—otherwise along the cliff,—we pass the sandstone reef of *Shipledge*, and next arrive at *Barnes*, where recent landslips have exposed to the curiosity of archæologists highly interesting traces of a Romano-British pottery. *Barnes Chine* will attract the tourist's attention. At *Dutchman's Hole*, a cavern into which it is said a Dutch vessel was once sea-driven, gold coins are occasionally discovered at certain turns of the tide. The low red cliffs of the Wealden formation continue as far as *Atherfield Point*, where we come upon the lower Greensand. Both *Cowleaze* and *Shepherd Chines* were formed by one little rivulet which rises near Kingston, and formerly fell into the sea at Cowleaze ; but its course having been diverted by an eel-loving shepherd, and its waters augmented by heavy rains, it wrought a new channel through the yielding strata, and created the ravine through which it now leaps and foams. These chines, as well as the three succeeding ones, while comparatively neglected by strangers, are pronounced by some better worth seeing than that "lion" of the island and hackneyed show-place, *Blackgang*.

Atherfield Point, a superstructure of clay on a foundation of rock, is a good locality for the fossil-hunter. It throws out far into the sea a ledge of "blue slaty clay," forming the dangerous *Atherfield Ledge*, where in 1892 the German Lloyd steamer *Eider* struck in a fog, all hands being saved, and the vessel remaining stuck fast for several weeks, so as to give the island the excitement without the horror of a great shipwreck.

Our next point of interest is *Whale Chine*, 180 feet wide at the mouth ; and just beyond it is *Ladder Chine*, an excavation in the black clay cliffs which dips deep into the land, and throws out, as it were, numerous ramifications. "The most striking peculiarity of its character is the copious exudation of the chalybeate springs from its sides, which are stained with ochreous tints to a very great extent, and their dusky red on the black clay ground gives the appearance of a vast extinguished furnace to the deep hollow" (Englefield). All these chines originate in the action of small streams of water upon the more pliable strata of the Wealden and Greensand formations. The cliffs gradually increase in height as we advance, and *Walpen Chine* assumes, therefore, a character of wild sublimity, its sides broken up into a variety of striking formations. We are now close upon *Chale Bay*, beyond which lies the more famous Blackgang Chine.

The walk may also be done by the line of the straight military road from Brook to Chale, which is not open throughout for driving, and where pedestrians may find reason to complain of the want of any opportunity for refreshment on a hot day.

The coach road, to which we now return, keeps more inland. Half-way between *Brixton* and *Shorwell*, *Lymerston* lies at the foot of its Down ; and we also pass two venerable old manor-houses.

SHORWELL (*Five Bells Inn*), 2 miles from Brixton, is a finely-situated village, with a restored church containing some remarkable relics and memorials. The font and the stone pulpit are of the fifteenth century ; and there has been preserved an iron hour-glass frame of Puritan days. The chalice and paten are curious and interesting. The latter was purchased abroad by the late vicar, and is a singular piece of workmanship. Twelve medallions of the Cæsars encircle a representation of Eve's temptation of Adam, also surrounded by an emblematic border, allegorising "Musique, Grammatique, Arithmetique, Astronomic, Minerve, and Retorique." The chalice is dated 1569.

From Shorwell it is an easy walk to *Rowborough* Farm, with its remains of an ancient British settlement ; but this visit we propose to make from Newport, which is only 5 miles off the road we are now following. The Newport road, diverging here, would at once bring us past *Northcourt*, a Jacobean mansion, the terraced gardens of which are particularly fine.

Two miles more and we are at KINGSTON, whose little church, carefully rebuilt from the old model, holds hardly a hundred worshippers, yet is too large for the number of the parishioners. From this it is 3 miles to *Chale*, and little more to *Blackgang*, where we enter upon the Under-cliff proper, and take our readers at once to Ventnor, over

7 miles of rarely picturesque road, which must be returned to for fuller description.

THE UNDERCLIFF

The famous UNDERCLIFF extends from *St. Catherine's* to *Dunnose*, a distance of about 10 miles by road, along which lies a platform varying from half a mile to a quarter of a mile in width, bounded on the south by the bays and promontories of the Channel, and on the north by gray rocks, forming buttresses to a range of high downs. Words give a poor idea of the charms of this English Riviera, its hillsides and terraces covered with groves, gardens, and tangles of shrubbery. Between the wall of deeply-grooved cliff shutting it in to the north, and the sea dashing at its foot, the foliage runs as wild as in a giant's greenhouse, beautifully displayed by the accidents of the irregularly sloping ground—

> "Crags, knolls, and mounds confusedly hurl'd,
> The fragments of an earlier world."

This line of cliffs has indeed reminded us of the Trossachs, with one side opened out to the sun and a richer vegetation at its base. Hawthorns, elders, and other bushes grow here to a huge height, dappling the green of the woods with their blossoms. There are many pink hawthorns, which in spring give the scene something of a continental touch. Myrtle and other semi-tropical plants flourish hardily; everywhere there are flowers growing like weeds, notably the red Valerian flourishing on walls and broken edges. Huge boulders are half hidden in ivy, heaps of old ruins are buried in almost impassable thickets. It is hard to say when this huge bank of greenery is most beautiful, whether in spring with all its blossoms and tender buds; or in summer wearing its full glory of leafage; or again in autumn brilliant with changing tints and spangled by bright berries: even in winter there are evergreens enough to make us half forget the cold winds from which this favoured spot is sheltered. Mansions and cottages nestle among the trees, sometimes clustered into knots that only from above are seen to form villages, for this is a tamed and populated wilderness. The one blot on such a paradise seems the many notices to trespassers, warning that its most tempting nooks are "private," and the still more ominous placards of "valuable building land to let on lease." At perhaps the finest point, from St. Lawrence to Bonchurch, where the overhanging cliffs give way to the towering mass of St. Boniface Down, nature has had to make room for a widely-scattered town, still mixed up with patches of green and banks of ivy. This is Ventnor, the capital of the Undercliff, and the chief resort of the island.

VENTNOR

Hotels : *Marine, Crab and Lobster* (C.), *Royal, Bonchurch—Queen's, Esplanade, Commercial, Freemasons', Solent, Rayner's Temperance, etc.* These are all towards the lower part of the town, except the *Bonchurch Hotel*, which stands in an elevated situation, a little way out of it towards Shanklin.

Boarding-Houses : *Hillside, Clarendon, Yarborough Villa, Undercliff, Belmont* (in the upper quarter)—*Esplanade, Balmoral, Marine, Trafalgar, Eversley, Holyrood, etc.* (by the sea).

The growth of Ventnor from an obscure fishing hamlet to a fashionable watering-place is a matter of the last half-century or so ; and seems well epitomised in the spacious structure of Cass's Hotel standing beside the quaint little "Crab and Lobster" tavern from which it developed. The fortune of this sheltered shore was made by Sir James Clark, an esteemed physician of his day, who pronounced it the English Madeira. It claims to enjoy the mildest climate in England, a question we leave Ventnor to settle with Torquay and other jealous rivals. Statistics published by the Royal Meteorological Society show for ten years a record of 50·88 as its mean annual temperature : 57·68 in summer ; 44·07 in winter. Here, then, have been established various charitable sanatoriums, such as the St. Catherine's Home for Consumptives, the Royal Hants Convalescent Home, the Seaside Home of the London City Mission, and the Royal National Hospital for Consumption at St. Lawrence. Already, in its short history, the neighbourhood

can boast several residents known to fame—among them the
Rev. James White, dramatist and historian ; Miss Sewell,
authoress of *Amy Herbert ;* the late Dr. Martin, whose
book on the *Undercliff* is worth reading ; and John
Sterling, Carlyle's friend, who ended his life at Hillside, a
cosy-looking house overlooking the town from its shady
garden, now occupied as a boarding establishment.

"Ventnor Cove," as it used to be called, has now grown
into a town of six thousand inhabitants, a number considerably increased in the season.   Unfortunately, in some ways
nature never meant herself here to be laid out in streets, and
eligible plots of building land have to be taken as they can
be found on the steep slope.   This fact, however favourable
to picturesqueness of general effect, proves a little trying to
those feeble folk who make so large a part of the population.
Communication with the different levels of the town, where
the climate varies according to their degree of elevation and
protection, has to be effected by steep stairs, winding ascents,
and devious roads ; and often one's goal seems provokingly
near, while it turns out to be tiresomely far by the only
available access.   To some of the houses one has to climb
up to the front, and climb down into the back premises.
One thoroughfare is so precipitous that a railing has been
provided for the aid of those risking its descent.

The twisting High Street debouches into a hollow,
prettily laid out, about which are the most sheltered parts
of the town.   Here stands the pier with its shelters and
pavilion ; and a short esplanade curves round the little bay
to a rocky point, from which other zigzags remount to the
higher quarters.   There has been a proposal to extend this
esplanade along the Bonchurch side of the shore, where
the gasworks certainly do not form a very pleasant or
convenient obstruction ; but on the whole it appears better
to leave Ventnor as it is.   Its great charm, says a
writer in the *Daily Graphic,* consists of being as unlike as
possible to the "ordinary Saturday-to-Mondayville" ; and
its irregular architecture, wilful roads, and provoking *im-
passes* are at least in harmony with each other.

The modern parish church of *St. Catherine's* stands down

town near the Post Office, and is understood to be appropriately "low" in its services, according to the present
standard of these matters. *Trinity Church*, higher up in
the eastern quarter, takes a medium tone, as seems fit. *St.
Albans*, though as yet a very unpretending structure, is
"high" in every respect, and will be found near the loftily
perched railway station. While on this head we may
mention the new church of *Bonchurch*, with its beautiful
cemetery, a saddening show of tombstones to the young,
and the tiny little old church below, now no longer used
for worship. *St. Lawrence*, on the other side, has also a
new church, and an old one, the latter distinguished as one
of the smallest in England. At Ventnor there are a Catholic
and various dissenting chapels. The town possesses *Assembly
Rooms* and other halls, a *Literary Institute* with free library
and reading-room, and a Club open to residents and visitors.
Frequent performances of various kinds take place on the
pier and in the concert halls; but it seems unfitting that a
place of so much quiet dignity should show such a strong
taste for nigger minstrels, who are in high favour here,
while more pretentious performers have often to complain
of a thin audience. The Park, on the western cliff, is very
pleasantly laid out with bowling-green and tennis-courts
among its leafy mazes.

The bathing must be called poor, the coast on this side
of Dunnose being much rougher than round the Shanklin
corner. The beach before the esplanade has been tamed a
little and brought under the yoke of bathing machines, but
one has usually some cautious walking to do before getting
into water for a swim, and even then must steer one's way
by posts indicating practicable channels. A little way
farther west, beneath the cliff, a shed has been erected to
afford a plunge at high water; but by last advices this
enterprise is in a state of closure, if not of collapse.
Steephill Cove, within a mile westwards, is used as a
bathing place by the local youth; and farther along
the shore there are here and there tempting strips of
sand; but visitors may be cautioned as to launching
forth from untried spots. The same hint applies to boat-

ing, this coast being best navigated with the help of some one who knows its reefs and eddies. The currents above Blackgang Chine are spoken of as specially dangerous.

Ventnor visitors are perhaps more ready to take their pleasure by land than by sea ; and the leading amusement is supplied by the coaches, brakes, and other vehicles which carry them to all parts of the island. There are daily excursions in the season to Freshwater, Cowes, and other remote points ; besides morning and afternoon trips to Blackgang, Shanklin, and such nearer goals ; and the stranger will have much ado to deny the insinuating recruiters who at every corner of the High Street lie in wait to enlist him for their crew of pleasure-seekers.

Building still goes on in and around Ventnor, which does not appear to suffer from the shift of medical opinion as to the treatment of consumption. It has two seasons, or indeed flourishes all the year, except perhaps at the most beautiful midsummer month. In early spring, when visitors of the best class are thickest, the town has recently tried to justify its pretensions to Mentoneship by holding a Carnival or Battle of Flowers, which seems to have been so successful as to bid fair to become an annual institution— weather permitting. In spite of its poor bathing, it does not want for guests in July and August, when the climate, so mild in winter, has a fair chance of being kept cool by the sea breezes. Such places, it should be remembered, keep their temperate character all the year round.

Even if the town be baked by a flaring sun full in its face, a refreshing coolness falls when the sun sets over ST. BONIFACE DOWN, and the nights are always endur- able. However stuffy it may be below, seldom will the perspiring climber fail to find bracing air on the top of this huge bank, rising at one point, the highest in the Island, to nearly 800 feet. Its steep sides are gained by a road near the high-placed railway station, and by other entrances from the top of the town ; and chalky paths lead to the summit, while gentlemen in knickerbockers and ladies in summer-like frocks will not always admire the scrambling upon some of its prickly slopes. For goal of the ascent there is a *Wishing Well*, as to which old tradition has it that, if you reach the spot, Orpheus-like, without casting a backward glance, the wish you may form while drinking of its welcome spring will speedily be fulfilled. Certainly no finer view could be wished for than one gains from the summit and along a wide stretch of open rambles on either hand.

On the adjacent REW DOWN, beyond the station, not to be behind the age, Ventnor has now laid out a new nine-hole golf-course, which seems to want hazards, unless the chance of sending one's ball down the abrupt slope, and will try the knees of elderly devotees by the preliminary pilgrimage needful to that lofty spot where the small club-house stands out like an Alpine chapel. But the climb, which may be made by carriage to beyond the cemetery, is well worth the labour, if only for the views of sea and land here disclosed. A breezy walk is round the wide horseshoe hollow between the two downs, from which the ramble may be extended to Shanklin on one hand, and on the other to St. Catherine's, or turning inland to the heights of Appuldurcombe, on which the conspicuous Worsley monument serves as a beacon. In the dip between run the railway, and the high road to Ryde, which from Ventnor is some three or four hours' smart walking.

EXCURSIONS FROM VENTNOR

THE LANDSLIP

The walk which every one must take from Ventnor, who has no time for more, is to the Landslip at the end of the Undercliff, so called *par excellence* as being comparatively recent and most exquisite in its effect of overgrown ruin, through which he can pass on to *Luccombe Chine* (about 2 m.), or even to *Shanklin*, another half-hour's walk over the cliff. Unless one follows the sea walks, the road leads along the face of St. Boniface Down, passing through BONCHURCH, that charming suburb of Ventnor, where the myrtle and the fuchsia, the verbena and the clianthus, grow rankly in the open air, demanding from the gardener but little attention.

In all sorts of odd nooks, either reposing against the mighty wall of the Undercliff, or hiding away in leafy hollows, are perched its picturesque cottages and handsome villas. The mildness of the climate is notably attested by fuchsias like trees, with trunks as thick as a strong man's wrist, and scarlet geraniums of such wonderful growth that a single plant will cover several square yards of wall in front of a house. This one fact, more than any word-painting, gives an idea of the way in which Bonchurch, and indeed most parts of Ventnor, are embowered by foliage.

The Bonchurch pond will be noticed, overhung with a rich bank of trees and shrubs, among them huge arbutus trees recalling those of Killarney. Many of the finest spots here are enclosed in private grounds; for instance, the *Pulpit Rock*, a towering mass of sandstone surmounted by a cross, which can be reached by a path from a drinking fountain near the pond; but permission must be obtained. The road also is somewhat shut in by the walls of adjacent mansions. Threading his way between these private paradises, instead of following the high road to Shanklin up-hill by the *Bonchurch Hotel* and the new church, the pedestrian turns steeply to the right by a lane leading past the tiny old church now disused, then joining a walk from the sea, and skirting *Monk's Bay*, soon passes into the Landslip, a wilderness of overgrown knolls and hillocks sloping down from the crags above.

This scene has a beauty all its own. At first our steps are over daisied turf; but soon we have to take a broken and twisting path for guide, that leads us by banks of bracken and bramble, into bowers of gnarled hawthorn, with masses of gray rocks half buried in green, where progress is not so easy. We may be content to lose ourselves in these tangled thickets, with occasional glimpses of the sea for direction, till we run against a wall that firmly guides us upward to the main track. The labyrinth opens out, and passing above the private grounds that have brought us up, we come round to LUCCOMBE CHINE. This is a little difficult to find, a fact probably related to that of there being no charge for admission; but by hugging the enclosure, we reach a stile below some cottages, and thus can descend through the Chine. After Blackgang or Shanklin this chasm seems in the right of it to be so modestly retiring, yet there are some who profess to admire it as superior.

At the bottom, by a rough coast path, we can get round the point to scramble back into the Landslip ; or, at low water, can pass along the shore to Shanklin. Those who are pressed for time may be advised merely to look into the Chine, then follow the open cliff walk to Shanklin, from which a return can be made by train or by road. At Shanklin they will find it difficult to escape its more famous Chine, so many are the notices directing one to it.

BLACKGANG CHINE

The excursion next in favour here is that to *St. Catherine's* and *Blackgang Chine*. The distance is 7 miles by road ; and in the season there are several brakes running both morning and afternoon, the trip taking about three hours. Even if there be not enough passengers to fill one of these sociable caravans, the rival proprietors will among them usually manage to make up a small party, carried at the return fare of two shillings. A public vehicle also runs to the Blackgang Hotel ; and the coaches bound on some longer excursions, such as that to *Carisbrooke*, will probably make a halt here. The pedestrian has the choice of two other routes, by the edge of the Downs, and along the winding shore.

The high road leads out between the Park and the grounds of Steephill Castle, once the heritage of that unfortunate Mr. Hambrough whose death gave rise to a *cause célèbre*. Near this will be the station of the new line to Newport, which is to tunnel through the cliffs of St. LAWRENCE, a parish becoming an *annexe* of Ventnor to the west, as Bonchurch to the east. Passing the cricket-field, a characteristically unlevel one, we drive by the Hospital for Consumption, which Ventnor people insist on reminding you belongs to St. Lawrence, modern medical theories as to germ infection making some look on such a neighbour with suspicion as likely to scare away more profitable guests. Yet any town might be proud of this model hospital, like a lordly terrace rather than an institution, whose temporary inmates have such good quarters as not every seaside visitor can command. The new church and hotel of St. Lawrence are next passed, signs of a larger population than might be guessed from the road. Till one has climbed the cliff and looked down into these groves and gardens, one has no idea how many houses are hidden away behind them.

Up and down winds the road, but our horses mount its turns with a will, for they know the journey, and that the sooner it is over, the sooner comes their hour's rest at Blackgang. Instead of enumerating the various half-hidden mansions passed, let us rather supply the reader here with one or two quotations as to the general character of this scenery.

"The cliffs," writes Lord Jeffrey, "are in some places enormously high—from 600 to 700 feet. The beautiful places are either where they sink deep into bays and valleys, opening like a theatre to the sun and the sea, or where there has been a terrace of low land formed at their feet, which stretches under the shelter of that enormous wall, like a rich garden plot all roughened over with masses of rock fallen in distant ages, and overshadowed with thickets of myrtle, and roses, and geraniums, which all grow wild, in great luxuriance and profusion." Miss Sewell, who has described this neighbourhood in her novel, *Ursula*, tells us : "The ground is tossed about in every direction, and huge rocks lie scattered upon it. But thorns and chestnuts and ash-trees have sprung up amongst them upon the greensward ; ivy has climbed up the ledges of the jagged cliffs ; primroses cluster upon the banks ; cowslips glitter on the turf ; and masses of hyacinths may be seen in glades, half hidden by the foliage of the thick trees, and through which the jutting masses of gray rock peep out upon the open sea, sparkling with silver and blue some hundreds of feet beneath them."

A more scientific account of the Undercliff has been

6

given in our Geological Article (see p. 58). Several fresh landslips have occurred in the present century ; and though it is said that we have no reason to apprehend any further serious disturbance, occasional falls of rock from the cliff above still remind us how this gracious ruin of nature may be renewed.

The next landmark is the *Sandrock Hotel* (5½ m.), where the road to *Niton* turns off. A little way beyond, on a shaded knoll to the right, some local worthy has thought well to erect a small temple by way of a monument to Shakespeare, which may perhaps serve to remind Ventnor visitors that nigger minstrelsy is not the highest form of the dramatic art. Below is a little fountain bearing the motto : "The water nectar, and the rocks pure gold." We have already at St. Lawrence and at Sandrock passed springs once of renown. The road now comes out of shade, mounting under the cliffs, by a bare turn that suggests Switzerland. Soon we reach the first houses of ST. CATHERINE'S, and descend to the *Blackgang Chine Hotel*.

Entrance to the Chine is through a bazaar, where one must either make a purchase or pay sixpence before he descends to explore this great chasm, echoing the ocean waves that break on the beach below. Description is to some extent out of place, as the bare sides change considerably, crumbling away year by year. Dr. Mantell's, however, will still be found true enough in its general outline :—

"The cascade falls in a perpendicular column from a ledge of 70 feet high, down the midst of a deep chasm formed in dark ferruginous clays and sands, and surmounted by broken cliffs 400 feet high ; and towering above all is the majestic escarpment of St. Catherine's Hill, rising to an altitude of between 800 and 900 feet.[1] The bands of greenish-gray sand and sandstone, which alternate with ferruginous clays in this division of the greensand system, appear very prominent, owing to the wearing away of the soft and friable intermediate beds. As the face of the sandstone, after long exposure to the atmosphere, separates into square blocks, the appearance of the projecting bands of

---

[1] Rather under 800 feet, by last Ordnance Survey.

stone, which are from 10 to 15 feet thick, is very singular, and is not unaptly compared by Sir Henry Englefield to courses of masonry built up at different heights to sustain the mouldering cliffs. The thin layer of ironstone grit which is very constantly found in this division of the green-sand, constituting, as it were, a line of demarcation between the upper arenaceous deposits and the lower more argilla-ceous group, intercepts the water that percolates through the upper porous strata, and projecting in a ledge, forms the bed of a stream.

This Chine wants the charm of luxuriant greenery found in the narrower ravine of Shanklin ; on the other hand, its nakedness enables one better to study the characteristic formation of those recesses so frequent on the southern coast of the island. There is a covered shelter on the cliff, from which one may look down into the depths of the Chine, and along the high coast-line, scene of more than one famous shipwreck. The *Clarendon*, West Indiaman, was wrecked here in 1836, before the building of St. Catherine's Light-house, only three lives being saved. View-hunters who may be a little disappointed in the Chine, after all they have heard of its renown, should not neglect to seek the cliff walk opening from it. But, indeed, the hour usually allowed to excursion parties is little enough for thoroughly examining a scene at once so striking and so instructive. A museum at the bazaar offers some curiosities, such as the skeleton of a large whale washed ashore on the island.

If the visitor have time and breath to spare, he may hence or from *Niton* ascend St. CATHERINE'S HILL, in height only a few feet short of St. Boniface Down, and commanding a view landwards and seawards, which Miss Sewell details for us : " The shore is closed in with red sand-cliffs, rather low, broken and jagged ; but away to the west the red sand changes into chalk, and the cliffs become very steep, and rise to a great height, standing out against the sky when the sun shines on them, until they almost dazzle the eye ; and at other times, covering themselves, as it were, with a bluish veil of mist, and looking out proudly from behind it. . . . Below the ridge the ground is very flat for a long

way. From the edge of the cliff it is level for miles, cut
up into cornfields and pastures, with a few trees dotting the
hedgerows. We can see as far as Newport, and beyond it ;
away, indeed, to where the river, which has its source close
to us, and is there only a tiny brook, becomes quite a broad
stream, and deep enough to float vessels." The coast of
Hampshire is also visible across the thin bright line of the
Solent. It is said that in clear weather the hills about
Cherbourg can be seen over the Channel. A landmark
here is the pillar erected by a Russian merchant in com-
memoration of the Czar Alexander's visit to England in
1814, to which has been affixed, not very appropriately, a
tablet to the memory of British soldiers who fell in the
Crimean war.

A less arduous finish of our excursion would be to CHALE
(*Clarendon Hotel and Boarding-House*), which may be called
the end of the Undercliff. It lies half a mile inland, the
square tower of its weather-worn church rising from among
the grass-grown graves of many a shipwrecked mariner,
where man's hand seems to imitate in little the half-hidden
rocks and mounds of the Undercliff.

On the drive back to Ventnor, it is usual to turn
down by the lower road, past the *Buddle Inn*, an old haunt
of smugglers, and Lloyd's signal station, so as to give at
least a glimpse of ST. CATHERINE'S LIGHTHOUSE, for a
visit to which we must go down to the shore, well
worth inspection as it is, its light being called the most
powerful in the world. The first beacon on this dangerous
coast was the lamp of a Hermitage on the Down above,
still preserved as a landmark. Last century the Trinity
Board began to erect a lighthouse on these misty heights,
but gave it up as useless. The wreck of the *Clarendon*
called fresh attention to the urgent need of some warning
signal here ; and the present lighthouse was completed in
1840. It measures 122 feet from the level of the ground,
and 204 feet from sea-level. The light was originally
equal to 740 candles, increased by means of a lens to
17,600 candles, produced by an oil lamp with six concentric
wicks. The electric light was first used in 1888, and is

capable of throwing a beam of light over the sea equal to more than 6,000,000 candles. This extraordinary light is produced by one of De Meritan's arc-lamps holding two fluted carbons 18 inches long and 2½ inches in diameter. It is surrounded by a revolving circular drum, 4 feet in diameter and 5 feet high, which is divided into sixteen panels or vertical lenses of wonderful magnifying power; each of these consists of a central bull's-eye, with thirty horizontal sectional prisms so arranged, above and below the centre, as to concentrate the rays of light into one powerful horizontal beam. The rotation of the drum is effected by means of a small compressed-air engine, the flash from each of the sixteen lenses passing a given point every half-minute. For lighting purposes two magnetic-electro engines are provided, each containing sixty bunches of permanent magnets. Near the lighthouse is another building which contains the fog-horn, or siren, whose hoarse note of warning in foggy weather is heard at Ventnor. It gives two blasts, a high note and a low note, every minute, and is worked by compressed air. The utility of these works is shown by the fact that wrecks are now rare on such a dangerous coast, whereas formerly they were common, fourteen vessels gone ashore in Chale Bay being the record of a single night.

From this point, the walk along the shore might be extended to *Rocken End*, where the Undercliff seems to tumble into the sea in a chaos of blocks of chalk and sandstone, upon which the waves burst with freshly ruinous fury.

We have already suggested to the pedestrian that he may return to Ventnor by a path rising and falling along the low cliffs of the shore. We are in doubt only as to the strip between *Puckaster Cove* and *Binnel Point*, where, however, we should not expect to find any serious obstacle. At more than one point he can also leave the high road to gain the edge of the Downs, by the roads through *Niton* or *St. Lawrence*, or by the *Cripple Path*, turning off to the left by steps as we come in sight of *Mirables*, a red-roofed mansion to the right below, which looks not yet toned down into keeping with the scenery. At the top, he has all the Undercliff beneath him, and a wide inland view of rolling agricultural country with villages and farms nestling in the hollows. A track, following the cliff almost all along, then leads to the highest level of Ventnor, gaining the road above the railway station.

NITON AND WHITWELL

From the *Royal Sandrock Hotel*, a short divagation might well be made to the pretty village, sometimes called *Crab Niton*, to distinguish it from K-nighton (whose K is strongly sounded however), a small hamlet near Newchurch. The valley of NITON breaks through the chalk hills to open out upon the sea at Wreath Bay. The Church stands at the base of St. Catherine's Down, near the meeting point of two roads—one ascending the eastern slope of the Down to its beacon-crowned summit, the other skirting the southern face, and joining the Chale road at Blackgang. It was restored in 1864, and contains some good painted glass. There are two inns in the village, where lodgings also can be had.

A lane from Niton leads in a north-easterly direction across the fields (where rises the tiny stream of the Eastern Yar) to WHITWELL. The Church, restored in 1868, is particularly interesting. It consists of a nave and south aisle, chancel and south chapel, a low square tower at the west end of the aisle, and a south porch. The south chapel was originally the chancel of the parish church, and was dedicated to Our Lady ; the present chancel was originally a chapel dedicated to St. Rhadegund, belonging to the parish of Gatcombe. Some vestiges of this peculiar arrangement are still preserved in the two altars. Nearly all the windows are filled with fine painted glass.

WHITWELL's natural access is by a steep road descending to St. Lawrence; and we may also get back to Ventnor over the Downs. The railway now in construction will be a great convenience for this part of the country.

APPULDURCOMBE

This finely-situated park, and the points reached from it, make the chief goal of inland pilgrimage from Ventnor. The railway serves us as far as *Wroxall*, but by the high road in the same valley or over Rew Down it is an hour's walk or so to the grounds of APPULDURCOMBE (pronounced with a strong accent on the last syllable).

The house, now a boys' school, was formerly a seat of the Yarborough family, who have left the island, carrying away the collection of art and antiquity for which Appuldurcombe used to be renowned. Old Lord Yarborough, Commodore of the Royal Yacht Squadron, who died in 1847, was the most determined opponent of railways in the Isle of Wight. He employed a large staff of men to keep guard over all his estate, and to take into custody anybody with a theodolite, or who looked in the least like a railway engineer. Upon one occasion, a man newly appointed to the post, meeting his master in a secluded part of the estate, at once collared his lordship and took him into custody, an incident to be paralleled by Mr. John Mytton's famous fight, in the disguise of a sweep, with his own keeper.

The manor was originally bestowed upon a Benedictine Abbey, but fell into possession of the Worsley family, by whom the present imposing mansion was built in 1710. The ground rises in the rear of this classical pile, exhibiting a fine mass of deep dense woods. On the crest of the hill stands the WORSLEY OBELISK, of Cornish granite, dedicated by Sir Richard Worsley, in 1774, to his ancestor Sir Robert. This massive structure, partially destroyed by lightning, some of the huge blocks of granite having been hurled right down the hillside into a hollow below, is a conspicuous landmark for many miles around. From the point on which it stands may be enjoyed a prospect perhaps the most extensive in the island, whose entire length and breadth are commanded from this spot, the white chalk cliffs of Freshwater at the extreme west and

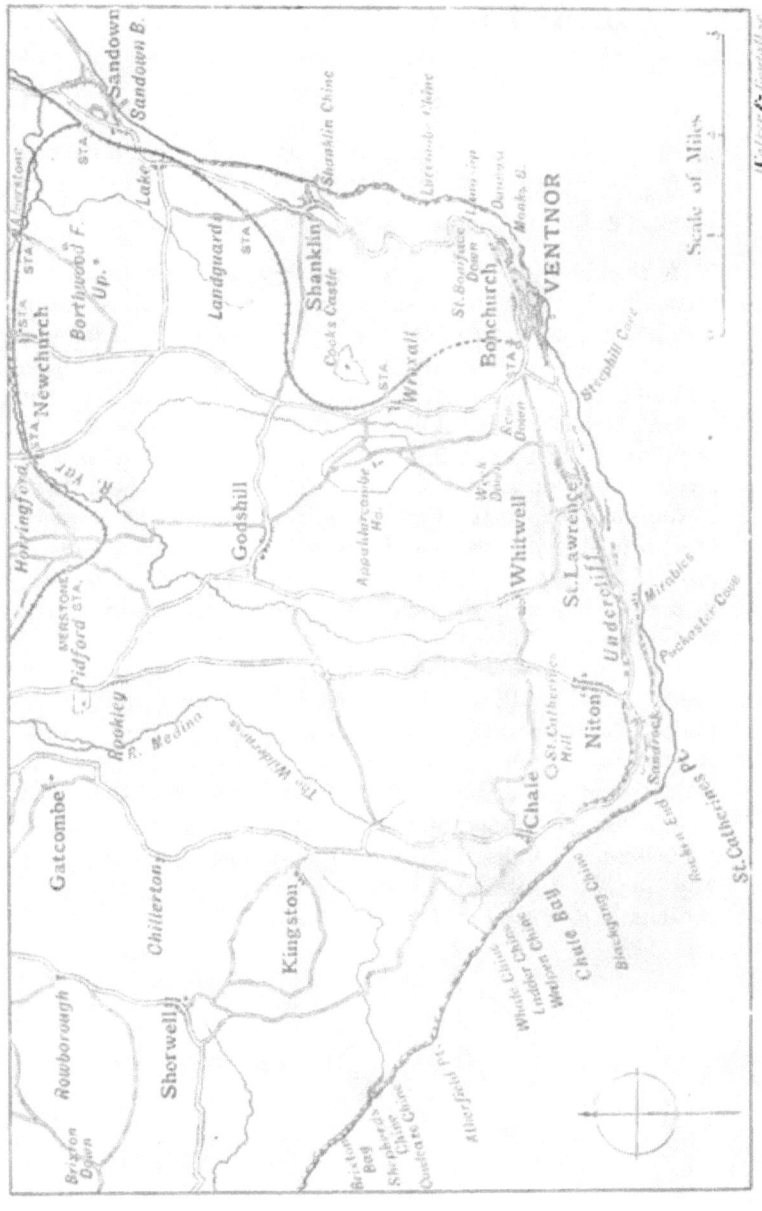

VENTNOR AND BACK OF ISLAND

SHANKLIN AND SANDOWN

SHANKLIN

Hotels : *Royal Spa* (on the Esplanade), *Daish's* and *Hollier's* (in the High Street), *Madeira* and *Clarendon* (near the cliff), *Marine* (at the station), *Chine Inn*, etc.
Boarding-Houses : *Cedars, Napier House*, etc.

THIS is one of the favourite watering-places in the island, attracting visitors earlier in summer than Ventnor, while it also has a good share of winter guests, to keep up a population of over three thousand. It somewhat resembles Lynton and Lynmouth in situation, consisting of two quarters, the esplanade below the cliff, and the old town above. A peculiarity is that the High Street, where the shops mostly are, hugging an inland hollow, runs almost on the outside of the place, connected with the edge of the cliff by more or less unfinished streets, which show how Shanklin means to grow. The esplanade and the upper district communicate by a steep winding road skirting the Chine, and by zigzag stairs from the pier, to which facilities have been lately added a particularly hideous Lift, more welcome to stiff limbs than to the artistic eye. The pier, also, is a pretentious structure, a little out of keeping with the tone of the place. For Shanklin is a choice resort, favoured by a good many permanent residents or constant visitors who form a sociable community. It has the air of no common watering-place, but seems unique by the charmingly irregular way in which its villas are scattered among blooming gardens and clusters of rich foliage. The antique little parsonage is characteristic, completely enclosed in enormous myrtles. The *Chine avenue* is a notably fine piece of greenery. Altogether, in spite of dubious "improvements," this place can have lost little of the beauty that struck Lord Jeffrey, when he described it as "all mixed up with trees, and lying among sweet airy falls and swells of ground which finally rise up behind the breezy downs 800 feet high, and sink down in front to the edge of the varying cliffs which overhang a pretty beach of fine sand, and are approachable by a very striking wooded ravine which they call the *chine*."

This popular sight, like other wonders of nature on the island, is enclosed, a small charge being made for admission, and in more than one respect rather suggests the tea-garden order of resort, but nothing can spoil it. It is to be entered at either end, but excursion coaches usually bring their passengers to the head of the Chine. At the top will be found a ferruginous spring. Here the chasm is at its narrowest, increasing till it has a breadth of nearly 300 feet, while the steep sides are in parts almost 200 feet high. Winding walks take one for some quarter of a mile down a deep glen, which differs notably from Blackgang Chine in being choked up with trees and a rich undergrowth of ferns, moss, and brushwood, wherever any shade-loving plant can take root. Into the top pours a little waterfall rushing to the sea at the bottom of this wilderness of greenery. Shanklin Chine is certainly, in its way, one of the finest bits in the Isle of Wight, the dispute between its admirers and those of Blackgang being quite a matter of taste.

Besides its Chine, Shanklin boasts of ferruginous springs, but we fancy these are not much regarded unless as curiosities, though they proclaim strong medical testimony as to their efficacy. The sands are capital for children, and display a goodly company of bathing machines. Under the new shelters at the end of the pier will be found a shed belonging to the Shanklin Swimming Club, open (for swimmers only) in the morning at a small charge. Posts on the sands mark the limits beyond which one is free to bathe "without the formality of an apparatus," as the

Oxford gentleman in *Humphrey Clinker* puts it. On fine
evenings the bay is alive with boats ; and the steamers will
not fail to call here on their frequent rounds, while, indeed,
Ventnor and Shanklin have now a steamboat enterprise
of their own. Near the High Street is an *Institute*, with
hall, reading-room and other accommodations open to visitors
at a small charge. The New Club and the Lawn Tennis
Club are likewise of a hospitable spirit.

While it is much frequented by excursionists from all
parts of the island, Shanklin has excursions of its own,
favourite ones being the coach drives to *Cowes* and to
Blackgang Chine, at a usual fare of 5s. But its guests have
not far to go for fine sights and views. Half an hour's
stroll over the breezy heights of *Dunnose* takes one over to
Luccombe Chine and so on to the *Bonchurch Landslip*, then
to *Ventnor* (4 m.). When the tide is not in, Luccombe
may also be reached along the shore. Many rambles will
be discovered on the wooded Downs, the slope of which
from Shanklin commands itself to less active pedestrians
as more easy than on the Ventnor side, while the height
here is only a little lower. One very pleasant path leads
through the fields beyond the churchyard, by which we
can gain various points. A favourite walk is thus to
Cook's Castle, an artificial ruin commanding a fine view, and
back through the woods below. The *America Wood* is
particularly admired.

Another charming spot is APSE CASTLE, the praise of which
has been invitingly proclaimed by Dr. Bromfield, whose *Flora
Vectensis* may be taken as a guide to the botany of the Island :
" A thick wooded eminence, about one mile west-north-west
of Shanklin, commanding a fine view, and flanked on one
side by a deep ravine, along whose bottom winds a clear
but shallow brook, overhung by precipitous banks covered
with trees and shrubs, the natural growth of the place. A
more delightful scene can hardly be imagined than is offered
by this fresh and verdant spot, when, on some radiant
morning in April or May, we tread the solitary mazes of
Apse Castle, a blooming wilderness of primroses, wood-
anemones, hyacinths, violets, and a hundred other lovely

and fragrant things, overtopped by the taller and purple-
stained wood-spurge, early purple orchis, and the pointed
hoods of the spotted-leaved wake-robin; the daisy-be-
sprinkled track leading us upward, skirted by mossy fern-
clad banks on one hand, and by shelving thickets on the
other, profusely overshadowed by ivy-arched oak and ash,
the graceful birch, and varnished holly." Passing over the
dip in which the railway runs, by *Wroxall*, we can gain
the farther heights of *Appuldurcombe*, and push on by the
grounds to *Godshill*, returning more directly by the road.

GODSHILL (*Griffin Inn*) is about equally distant from
Ventnor and Shanklin—say 4 miles as the crow flies;
but there are so many tempting rounds and by-ways, that
the visitor might as well make a day's excursion of it.
This is one of the prettiest of the island-villages, studded
with irregular cottages and trim gardens. The Church is
worth a visit, as well on account of its architectural merits
and interesting memorials, as of its admirable and striking
position. A fine view is to be obtained from the churchyard, embracing the Vale of Newchurch, the white cliffs
of Culver, and the Downs both north and south. Besides
several monuments of note, the Church contains a picture
said to be in whole or in part by Rubens, of " Daniel
in the Lions' Den." The name of the village is traced to
one of the wide-spread legends which connect the building
of the church with supernatural interference.

NEWCHURCH is about 4 miles from Shanklin, by
Landguard, *Cheverton*, and *Apse Heath*, where we turn to the
right through what was once the forest of BORDWOOD. A
small mound on the right is called *Queen Bower*, from which
Isabella de Fortibus, that famed Lady of the Island, is said
to have watched the chase of the deer. The stranger will
pause here for a very pleasant prospect of another kind,
then make for Newchurch by a steep lane to the left over
Skinner's Hill. This is a large village, its ancient church
prominent on an eminence in the centre, which, though
modest enough in appearance, is distinguished as the mother-
church of both Ryde and Ventnor. From Newchurch we

may return by rail, or vary the walk by taking the high road to Ventnor as far as the cross road for Shanklin.

One of the most frequented walks at Shanklin is that along the cliff to *Sandown* (2 m.). These two places seem destined to be united one day, though as yet their esplanades stretch out vainly towards each other. But while Sandown appears free to grow without objection, the operations and designs of the jerry builder on both sides of Shanklin are too often such as to make its most judicious admirers grieve. By the road they have already a connecting link in LAKE, a village distinguished by the sumptuous "Home of Rest" for women, lately established by private munificence, and as headquarters of Isle of Wight cricket. This village stands back from the sea, to which there is a descent from the cliff here, known as *Littlestairs*. Lake has a railway platform, where trains stop on occasion of great cricket matches or athletic gatherings.

SANDOWN

Hotels : *Royal Pier, Sandown, King's Head, York, etc.*
Boarding-Houses : *Esplanade, York, Child's, The Balconies, etc.*

In a break of the cliffs, backed by low lands once covered by the sea, stands Sandown, occupying the centre of the wide bay to which it gives its name. This has of course been compared to the Bay of Naples, by those who never saw the Bay of Naples, but indeed it has charms of its own, looking right out to the open sea between the white cliffs of Culver and the wooded heights behind Shanklin. It rejoices in a wide stretch of firm sands, which offer perhaps the best bathing and play place for children in the island. Sandown is then more of the conventional family watering-place than its neighbours, and though its pier be less pretentious than that of Shanklin it can boast a rather larger population. It has a long esplanade, with bathing machines at each end, and a pleasant lounge in the little covered arcade at the south, where a path leads up to the cliffs. Another feature of the place is the strong forts that frown on either hand,

having taken the place of more picturesque but less service-
able works. Two more such fortifications are visible on
the heights to the north, so that the troops of children
encamped here in summer have no want of models for their
sand engineering.

Sandown has grown rapidly of late years. August is
naturally the gayest time, when the regatta is held. A
good deal of boating goes on, beside yacht sailing. A recent
attempt to extend the pier and make it a better landing-
place for steamers has met with rough handling from the
winter storms; but this enterprising town will not give in
to the sea as easily as King Canute. Sandown is the junction of the lines to Ventnor, Ryde, and Newport, so that
all parts of the island may hence be conveniently visited.
Out of the season, as there are so many lodging-houses, it
ought to be easy to arrange for cheap quarters. The leading hotels are rather expensive. The boarding-houses
advertise terms at from about 6s. per day. The station,
as at Shanklin, stands some way back from the sea.

Since its old fort has been destroyed, perhaps the only
thing like an historical association the growing town can
boast is as once having been the residence of that notorious
demagogue John Wilkes, whose pursuits here were of a
more innocent character than might be expected. He was
given to rearing birds, we are told, and studying their habits.
If Shanklin wanted a name to set off against this worthy's,
it might proclaim how it was the favourite abode of Benson,
alias Count de Montague, hero of a notorious Turf fraud, and
still greater knaveries that never came to light. Son of a
respectable Jewish tradesman in Paris, he began his career
of crime in England by swindling the very Lord Mayor of
London, and at the height of it delighted in a charming
retreat at Shanklin, where he used to entertain the detectives
charged with quite a different errand to him. The way in
which this plausible scoundrel's turn for the genteel and
beautiful recommended him to local society must be still a
sore point in the neighbourhood; but in London also he
made influential friends among those who were not set on
their guard by his overdone elegance. After serving a long

sentence of penal servitude he took to his old tricks almost immediately on his release, and finally committed suicide in an American prison.

Though Sandown itself be not so much favoured by nature, it is within sight of many beautiful and interesting spots. Ashey, Bembridge, and Shanklin Downs, with their fine views, are all within an hour or two's walk. The Roman Villa (see p. 18) is almost as near it as to Brading. A walk of little over a mile by the Brading road, through the meadows lying along the course of the Yar, brings one before the chalk cutting in the face of the Downs, beneath which lies this curiosity, easily recognised from the ugly tarred sheds covering it. Once off the high road to the left, the intending visitor will find no want of direction posts. In returning to Sandown he may take another path to the left, into a deep lane beneath the Downs, reaching the prosperous-looking village of YARBRIDGE with its *Angler's Inn*, through which another road to Sandown (about 2 m.) may be followed by YAVERLAND, reached by a steep ascent from the bridge over the Yar.

The nucleus of Yaverland parish, on the southern slope of Bembridge Down, is a tiny Norman Church (with fine chancel-arch and south doorway), standing upon a mound, with an antique Jacobean Manor-House (A.D. 1620) in its rear, the latter a building of much interest, containing some curious carvings.

BEMBRIDGE DOWN to the north rises at one point to 355 feet, crowned by a large fort, to make room for which the conspicuous obelisk to Lord Yarborough has been moved a little way down. It was once an island, for at Sandown Brading Harbour opened into the sea up to the reign of Elizabeth. The round by the *Culver Cliffs* and the *Foreland* to *Bembridge* is a matter of 5 or 6 miles, to be diversified by a scramble on to the Down. Some caution is here and there desirable on these treacherous slopes, and the walk by the beach is not practicable at all states of the tide. Between the CULVER CLIFFS and the FORELAND, the eastern extremity of the island, curves the broken shore of WHITECLIFF BAY, where, as at Alum Bay, the chalk gives place to less imposing formations, already mentioned in our introduction as of special interest to geologists. The hotel, which did not flourish in this pretty spot, has recently been reopened as a boarding-house, under the style of *The Isle of Wight Hydro*, a title perhaps suggested by the chalybeate spring on the premises. At the Fore-land coastguard station (1½ mile from Bembridge) is a little fishing hamlet with a small inn, the *Crab and Lobster*. This is a dangerous part of the coast, through a long low-lying reef of rocks, known as the *Bembridge Ledges*, which projects far into the sea, either covered or exposed according to the state of the tide. Here we round the point of the promontory and come back to the limit of our walks from Ryde. We must now turn inland to conclude our tour at the centre of the island.

FROM SANDOWN TO NEWPORT

Sandown to Newport is a railway ride of half an hour or so, the line passing along the foot of the central Downs, their green face broken by chalk cuttings and patches of wood. Weather and other considerations permitting, the visitor would do well to make this journey on foot by the top of the Downs, a walk from Sandown of some 10 miles, where he could hardly miss the way, either keeping the high road or following the heights till they drop down into the Medina Valley. Ascending the Downs by the road between Yarbridge and Brading, or making a short cut over them by the Roman Villa, he will soon sight the stone pillar marking the height of ASHEY DOWN, one of the finest view points in the island, which is a favourite excursion from Ryde and Newport. The Ryde Waterworks at the foot of it will serve as another landmark. The prospect from above embraces the Solent, the harbours of Portsmouth and South-ampton, Ryde, Osborne, Brading Harbour, Sandown, Shanklin and the Downs to the south. Sir H. Englefield, in his description of the beauties of the island, speaks of this view as unsurpassed in richness and variety.

The railway stations are :

Alverstone, near the Roman Villa.

Newchurch, already visited from Shanklin. To the right lies *Knighton,* through which is the way to *Ashey Down,* about 2 miles off.

Harringford, a place of no note in itself, but the station for ARRETON village and Down, about a mile to the north. This is one of the favourite spots, to which the coaches from Ryde to Carisbrooke commonly make a detour on the return journey, halting to let the passengers visit the church-yard, where, among those of knights and men of war, the most famous monument is that to Elizabeth Wallbridge, the "Dairyman's Daughter," renowned in Legh Richmond's *Annals of the Poor.* Her cottage is also shown in the vicinity. The old manor-house, now a farm, contains some good carving. The landscape here is renowned, Arreton lying between the Downs and a pleasant vale of rich agricultural land. The scattered village (*Hare and Hounds Inn*) numbers some 2000 inhabitants. Its *Church* stands upon a slight ascent which rises gently from the road—a fine old building, containing traces of all the different styles of Gothic, from Norman of the eleventh century down to Perpendicular of the sixteenth. The windows of the chancel are good specimens of Early Decorated work of about 1300, and around one of these there are the remains of an ancient fresco. Some brass work is also noticeable. On the Downs above are some Saxon barrows.

Merston Crossing would be the nearest station for *Godshill,* already described ; but all trains do not stop here. To the south we see the Downs of the Undercliff within an after-noon's walk.

Blackwater, also a mere stopping-place, lies below *St. George's Down,* and among fine woods. Here we come upon the river *Medina.* This is the station for GATCOMBE, with its park, and the fine tower of its old church rising from a leafy grove. There is some good painted glass here, both old and new. On the north side of the chancel is a wooden cross-legged effigy of a crusader, dating from early in the thirteenth century. Blackwater is also half an hour's walk from *Carisbrooke Castle.*

7

Shide, with its bridge over the Medina, at the foot of *Pan Down*, is almost a suburb of Newport.

As the historical associations of the island cluster mainly round Newport and Carisbrooke, here seems the place for presenting a short sketch of its history, which may be skipped by the light-minded reader, yet might serve him to while away one of the wet days that too often spoil his tour.

HISTORY OF THE ISLAND

The ISLE OF WIGHT, known to the Romans as *Vecta* or *Vectis*, was first invaded by them A.D. 43, in the reign of the Emperor Claudius, and they retained possession of it till A.D. 530, when it was reduced by Cedric the Saxon. It suffered severely during the wars of the Saxon heptarchy, and was also frequently plundered and devastated by the Danes. The Saxons formed the nucleus of the feudal stronghold at Carisbrooke, where probably had stood a British camp, as later a Roman fortress. When the island fell into the hands of William the Conqueror, he gave it over to the lordship of one of his most valiant knights, William Fitz-Osborne. Once only the king himself visited this domain, his presence called for by rebellious designs on the part of his half-brother Odo, whom he seized at Carisbrooke and sent the ambitious prelate prisoner to Normandy.

Fitz-Osborne repaired and enlarged the fortress, adding what is called the *basecourt* to the Saxon *keep*, and constructing strong walls, which included a space of an acre and a half. In this castle he often held high revels, and, imitating the example of his royal master, he divided the surrounding country among his faithful vassals, who afterwards held their estates of "the Honour and Castle of Carisbrooke."

William Fitz-Osborne's honours passed to his son, Roger Fitz-Osborne, or de Bretuel, Earl of Hereford; but Roger was neither so prudent nor so able as his father. Rebelling against King William, he was cast into prison and deprived of his possessions. Thus the Castle of Carisbrooke fell into the hands of the king. For more than two centuries, however, the island continued to be governed by quasi-independent lords. But in 1293, Edward I. purchased the regalities for the sum of 6000 marks an amount nearly equal in purchasing power to £60,000 of our money, from Isabella de Fortibus, Lady of Wight; and since then the island has been governed by wardens, appointed by the Crown. Henry VI. conferred the title of King of the Isle of Wight upon Henry Beauchamp, Duke of Warwick, and crowned him with his own hands; but the empty title expired in 1445 with the nobleman who first bore it. The royal wardens afterwards came to be entitled governors or captains; and the office has now become a mere honorary one. It is at present held by Prince Henry of Battenberg.

In 1377, the first year of the reign of Richard II., Sir Hugh Tyrrell being Warden of the Isle of Wight, a large body of French rovers landed on the east shore, and encamped beneath the walls of Carisbrooke. Unprovided for a regular siege, they attempted to capture it by a *coup de main*, but fell into an ambuscade planned by Sir Hugh Tyrrell, the governor, and were cut to pieces. So great was the slaughter that the islanders (according to a tradition) called the fight thus easily won the battle of *the Noddies*, or simpletons, and the spot where the chief rush of the *mêlée* took place is still called *the Noddies*', or *Node Hill*. A lane near the castle, called Dead Man's Lane, is said to have received its name from the number of slain found in it after the fight; but this sinister appellation is also attributed to the ravages of the plague in 1582.

The castle received a distinguished prisoner in 1397, the Earl of Warwick, who had joined "the Fitzalan Conspiracy" against Richard II., and was saved from the scaffold by the earnest solicitations of the Earl of Salisbury, to be banished for life to the Isle of Wight. Humphrey the "good" Duke of Gloucester; Richard Duke of York who perished at Agincourt; Edmund Duke of Somerset; Anthony, valiant and accomplished Lord Scales; Sir Edward Woodville, a gallant and courteous gentleman, who kept up a brave splendour at Carisbrooke; and Richard Worsley, a favourite councillor of Henry VIII., were among the captains of Carisbrooke Castle in Plantagenet and Tudor times.

In the middle of the sixteenth century another invasion was attempted by the French, who landed at different points to be everywhere repulsed. A greater calamity was an outbreak of the plague in 1582, which at Newport especially exacted an appalling tribute of victims. Among them was Sir Edward Horsey,

Captain of the Island, who left his mark on its records as a stout soldier of fortune that kept a sharp eye on French and Spanish enemies, yet no saint in private life, and not untainted with suspicion of piracy such as then often counted for a patriotic virtue.

Carisbrooke Castle now becomes more than ever the centre of the island's history. In Elizabeth's reign, during the panic caused by the fitting out of the Spanish Armada, the castle was repaired, strengthened, and enlarged. It was once visited by James I. and twice by Prince Charles, who "hunted in the parke, and killed a bucke," and otherwise amused their idle hours during their brief excursions. At the outset of the great Civil War it was garrisoned by a small detachment of Royalist troops under a chivalrous Cavalier, Colonel Brett. The wife of the Governor of the Island, the Countess of Portland, and her five children were entrusted to their loyal care, and all hoped, in the stout castle, to secure a pleasant asylum. But the inhabitants of Newport were fiercely Parliamentarian, and, assisted by 400 naval auxiliaries, resolved upon seizing the castle, and holding it for the Parliament. The besiegers were numerous, well provided with artillery, and easily supplied with stores. The garrison consisted of a few invalided soldiers, and had but three days' provisions. There seemed no alternative but an unconditional surrender. In these critical circumstances the Countess took her lord's place to play the hero. Appearing on the ramparts, a lighted match in hand, she demanded the lives and freedom of the defenders, or she herself would fire the first cannon and hold out till they were buried beneath the walls. The besiegers, struck by admiration of such courage, granted her demands, and the Countess retired from the castle with honour.

Thirty years had elapsed since Prince Charles hunted the buck in Parkhurst Forest, when, a powerless king, he passed again under the massive archway to the solitude and sorrow of a prison. At first he was treated with all the respect due to his rank. He rode out whenever he pleased, and again hunted the deer in Parkhurst, though Colonel Hammond, the Parliamentary Governor, rode at his side. The Parliament allowed him a yearly revenue of £5000, and he lived in the state apartments of the castle, long shown as *King Charles's Rooms*. But he was gradually stripped of the ceremonials of royalty. His chaplains and faithful attendants were removed, and others forced upon him, of whom he only knew that they had been chosen by his enemies. He no longer rode abroad, but was constrained to view the forest and the downs through the bars of his prison window. Thus confined, the unhappy monarch became careless of his attire, iu which once he had so fine a taste, allowed his beard to grow, was wan and haggard,—a "gray discrowned king."

How the imprisoned king passed his days has been duly recorded by his faithful attendants. He rose early. He took moderate exercise, walking round the ramparts, or pacing to and fro the narrow bowling-green, into which Colonel Hammond had converted "the place of arms." Of food he ate sparingly, and his drink at dinner was sack, diluted with two parts water. He chiefly employed his leisure hours in reading, writing, and meditating, or in conversation with those who waited about his person. The principal books he read were Bishop Andrew's Sermons, Hooker's "Ecclesiastical Polity," Herbert's Poems, Fairfax's version of Tasso's "Gierusalemme Liberata," and Spenser's "Faëry Queen." In one of these books he penned a Latin distich, which vividly illustrates his peculiar cast of thought :—

> "Rebus in adversis facile est contemnere vitam ;
> Fortiter ille facit qui miser esse potest."

> In evil times, life we may well disdain ;
> He doeth bravely who can suffer pain.

Here also, according to some, he wrote or finished the famous *Eikon Basilike*, which is more credibly attributed to Bishop Gauden.

Two attempts were made by the Royalists to secure the monarch's freedom, both ineffectual. He carried on a correspondence with his chief adherents in cipher ; but the cipher was detected, and the letters were intercepted by the Parliamentarian leaders, who consequently could frustrate the plans contrived for his escape.

The first attempt was made on the night of the 20th of March 1648. Four or five gentlemen were on the watch to assist the king, whose purpose it was to get out through his prison window, cross the court of the castle, and reach the counterscarp. A horse, ready saddled and bridled, was there waiting for him, in charge of a trusty cavalier ; a ride across the island by night ;

then at the seashore a boat, well manned, to bear him to liberty. The scheme was well devised, but failed through the narrowness of the window, which prevented Charles from forcing his body through it.

Again the plot was laid for on Sunday night, May 28th, when the king removed the bars which had impeded him on the former occasion, and might have escaped, but that the whole details of the project were known to Colonel Hammond, the Governor of Carisbrooke, and double guards had been placed at convenient positions to fire upon any person leaving the castle. An attempt by Captain Burley, a half-pay naval officer, to rouse the inhabitants in his favour, met with no better fortune, being quickly put down, when the leader was hanged as a traitor, as "having made war against the king in his parliament."

Towards the end of that year, negotiations were held at Newport between the king and the Parliamentary Commissioners, by whom he was treated in a respectful spirit. These negotiations took place in the Grammar School, the king being seated in a chair of state under a canopy ; on either side of a long table were ranged the Commissioners ; behind the king stood his attendants, Sir P. Warwick, Sir Edward Walker, and others. The proceedings continued for sixty days. The king occupied the house of a private citizen, his attendants being accommodated at the George Inn on the south side of High Street (now destroyed), and the Commissioners staying at the Bull (now the Bugle) Inn.

The treaty proved abortive to some extent through the curious mixture of conscientiousness and crookedness which marked this king's character. And now power passed out of the hands of the more moderate party. Cromwell's victorious army overrode all scruples. The parliament was "purged" by military violence. The king soon learned the disposition of his new masters. In the middle of the night, hesitating to make another venture for escape which here seemed open to him, he was seized by Roundhead soldiers at Newport, hurried away to the north-western corner of the island, and carried across the strait to Hurst Castle. A brief entry in the register of Carisbrooke Church records the king's removal :—"The last day of November he went from Newport to Hurst Castell to prison, carried away by two troops of horse." Another pithy passage sums up the ill-fated monarch's history :—"In the year of our

Lord God, 1649, January the 30th day, was Kinge Charles beheaded at Whitehall Gate."

The next prisoners in this castle were recommended to the humanity of their gaolers by their innocent youth as much as by their royal blood. The Princess Elizabeth and the Duke of Gloucester, the daughter and son of Charles I., were removed here on the 16th of August 1650. The Princess Elizabeth was "a lady of excellent parts, great observation, and an early understanding," but deformed and bowed down by an unconquerable malady. Her brother has been described by Clarendon as "a prince of extraordinary hopes, both from the comeliness and gracefulness of his person, and the vivacity and vigour of his wit and understanding." While residing at Carisbrooke he was addressed as "Master Harry," and a yearly allowance of £1000 was granted both to him and the princess.

But within a week after their arrival, the princess "being at bowls, a sport she much delighted in, there fell a sudden shower, and being of a sickly constitution, it caused her to take cold, and the next day she complained of headache and feverish distemper, which by fits increased upon her." In spite of all that could be done by the medical science of that day, she "took leave of the world on Sunday the 8th September 1650." It is said she was found lying upon her couch, as if sleeping, her face resting upon an open Bible, her royal father's gift. She was buried in Newport Church, September 20, 1650.

The young Duke of Gloucester remained a prisoner in the castle until 1652, when, by permission of Cromwell, he was released and departed into Holland.

After this, the Isle of Wight seems to have been happy in having no history to speak of, though at the beginning of our century it was kept in alarm, even more than most parts of the kingdom, by dread of that old calamity, French invasion. Its next great event was a royal residence under happier auspices, when in 1844, Queen Victoria, conjointly with the late Prince Consort, purchased Osborne and has since made her winter home there.

If it has gained in royal favour, the island has lost in political influence. Before the Reform Bill of 1832, it was much over-represented, the boroughs of Newport, Newtown, and Yarmouth returning each two members to Parliament, but Newtown and Yarmouth were then disfranchised, one member being given to the Isle, and two for the borough of Newport. By the Reform Bill of 1867, Newport was deprived of one of its members and in 1885 it was disfranchised. There is therefore now just one member for the Isle of Wight, which for the purposes of the Local Government Act forms a separate administrative county.

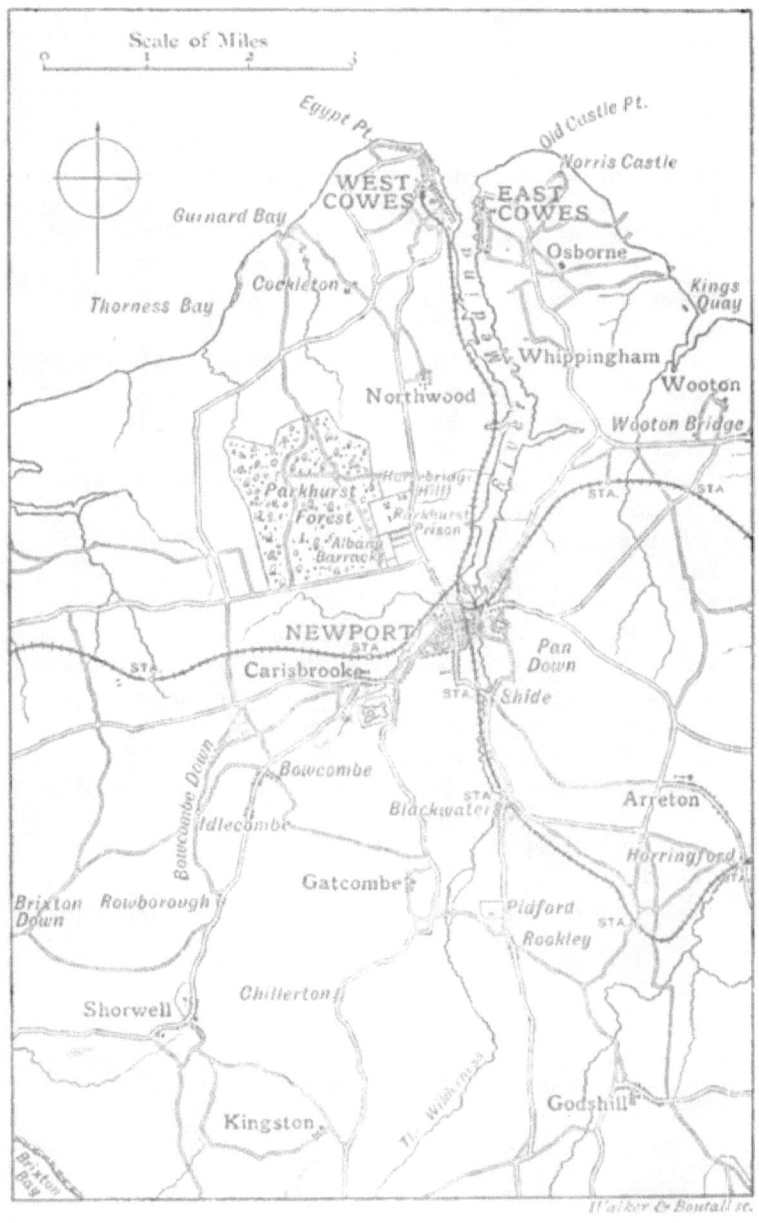

NEWPORT

Hotels : *Eagle* (C.), *Swan*, *Warburton's*.
Inns : *Star*, *Wheatsheaf*, *Rose and Crown*, *St. James' Temperance, etc.*
Banks : London and County ; National Provincial ; Capital and Counties.

THE capital of the island is a prosperous-looking borough of some 10,000 inhabitants, with many smart shops in the long High Street, and its openings of *St. Thomas'* and *St. James' Squares*. The place is believed to be of Roman origin. It was incorporated in 1603. With various ups and downs of fortune, it has grown into its present flourishing state, the main source of which is the river Medina, navigable up to this point for small vessels, which carry on a trade in timber, malt, wheat, and flour. Newport is now important also as the meeting-point of the railways from all parts of the island, of which its situation, where the Medina cuts through the dividing Downs, makes it a natural centre.

A few minutes by the road from the railway station brings us to *St. Thomas' Church*, built in 1854-7 to replace the old church dating from 1175, when it was erected by Richard de Redvers, and dedicated to the recently canonised Archbishop of Canterbury, Thomas à Becket. The memorials it contained are preserved in the present building—an Early Decorated structure of some size. The tower at the west end contains the fine peal of bells from the old church. The nave is clerestoried, and there are gabled aisles and a chancel. The *Pulpit* (from the old church) dates from 1633. Its carvings were the work of one Thomas Caper, whose device—a goat, in allusion to his name—may be seen on its back. Justice and Mercy figure

on the sounding-board, around which is a sentence from
the Psalms, "Cry aloud, and spare not : lift up thy voice
like a trumpet." On the sides are sculptured a curious
personification of the Three Graces, the Four Cardinal
Virtues, and the Seven Liberal Sciences—grammar, dia-
lectics, rhetoric, music, arithmetic, geometry, astrology.
There is a monument to *Sir Edward Horsey*, formerly
captain of the island (1565-82), representing his effigy, clad
in armour, beneath a rich painted and gilded canopy, and an
epitaph which ascribes to him more virtues than we fear he
possessed. The memorial (by Marochetti) erected by Queen
Victoria to Charles I.'s ill-fated daughter, the *Princess
Elizabeth*, is a lovely piece of sculpture, and ought to be visited.
It represents her as, according to tradition, she was discovered
by her attendants, reclining in death upon her couch, with
her face resting on the pages of an open Bible, a gift from
her royal father. Her body was buried in the chancel of
the old Church on September 20, 1650, but its resting-
place was forgotten until, in 1793, some labourers engaged
in digging a grave discovered the royal maiden's coffin.
This has of late years been moved and opened. A deformed
rib bone and a lock of fair hair taken out of it are shown at
"Ye Olde Curiosity Shoppe," near the railway station.
There is a good deal of painted glass in the church, and
in the north aisle is a medallion likeness, in white marble,
of the late Prince Consort by Marochetti.

St. Thomas' stands in a square off the High Street, which
forms the central point of the town, though St. James' Square,
a little farther on, may show more bustle on market days.
The new red building, which at one corner makes such a
contrast with its old-fashioned neighbours in St. Thomas'
Square, is a factory of the mineral waters so much used
over the island. There are two other churches in the town,
of no great interest, and various chapels, including a characteristically sober Friends' Meeting-house.

The most remarkable old building is the *Grammar School*
at the corner of Lugley and St. James' Streets. It dates
from 1612, and the old schoolroom is notable as having
been occupied for a time by Charles I. during the negotia-

tions which resulted in the abortive treaty of Newport. A new schoolroom has now been added ; but as the old room is in part adapted for use as the boys' dining-hall, visitors will do well to choose a convenient hour for inspection, which is permitted by the courtesy of the headmaster. The old portion makes a fine specimen of a Jacobean mansion. Here on November 30, 1648, the king was seized and hurried to the mainland on the last stage of his un-fortunate career.

The *Town Hall*, as to which, perhaps, the less said the better, forces itself on one's attention in the High Street, near St. Thomas' Square. The style bespeaks the date— 1816. It contains a statue of Lord Chief Justice Fleming, and a medallion of Guido Fawkes. The foundation stone of the Clock Tower was laid in 1887 to commemorate the Jubilee of Queen Victoria. The *Isle of Wight County Club* now occupies the buildings formerly belonging to the Literary Institution at the corner of High Street and St. James' Square. The *Isle of Wight Museum*, on the premises of the Newport Literary Society in Quay Street, opposite the Town Hall, is a very creditable institution, and contains among other things an excellent and well-arranged series of local fossils. In Lugley Street is the *Newport Jubilee Free Club*, established at the expense of the late Charles Seely, M.P. for Lincoln, with a library of from two to three thousand volumes, which may be borrowed by any resident on three days of the week.

The great sight of Newport is of course Carisbrooke Castle.

CARISBROOKE

It is only a mile or so from Newport to Carisbrooke, which the excursion coaches usually take as their goal here. From the end of the High Street, turning to the right as we reach it from the station, our way lies by the *Mall*, a parade suggesting some dignified watering-place rather than a quiet country town. The road branches at a Cross erected to the memory of Sir John Simeon, Tennyson's friend. Here the pedestrian may hold to the left, and will

soon be guided by the Castle Keep peeping out among trees
on an eminence.   The road to the right leads to the
village, which, as becomes this Windsor of Newport, has
many hostelries that, in the matter of terms, are in the way
of making hay while the sun shines.   We find the *Red
Lion*, the *Carisbrooke Castle* in the middle, and the *Waverley*
at the top of the village, which take brevet rank as Hotels,
and answer to that designation in point of charges.   The
Eight Bells, Bugle, etc., more modestly style themselves Inns.
There is a Temperance House also and much tea-garden
accommodation, which must be hard beset on occasion of
great popular excursions, for one Whit Monday holiday of
late brought about ten thousand visitors.   The coach
excursionist will be saved the trouble of choosing his
quarters, as the coaches usually set him down at the
Carisbrooke Castle or the *Eight Bells*.   These are all in the
village street, mounting a hollow between the Church and
the Castle.   An omnibus runs from Newport Station to
Carisbrooke, which has a station of its own on the Freshwater line.

The *Church*, originally belonging to a Priory, of which
a few gray stones remain, is a very stately building, with a
remarkably fine Perpendicular tower, of the same date as
the towers of Gatcombe, Chale, and Godshill.   The south
aisle is separated from the nave by a Transition-Norman
arcade.   An ancient slab, broken into two pieces, com-
memorates one of the monks, vicars of Carisbrooke.   There
are several interesting monuments, particularly one to Lady
Dorothy Wadham, Queen Jane Seymour's sister.   Against
one of the pillars of the nave is the monument with rhym-
ing inscription to *William Keeling*, d. 1619, groom of the
chambers to King James I., and general to the East India
Company.   There is also a tomb to Charles Dixon, a black-
smith, with quaintly figurative verses, ending with the
lines :—

> " My fire-dried corpse here lies at rest ;
> My soul, smoke-like, soars to be blest."

In the porch is an ancient stone coffin, dug up in the

churchyard. Another relic is a curious old Peter's Pence box.

Near the parsonage are the ruins of a ROMAN VILLA unearthed in 1859, which it would seem included an area of 120 feet by 55, and contained several apartments, the largest 40 feet by 22, a semicircular bath, hypocaust, etc. A mosaic pavement, some coins, and other relics have been carefully preserved. The remains are, however, nothing like so extensive or so interesting as those more recently discovered near Brading. The charge for admission is 6d.

These minor lions duly disposed of, we can devote ourselves to the dominant attraction of the place.

CARISBROOKE CASTLE stands beautifully situated on a wooded mound, its moat choked with trees, its crumbling bulwarks overgrown with creepers, but still in sufficient preservation to show how in Charles I.'s day it was a not unworthy royal residence. Its touching associations with that king's last days taken into account, it makes perhaps the most romantic ruin in England, and many an hour might by poetic souls be dreamed away within this

> "Chiefless castle, breathing stern farewells
> From gray and ivied walls where Ruin greenly dwells."

The walls enclose an area of about an acre and a half, the greatest length being from east to west. It is said that a fortress existed here before the Roman occupation; but it is quite certain that Carisbrooke was fortified and held by the Romans in the reign of the Emperor Claudius. The most ancient part of the existing castle is the Keep, probably of the eleventh century; the handsome entrance gateway was erected in the fifteenth century; the small outer gate during the reign of Queen Elizabeth; and most of the buildings in the courtyard belong to various periods since that date. The present ground-plan of the castle, with its pentagonal arrangement, represents the additions to its fortifications made in the reign of Elizabeth, under the direction of an Italian engineer named Genobella. A dilapidated window, with a few rusty bars, brings back the shadow of the Civil Wars, being pointed out as that through which Charles I. vainly attempted to escape. Thus almost every era of English history has some association with the ruined stronghold.

Our first step must be the prosaic one of ringing the bell and paying the charge of a groat for admission at *Queen Elizabeth's Gate*, after, if we please, making the circuit of the grassy moat, in itself a very agreeable stroll, and surveying the walls from the outside through the rich copse that has grown up around them. We will now pass under the fine machicolated Gateway, erected by Anthony Woodville, afterwards Lord Scales, about 1464. A portcullis defends it, and on each side it is strengthened by a round tower. The stout wooden gates are very ancient. Entering the Great Court we observe, on our left, the Elizabethan building occupied by Charles I. after his first attempt to escape. Here too is the chamber in which it is said that the Princess Elizabeth breathed her last.

The buildings facing the entrance were formerly the *Governor's Residence.* Recent repairs have brought to light some ancient features of high interest. The great staircase appears to have been converted out of an Early English *Chapel*, built by William de Vernon, 1184-1217; and the *Great Hall* of Baldwin de Redvers, 1135-1156, was found to have been divided into two stories. The apartments occupied by Charles before his first attempted flight have been carefully renovated, and a good stone fireplace, and a hagioscope communicating with the chapel will attract attention in the royal *Presence-Chamber*. The *King's Bedroom* was on the upper story.

The *Chapel of St. Nicholas*, now an utter ruin, was built by Lord Lymington, Governor of the Island, in 1738, on the site of an ancient fane, which was supposed to be Saxon in its origin.

The *Keep*, occupying the site of the old Celtic stronghold, and the stout tower of William Fitz-Osborne, is still massive and imposing. The mound whereon it stands is scaled by 71 broken steps. In a ruined chamber to the left was a well, nearly choked with rubbish, but still deep enough to need protection. It failed during the siege of the castle

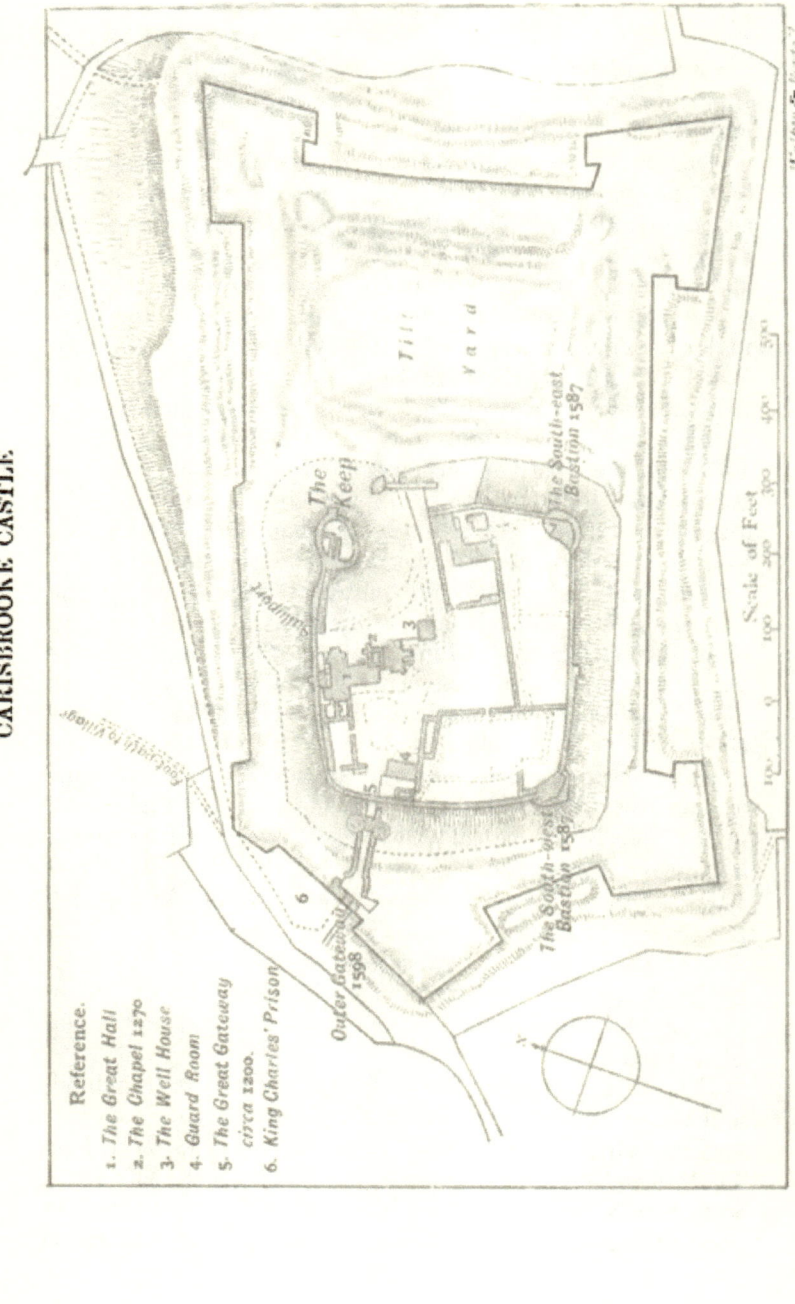

CARISBROOKE CASTLE

Reference.

1. The Great Hall
2. The Chapel 1270
3. The Well House
4. Guard Room
5. The Great Gateway
   circa 1200.
6. King Charles' Prison.

Tilt Yard

The Keep

The South-east Bastion 1587

The South-west Bastion 1587

Outer Gateway 1598

Footpath to Village

Scale of Feet

by King Stephen's forces in 1150, and Baldwin de Redvers was consequently forced to surrender. That a similar catastrophe might not again occur, Count Baldwin sank, in another part of the castle-area, the famous *Well*, so great an object of attraction to visitors, from whose depths (150 feet) the water is drawn up by means of an industrious donkey and a large wooden wheel. The donkeys thus distinguished have been remarkable for their longevity : one died in 1798, aged 32. A successor "paid the debt of nature" in 1851, after 21 years' toil. There are now two donkeys employed, the senior as yet a mere youngster in his teens. The water of this well is renowned for its refreshing purity and coolness, at such a depth remaining unaltered in temperature throughout the year. The *Well-house*, of the fifteenth century, has been restored.

The visitor should conclude his examination of the castle by a stroll round its outworks, and a visit to the *Tilt-yard*, and the *Mountjoy Tower*, which strengthens the south-east angle of the ramparts. He can walk all round the ramparts, except at one part beside the Keep, where the way is closed. The top of the Keep gives a glorious view over a great part of the island, from the towers of Osborne, peeping out over its woods, to the monument on Appuldurcombe. Only towards Freshwater is the prospect somewhat shut in by nearer heights.

The return to Newport might be made by the Node Hill road, passing the New Cemetery, and traversing the green slopes of Mountjoy. Behind the Cemetery, on the way to Gatcombe, is the large Dominican Priory, founded by the late Countess of Clare. This is a very fine range of buildings with a handsome chapel. In the rear of the convent are the gardens and orchards for the use of the nuns. The chapel and some of the rooms can be seen by visitors ; but this being an enclosed order, the public are not admitted into the convent itself.

OTHER EXCURSIONS FROM NEWPORT

As the excursion coaches usually put up at Carisbrooke, many visitors see nothing more of the chief town than a glimpse in rattling through its High Street. But those who are not devoted to the sea might oftener make their headquarters at Newport, which is an excellent centre for visiting the whole island, not to speak of the amenity of its immediate environs. Lodgings can be had on the Mall and elsewhere ; and in the hot season, we fancy, the hotel accommodation would not be found so crowded as at the coast resorts.

The Medina here is tidal, and at high water offers a very pretty picture that *ladet zum Bade*. Young mud-larks may be seen dabbling refreshingly in it at various states of the tide ; but as the sewage of Newport and Cowes must be bandied about between the two, more fastidious strangers will probably eschew this delight. The nearest point at which good bathing will be found is Gurnard Bay, about 5 miles off. The directest way is by the high road to Newport (see p. 33), skirting PARKHURST Forest, and passing the large barracks and prison which in themselves form a small town, where we have seen prisoners engaged in the idyllic occupation of making hay under a guard with fixed bayonets. This prison, formerly a military one, now ranks among convict establishments as a kind of sanitarium, to which delicate criminals are sent : a detail that, we trust, will be of interest to none of our readers. If in no hurry, one would do well to turn aside to seek the shady paths and lanes through the forest, just the scene for a ramble on hot days. This compact woodland begins a mile from Newport, stretching northward for a couple of miles or so.

A row or sail to Cowes and back, the tide being duly studied, might make another pleasant trip. Landing on the way, however, is not easy, when the slimy mud-banks are exposed.

On the other sides, Newport is enclosed by the "quarried downs of Wight," where the stranger can hardly go wrong in trying his fortune, and, by noting the many conspicuous landmarks, is in little danger of losing his way. Mounting *Pan Down*, for instance, he might cross its velvety turf to descend into *Arreton*, and return by the opposite side of the valley through *Carisbrooke*; or he might hold on over the central ridge to *Ashey Down*, and thence to *Bembridge Down*, a walk of 10 miles. Not quite so long would be a tramp southwards over *Bowcombe Down* to *Brixton* and the coast; and not much longer to keep on by the southern heights, with the sea for guide, till over *Afton Down* he reaches the Freshwater corner. Few English towns are so much favoured as Newport in having long stretches of open and breezy walking close at hand.

Excellent roads run to all parts of the island, and the less interesting stages can usually be got over by train. A few distances are: *Osborne* 4 miles, *Ryde* 7 miles, *Brading* 8 miles, *Bembridge* (by road) 12 miles, *Shanklin* and *Ventnor* about 10 miles, the other end of the *Undercliff* 9 miles, *Freshwater* 12 miles, *Yarmouth* 11 miles. A good walker, taking up his quarters at Newport, will thus have no difficulty in "doing" the whole island in a week.

In conclusion, we will indicate more in detail two or three of the outings from Newport, each of them half a dozen miles or less, which will take us to spots already dealt with, by some points of interest which have hitherto been passed over.

NEWPORT to GODSHILL

The road to Godshill is one of the most picturesque in this part of the Wight. Beyond the town, leaving behind us, on our right, the church of *St. John's*, we quickly descend to *Shide Bridge*, on the Medina, a spot of some importance in the earlier history of the island, cross the Medina, and traverse the valley that here breaks through the central range of chalk hills. We follow the course of the river with but little variation until

Blackwater is reached. Here the valley opens upon a wide expanse of meadows and cornfields, and the undulating downs stretch far away to the east. At the base of *Pan Down* may be noted the plain brick building of *Standen House*. To the right extends the well-timbered park of *Gatcombe*, situate in a pleasant valley, and watered by the winding river. Then we reach *Pidford House*, about 3 miles from Newport, where a road diverges to Gatcombe, and another road, or lane, a short distance beyond, to Sheat Farm, and thence southward to *Chillerton*. *Rookley* and its little school-house is our next point. Here we have a choice of routes. The road to the left skirts the sloping sides of *Rookley Down*, and passes some sequestered farmsteads on its way to Godshill, affording some fine views of the southern downs, and the distant hill, of ferruginous sand, upon which stands *Godshill Church*. The other road at the *Chequers Inn* divides again,—one branch, by a circuitous route, reaching *Godshill* (for which a straighter field-path goes off just beyond the inn), the lane to the right crossing *Bleak Down*, and proceeding by way of *Lashmere Pond* and *Appleford* to *Niton*. This is an excellent locality for the botanist, who should have little difficulty in making some interesting finds.

NEWPORT to CALBOURNE

Leaving Newport by the Carisbrooke road, passing between the church and the castle, at the top of the village take the right-hand road and so gain Bowcombe Down (*Beaucombe*, fine valley). In the hollow beneath lies the manor-house of Alvington, and beyond, appear the dark fir clumps of Parkhurst Forest. At *Park Cross*, 2½ miles, a road, right, branches off to *Thorness*, and from thence by Tinker's Lane and Lower Cockleton into West Cowes; another, left, crosses the chalk hills to Bowcombe Farm. Continuing our route we reach (at 4 miles from Newport) the grounds and mansion of *Swainston*, once attached to the see of Winchester. The house, a square stone mansion, about half a century old, contains some mediæval fragments of

the ancient episcopal residence. The demesne is richly
wooded. To the north lies *Watchingwell*, a portion of the
old royal chase of Parkhurst Forest. Southward runs a
picturesque lane to *Rowbridge* (where, in the neighbouring
copses, may be found the beautiful *Calamintha sylvatica*,
and on the downs several varieties of orchises) and across
the hills to Gallibury and Rowborough, the sites of some
ancient Celtic pit-villages. At a mile and a half from
Swainston we gain the interesting village of Calbourne,
where we are about half-way to either Yarmouth or
Freshwater.

THE ROWBOROUGH REMAINS

For a more direct way to these traces of antiquity, we
leave Newport by the High Street to follow the road through
the village of *Carisbrooke*, having then *Bowcombe Down* on
the right hand. We pass Bowcombe Farm on the left,
Idlecombe Farm on the right, and after walking just 3
miles from Carisbrooke Church, reach *Rowborough Farm*.
Here a little lane turns up from the main road to the right
to an Ancient British Settlement, lying in the hollow between
Gallibury and Rowborough Downs, well worth examination,
though the eye of an antiquary be needed to make much of
its half-effaced outlines.

After leaving the main road keep to the right up to the
Down, where a turn to the left should be taken. Following
the footpath a gate is reached which leads into the first of
the valleys containing the pit-dwellings. The lower portion
of this valley is terraced roughly across, with about one pit
to each terrace ; higher up the valley the pits are closer together. There are here in all ten pits, each 20 to 30 feet
wide, and more or less circular in outline. Some of them
are now filled up to a greater or less extent with a growth of
brushwood. Above the last pit a long excavation runs up the
valley for some 20 or 30 yards, inclining a little to the left ;
probably this is the bottom of an old road. A good deal
higher up on the left slope, at the very top of the valley
and just below the ridge which divides it from the next

valley, is a much larger excavation, basin-like, with an embankment towards the first valley. This excavation now contains water, presumably supplied by a spring in the chalk formation. Above lies another shallow excavation, much larger than the pit-houses below.

Reached over the ridge on the left, the next valley may be recognised by the presence of a large barn at its upper end. Now turning to the left down the valley, we keep on the right-hand side of the hedge. After passing seven more or less distinct pits, the last three on the left-hand side of the hedge, a gate is reached which faces the opening of a third valley running up to the right. In this lies the best series of pit-dwellings. There are about eighteen of them, arranged for a long distance up the valley in a single series. After passing the first two excavations, the second of which is much elongated in the direction of the valley, a very large, transversely-elongated excavation is reached, from which a raised dyke may be traced, running up the slope of the Down on the right-hand side. The other pits are similar to those described.

The main road may be regained by following a footpath which leads straight from the gate at the bottom of this valley into the lane by Rowborough Farm ; but the visitor, if returning to Newport, is recommended to find his way back along the tops of the Downs, whence a magnificent prospect may be enjoyed.

One expedition we mention with reserve, as, in damp weather especially, like to prove too adventurous. Yet some undaunted and well-shod explorer might venture to find his way up the Medina, through the peaty bogs of the *Wilderness* to where it takes its obscure rise near the heights of the Undercliff. He who tracked it from shore to shore would have seen almost every kind of scenery displayed by the Isle of Wight.

ITINERARIES

The following itineraries are suggested for the convenience of those who intend spending a few days on the island :—

NOTE.—Although these are intended as walking tours, yet in one or two places the tourist is recommended to take the train, as it will prevent his wasting his time and strength in the least interesting portions of the journey.

FOUR DAYS' ITINERARY.—FROM RYDE

FIRST DAY.—To Brading by train, 10 minutes ; walk to Yaverland, 1 m. ; on to the top of Bembridge Down, by the Obelisk, 1 m. ; along the cliffs to Sandown, 2 m. ; to Shanklin 2 m. ; along the cliffs to Luccombe Chine, 1½ m. ; through the Landslip to Bonchurch, 2 m. ; to Ventnor, 1 m.

SECOND DAY.—To St. Lawrence, 2 m. ; through the Undercliff to Blackgang, 5 m. ; Chale, 1 m. ; Kingston, 2½ m. ; Shorwell, 2 m. ; Brixton, 2 m. ; Mottistone, 1½ m. ; Brook, 1 m. ; Freshwater, 3 m.

THIRD DAY.—To the Needles, 3 m. ; Alum Bay, 1 m. ; Yarmouth, 4 m. ; Thorley, 1 m. ; Calbourne, 4 m. ; Carisbrooke, 4 m. ; Newport, 1 m.

FOURTH DAY.—To Cowes by train, 15 minutes ; East Cowes, 1 m. ; Whippingham, 2 m. ; Arreton, 5 m. ; along the top of the downs to Ashey sea-mark, 3 m. ; Ryde, 4 m.

THREE DAYS' ITINERARY.—FROM RYDE

FIRST DAY.—Cowes by steamer, half an hour ; train to Newport, 15 minutes ; Carisbrooke, 1 m. ; Calbourne, 4 m. ; Freshwater Gate, 5 m. ; the Needles, 3 m. ; Alum Bay.

SECOND DAY.—Freshwater, 3 m. ; Brook, 3 m. ; Mottistone, 1 m. ; Brixton, 1½ m. ; Shorwell, 2 m. ; Kingston, 2 m. ; Chale, 2½ m. ; Blackgang, 1 m.

THIRD DAY.—Through the Undercliff to St. Lawrence, 5 m. ; Ventnor, 2 m. ; Bonchurch, 1 m. ; through the Landslip to Luccombe, 2 m. ; Shanklin, 1½ m. ; Sandown, 2 m. ; from Sandown take the train to Ryde, 15 minutes.

FOUR DAYS' ITINERARY.—FROM WEST COWES

FIRST DAY.—To Gurnard Bay by the shore, 1½ m. ; Thorness Bay, 2 m. ; Shalfleet, 4 m. ; Yarmouth, 4 m. ; Alum Bay, 4 m. ; the Needles, 1 m. ; Freshwater Gate, 3½ m.

SECOND DAY.—To Brook, 4 m. ; Mottistone, 1½ m. ; Brixton, 2 m. ; Shorwell, 2 m. ; Carisbrooke, 4½ m. ; Newport, 1 m.

THIRD DAY.—To Shide, 1 m. ; Gatcombe, 2½ m. ; Kingston, 3 m. ; Chale, 3 m. ; Blackgang, 1 m. ; through the Undercliff to St. Lawrence, 5 m. ; Ventnor, 2 m.

FOURTH DAY.—To Bonchurch, 1 m. ; through the Landslip to Shanklin, 3 m. ; along the cliff to Sandown, 2 m. ; Brading, 2 m. ; take the train to Ryde, 10 minutes ; Ryde to Binstead, 1 m. ; Wootton, 2 m. ; Whippingham, 3 m. ; Cowes, 2 m.

THREE DAYS' ITINERARY.—FROM WEST COWES

FIRST DAY.—To Whippingham, 2 m. ; Wootton Bridge, 3 m. ; Binstead, 2 m. ; Ryde, 1 m. ; take the train to Brading, 10 minutes ; walk to Sandown, 2 m. ; Shanklin, 2 m. ; through the Landslip to Bonchurch, 3 m. ; Ventnor, 1 m.

SECOND DAY.—To St. Lawrence, 2 m. ; through the Undercliff to Blackgang, 4½ m. ; Chale, 1 m. ; Kingston, 3 m. ; Shorwell, 2 m. ; Brixton, 2 m. ; Mottistone, 2 m. ; Brooke, 1½ m. ; Freshwater Gate, 4 m.

THIRD DAY.—To the Needles, 3 m. ; Alum Bay, 1 m. ; Yarmouth, 4½ m. ; Calbourne, 6 m. ; Carisbrooke, 5 m. ; Newport, 1 m. ; take the train to Cowes, 15 minutes.

THREE DAYS' ITINERARY.—FROM NEWPORT

FIRST DAY.—To Carisbrooke, 1 m. ; over Alvington, Bowcombe, Gallibury, Brixton, Mottistone, Shalcomb, and Afton Down to Freshwater Gate, 10 m. ; commanding glorious views of the island ; along the top of the High Down to the Needles Fort, 3 m. ; Alum Bay, 1 m. ; round the base of Headon Hill to Totland Bay, 2 m. ; inland to Freshwater Gate, $2\frac{1}{2}$ m.

SECOND DAY.—Along the Military Road to Brook, $3\frac{1}{2}$ m. ; Mottistone, 1 m. ; Brixton, 2 m. ; Shorwell, 2 m. ; Kingston, 2 m. ; Chale, 3 m. ; Blackgang, 1 m. ; through the Undercliff to St. Lawrence, 5 m. ; Ventnor, 2 m. (This day's walk may be shortened by continuing along the Military Road from Brook to Chale.)

THIRD DAY.—Bonchurch, 1 m.; through the Landslip to Shanklin, 3 m. ; Sandown, 2 m. ; Brading, 2 m. ; over Brading, Ashey, and Arreton Down to Newport, $7\frac{1}{2}$ m.

FOUR DAYS' ITINERARY.—FROM BEMBRIDGE

FIRST DAY.—To the Foreland, and thence along the cliffs to Whitecliff Bay, $2\frac{1}{2}$ m. ; over Bembridge Down to Yarbridge, 2 m. ; over Brading, Ashey, Arreton, and St. George's Downs to Shide, $7\frac{1}{2}$ m. ; Carisbrooke, 1 m. ; Newport, 1 m. ; West Cowes, 5 m.

SECOND DAY.—Gurnard Bay along the shore, $1\frac{1}{2}$ m. ; Thorness Bay, 2 m. ; Shalfleet, 4 m. ; Yarmouth, 4 m. ; Alum Bay, 4 m. ; the Needles, 1 m. ; Freshwater Gate, $3\frac{1}{2}$ m.

THIRD DAY.—Along the Military Road to Brook, $3\frac{1}{2}$ m. ; Mottistone, 1 m. ; Brixton, 2 m. ; Shorwell, 2 m. ; Kingston, 2 m. ; Chale, 3 m. ; Blackgang, 1 m. ; through the Undercliff to St. Lawrence, 5 m. ; Ventnor, 2 m.

FOURTH DAY.—Over the tops of the Downs to the Worsley Monument, $3\frac{1}{2}$ m. ; Godshill, $1\frac{1}{2}$ m. ; Shanklin, 4 m. ; along the cliff to Sandown, 2 m. ; Brading, 2 m. ; Bembridge, 4 m.

THREE DAYS' ITINERARY.—FROM YARMOUTH

FIRST DAY.—Shalfleet, 4 m. ; Calbourne, 2 m. ; Carisbrooke, 4 m. ; Newport, 1 m. ; West Cowes, 5 m. ; Steamer to Ryde.

SECOND DAY.—Brading by train, ten minutes (see the Roman Villa) ; Sandown, 2 m. ; Shanklin, along the cliffs, 2 m. ; through the Landslip to Bonchurch, 3 m. ; Ventnor, 1 m. ; Blackgang, through the Undercliff, 7 m. ; Chale, 1 m.

THIRD DAY.—Along the Military Road to Brook, 8 m. ; Freshwater Bay (along the Military Road), 3½ m. ; along the top of the High Down to the Needles, 3 m. ; Alum Bay, 1 m. ; Yarmouth, 4 m.

THREE DAYS' ITINERARY.—FROM VENTNOR

FIRST DAY.—Bonchurch, 1 m. ; through the Landslip to Shanklin, 3 m. ; along the Cliff to Sandown, 2 m. ; take the train to Bembridge ; to the Foreland, and thence along the Cliffs to Whitecliff Bay, 2½ m. ; over Bembridge Down to Yarbridge, 2 m. (see the Roman Villa) ; over the Downs to Newport, 8 m.

SECOND DAY.—Carisbrooke, 1 m. ; Calbourne, 4 m. ; Shalfleet, 2 m. ; Yarmouth, 4 m. ; Totland Bay, 3 m. ; round the base of Headon Hill to Alum Bay, 2 m. ; Needles, 1 m. ; over the High Down to Freshwater Gate, 3 m.

THIRD DAY.—Along the Military Road to Brook, 3½ m. ; Mottistone, 1 m. ; Brixton, 2 m. ; Shorwell, 2 m. ; Kingston, 2 m. ; Chale, 3 m. ; Blackgang, 1 m. ; through the Undercliff to Ventnor, 7 m.

INDEX

THE END

Printed by R. & R. Clark, Edinburgh.

THE
DRYBURGH EDITION

OF THE

WAVERLEY NOVELS.

In Twenty-five Volumes, Large Crown 8vo, Cloth.

Price 5/-

EACH VOLUME CONTAINING A COMPLETE NOVEL.

THIS EDITION contains the latest revised text, with ample Glossaries and Indices, and is Illustrated with 250 Wood Engravings, specially drawn for this Edition, and Engraved by Mr. J. D. Cooper.

LIST OF ARTISTS.

CHARLES GREENE . .	WAVERLEY.
GORDON BROWNE .	GUY MANNERING.
PAUL HARDY . .	THE ANTIQUARY.
LOCKHART BOGLE .	ROB ROY.
WALTER PAGET .	{ BLACK DWARF.
LOCKHART BOGLE .	{ LEGEND OF MONTROSE.
FRANK DADD, R.I. .	OLD MORTALITY.
WILLIAM HOLE, R.S.A. .	HEART OF MIDLOTHIAN.
JOHN WILLIAMSON .	BRIDE OF LAMMERMOOR.
GORDON BROWNE .	IVANHOE.
JOHN WILLIAMSON .	THE MONASTERY.
JOHN WILLIAMSON .	THE ABBOT.
H. M. PAGET . .	KENILWORTH.
W. H. OVEREND .	THE PIRATE.
GODFREY C. HINDLEY .	FORTUNES OF NIGEL.
STANLEY BERKELEY .	PEVERIL OF THE PEAK.
H. M. PAGET .	QUENTIN DURWARD.
HUGH THOMSON .	ST. RONAN'S WELL.
GEORGE HAY, R.S.A. .	REDGAUNTLET.
GODFREY C. HINDLEY .	{ THE BETROTHED.
GODFREY C. HINDLEY .	{ HIGHLAND WIDOW.
GODFREY C. HINDLEY .	THE TALISMAN.
STANLEY BERKELEY .	WOODSTOCK.
C. M. HARDIE, A.R.S.A. .	FAIR MAID OF PERTH.
PAUL HARDY . .	ANNE OF GEIERSTEIN.
GORDON BROWNE .	COUNT ROBERT OF PARIS.
PAUL HARDY . .	{ THE SURGEON'S DAUGHTER.
WALTER PAGET .	{ CASTLE DANGEROUS.

A. & C. BLACK, SOHO SQUARE, LONDON.

THE

NORTH BRITISH RUBBER COMPANY

(LIMITED).

General Indiarubber Manufacturers.

WORKS:
CASTLE MILLS,
EDINBURGH.

Large Stock to select from, and being bona-fide Manufacturers, their products can be warranted first quality.

WATERPROOF	Coats and Capes.
WATERPROOF	Walking Coats. Driving Coats.
WATERPROOF	Fishing Coats.
WATERPROOF	Shooting Coats. Fishing Trousers.
WATERPROOF	Fishing Stockings. Brogues.
WATERPROOF	Gaiters. Sea Boots.

PRICES STRICTLY MODERATE.

WAREHOUSES		
LONDON	57 MOORGATE STREET, E.C.
MANCHESTER	69 & 71 DEANSGATE.
LIVERPOOL	9 LORD STREET.
LEEDS	65 & 66 BRIGGATE.
NEWCASTLE	39 GRAINGER STREET.
GLASGOW	60 BUCHANAN STREET.
EDINBURGH	106 PRINCES STREET.

1

ABERDEEN.
IMPERIAL HOTEL

Personally Patronised by their Royal Highnesses

The Duke of Edinburgh,

The Duke of Connaught,

The late Duke of Albany,

Princess Beatrice,

The late Prince Henry of Battenberg,

Princess Louise (Marchioness of Lorne),

Prince and Princess Christian,

The King of the Belgians,

Prince Frederick William of Prussia,

and other distinguished Visitors.

THIS well-known Hotel has been recently very much enlarged, redecorated, and refurnished throughout; a Patent Safety Hydraulic Lift, the Electric Light, and all the latest improvements have been introduced, and the house will now be found replete with every comfort for Visitors and Families.

The Hotel occupies the most central position in the City, close to the Station, Post and Telegraph Offices, Docks, and Golf Course; and within easy access of the fishings on the Dee and Don.

The Coffee Room is the largest and most handsome in the City. Separate Tables for Table d'Hote. Private Suites of Rooms, handsomely and comfortably furnished, for Families.

LADIES' DRAWING ROOM, READING, BILLIARD, AND SMOKING ROOMS.
BATH ROOMS ON ALL THE FLOORS.

CUISINE AND WINES OF THE CHOICEST DESCRIPTION.
TARIFF ON APPLICATION.

ABERGAVENNY.

ANGEL FAMILY AND COMMERCIAL HOTEL.

FISHING and Sporting quarters. The above Hotel affords some of the best Salmon and Trout water on the famous river Usk, sufficient private water for twenty rods, also tickets for the Abergavenny Association water close to Hotel, the upper Usk within three miles. Large Coffee Room. *Table d'Hôte.* Charming drives to Raglan, Llanthony, Crickhowell Valley. Near Monmouthshire Golf Links.

JOHN PRICHARD, *Proprietor.*

AMBLESIDE.

THE WINDERMERE WATERHEAD HOTEL.

STANDING in its own grounds on the margin of the Lake, adjoining Steamboat Pier, the Terminus of the Furness and Midland Railway Systems.

M. TAYLOR & SON, Proprietors of the Salutation and Queen's Hotels (both of which will be carried on by them as heretofore), have taken over the above First-Class Hotel, recently enlarged and refurnished, which will be conducted on a liberal and popular tariff.

Taylor's Four-in-Hand Stage Coaches run from the Hotel, also from the Salutation and Queen's, to **Keswick, Coniston, Ullswater,** and the **Langdales,** two or three times daily during the season (Sundays excepted), affording special facilities for exploring the district in every direction.

N.B.—*Boats, Fishing Tackle, &c., supplied.*

ARDARA, DONEGAL HIGHLANDS.

NESBITT ARMS HOTELS.

The above Hotels having been rebuilt and furnished in the most modern style, will be found most comfortable for Tourists visiting the Donegal Highlands. Cars meet trains (6 miles distant) by appointment. Splendid Fishing and Charming Scenery **in the** Neighbourhood.

TERMS MODERATE.

Sea Bathing Convenient.   N. McNELIS, *Proprietor.*

DONEGAL COTTAGE INDUSTRY.

The Proprietor has a depôt for the sale of Home-spun and Hand-wove tweeds in the village, and a special selection is always on exhibition at the Hotel.

ASHBOURN NEAR DOVEDALE.

FANNY WALLIS.

Family & Commercial Posting House,

GREEN MAN & BLACK'S HEAD HOTEL.

BILLIARDS. CHOICE WINES & SPIRITS. OMNIBUS TO AND FROM EVERY TRAIN.

ASHBURTON, DEVON.

GOLDEN LION HOTEL.

E. JNO. SAWDYE, Proprietor.

THIS Hotel, the principal one in the Town, is replete with every convenience for the comfort of Tourists and Travellers. It contains spacious Suites of Private Apartments, has an extensive Garden attached, and is in the immediate neighbourhood of the finest of the Dartmoor Tors, Haytor Rocks, the Buckland and Holne Chase Drives, the upper reaches of the celebrated river Dart, and some of the most picturesque of the world-famed Devonshire Scenery.

Posting Horses and Carriages of every description.

Excellent Trout and Salmon Fishing may be had in the neighbourhood on payment of a small fee. Particulars can be obtained on application to the Proprietor of the Hotel.

AUCHANAULT.

AUCHANAULT HOTEL.

THIS HOTEL IS

NOW OPEN TO RECEIVE VISITORS

Who may wish for a quiet retreat or for

FISHING ON LOCH AUCHANAULT.

Whereon Boats can be had.

The House has lately undergone a thorough repair and refurnishing.

Mrs. JANE M'IVER, *Proprietrix.*

AUCHNASHEEN HOTEL

Connected with the Auchnasheen Station of the Dingwall and Skye Railway.

THIS HOTEL is situated amid very fine scenery, varied with mountain, loch, and river, and is the starting-place of Tourists for Loch Maree, Gairloch, &c. The Coach for these places starts from the door daily, and seats can be secured by letter or telegram addressed to Mrs. M'Iver, the Proprietrix of the Hotel and Coach. Comfortable and well-aired Bedrooms, and careful attention in every way.

Posting in all its Branches.

Mrs. M'IVER, *Proprietrix.*

AYR.
THE AYR STATION HOTEL.

Adjoins the Railway Station.

FIRST-CLASS HOUSE FOR FAMILIES AND GENTLEMEN.
HANDSOME PUBLIC ROOMS.   SUITES OF APARTMENTS.
LARGE AND WELL-APPOINTED BEDROOMS.
PASSENGER ELEVATOR.   MODERATE TARIFF.

PHILIP BLADES, Hotel Manager.
Glasgow and South-Western Railway.

BALLATER (NEAR BALMORAL).

INVERCAULD ARMS HOTEL

THE Hotel is pleasantly situated on the Banks of the Dee in the midst of the finest Scenery in Deeside, and most centrically and conveniently situated for parties visiting the Royal Residence, neighbouring Mountains, and other principal places of interest on Deeside.

The Hotel has recently undergone extensive alterations and improvements, and for comfort will compare favourably with any *First Class Hotel* in Scotland.

Parties BOARDED by the WEEK on SPECIAL TERMS, excepting from 15th July to 15th September.

POSTING IN ALL ITS BRANCHES.

(By Special Appointment Posting Master to Her Majesty the Queen.)

Coaches during the Season to Balmoral and Braemar.

Letters and Telegrams promptly attended to.

Telegraphic Address—   ALEX. M'GREGOR.
"Invercauld Arms, Ballater."   Proprietor.

BATH.

CASTLE HOTEL.

The Oldest Established and most Central for Families, Private and Commercial Gentlemen.

NIGHT PORTER.

JOHN RUBIE, Proprietor.

ALSO WINE AND SPIRIT MERCHANT,

24 & 25 NEW BOND STREET, BATH.

BELFAST.

LOMBARD CAFÉ

16, 18, and 20 LOMBARD STREET,

FIRST-CLASS TEMPERANCE RESTAURANT FOR LADIES AND GENTLEMEN.

Hot Luncheons and Dinners from 12 noon till 4.30 p.m.

OPEN FROM 7 A.M. TO 7.15 P.M.

BELFAST.

INTERNATIONAL TEMPERANCE HOTEL,

7 COLLEGE SQUARE, E.,

Opposite grounds of Royal Academical Institution, in the centre of the city. Breakfast or Tea from 1s. 3d. Apartments from 2s. Attendance, 9d.

Telegrams :—"Homely, Belfast." Telephone No. 974.

WM. WILKINSON, *Proprietor.*

BERKELEY.

BERKELEY ARMS HOTEL.

FAMILY AND COMMERCIAL.

Half-mile from Station. General Posting.

E. BROWN, *Proprietor.*

BETTWS-Y-COED.

ROYAL OAK HOTEL.

THIS celebrated Hotel, for which the signboard by David Cox was painted in 1847, has an unrivalled situation, and is very suitable as a centre from which the most beautiful scenery in North Wales may be visited. It contains every accommodation for visitors, considerable additions having been recently made.

POSTING.   FIRST-CLASS STABLING.

BILLIARDS.   TENNIS.

Private Road to Station.

OMNIBUS MEETS ALL TRAINS.

Well-appointed Four-horse Coaches are run daily by the Proprietor to Llanberis and back, Beddgelert and back, Portmadoc, and Bangor, through **the finest scenery of North Wales**, including the Passes of Llanberis, Gwynant, Aberglaslyn, and Nant Ffrancon.

E. PULLAN, Proprietor.

BIDEFORD.

Central for the whole of North Devon.

Including WESTWARD HO! CLOVELLY, HARTLAND, BUDE, ILFRACOMBE, and LYNTON.

COACHES IN THE SEASON TO ABOVE PLACES.

Adjoining Railway Station.

ROYAL HOTEL,

Overlooking the River Torridge & Old Bridge.

BIDEFORD.

The Most Modern Hotel in West of England.

Replete with every convenience and comfort.

COMPLETELY SHELTERED FROM E. & N.E. WINDS.

Lofty, perfectly ventilated, and handsomely furnished rooms.

Delightful Winter Resort—one of the mildest and healthiest in the Kingdom.

First-Class Horses and Carriages of every description always ready.

CONTINENTAL COURTYARD.

Finest Stabling and Lock-up Coach-house in Devonshire.

Specially reduced Winter Tariff.

Porters attend every Train.

SAVE OMNIBUS & PORTERAGE.

French and German spoken.

WINTER ATTRACTIONS.

Hunting (Wild Stag, Fox, Hare), Shooting, Fishing, Golfing.

The Royal Hotel, originally a private mansion, built in 1688, contains the interesting old oak rooms in which Charles Kingsley wrote portions of *Westward Ho!* and from its size and the admirable way in which it is fitted out must be regarded as one of the best Hotels in the West of England. For situation the Royal is probably unequalled in the North of Devon.—*Vide* PUBLIC PRESS.

" *Bideford*, chiefly remarkable for having a first-rate hotel."—*Punch*, 5th Oct. 1889.

BLAIR-ATHOLL.

ATHOLL ARMS HOTEL.

Adjoining the Railway Station.

THE SITUATION is unequalled as a centre from which to visit the finest Scenery of the PERTHSHIRE HIGHLANDS, comprising KILLIECRANKIE ; LOCHS TUMMEL and RANNOCH ; GLEN TILT ; BRAEMAR ; the FALLS OF BRUAR, GARRY, TUMMEL, and FENDER ; DUNKELD ; TAYMOUTH CASTLE and LOCH TAY ; the GROUNDS of BLAIR CASTLE, etc.

This is also the most convenient resting-place for breaking the long railway journey to and from the North of Scotland.

TABLE D'HÔTE daily during the season in the well-known magnificent DINING HALL, with which is connected *en suite* a spacious and elegantly furnished DRAWING ROOM.

Special terms for Board by the week, except during August.

Tariff on Application.

THE POSTING DEPARTMENT is thoroughly well equipped.

Experienced Guides and Ponies for Glen Tilt, Braemar, and Mountain Excursions.   *Telegraphic Address*—HOTEL, BLAIRATHOLL.

D. MACDONALD & SONS, *Proprietors.*

BOURNEMOUTH.
THE ROYAL BATH HOTEL.

Caution—The ONLY Hotel or Licensed Establishment on "EAST CLIFF."

PATRONISED BY
H.R.H. THE PRINCE OF WALES,
H.M. THE KING OF THE BELGIANS,
H.R.H. THE DUCHESS OF ALBANY,
H.I.M. THE EMPRESS EUGENIE,
T.R.H. THE CROWN PRINCE OF DENMARK AND
PRINCESS ROYAL OF SWEDEN,
THE LATE LORD BEACONSFIELD,
And all the most distinguished Personages visiting Bournemouth.

THE LEADING HOTEL IN BOURNEMOUTH.

"It has a unique and unrivalled position, being completely protected by Pine Woods from north and east winds. Standing in its own Grounds of 5 Acres, with a Sea Frontage of 1000 feet due south, and within three minutes' walk of the Pier and Post Office. The only Hotel on the East Cliff. The Cliff, par excellence."—*Court Journal*, 16th August 1879.

Moderate Fixed Tariff. Comparison Invited.
Table d'Hote at separate tables.

The Hotel private Omnibus meets Trains.

NIGHT WATCHMAN. SANITARY CERTIFICATES.

BILLIARD ROOM WITH TWO TABLES.

Tariff, &c. sent on application to Manager.

BRIDGE OF ALLAN.

PHILP'S ROYAL HOTEL.

THE finest Hotel in the district, about one hour by rail from Edinburgh and Glasgow, and 3 miles from Stirling. Most convenient for Tourists breaking their journey to and from the Highlands. Bus to and from Railway Station.

An extensive Carriage-Hiring Establishment.

Telephone No. 516.
Telegrams :—" Hotel, Bridge of Allan."   R. PHILP, *Proprietor.*

BRIDGE OF ALLAN

HYDROPATHIC ESTABLISHMENT,

NEAR STIRLING.

BEAUTIFULLY situated and sheltered by the Ochils, on a dry and porous soil. The House is replete with every comfort and convenience. Elegant Suite of Baths, including Turkish, Russian, Vapour, Spray, &c., all on the most approved principles.

Terms from £2 : 12 : 6 per week.

Qualified Medical man in daily consultation, who has studied Hydropathy at Smedley's, Matlock.

Massage Treatment.

Golf Course in Vicinity of Establishment.

Applications to be addressed to WILLIAM G. SPRUNT, *Manager.*

CHANNEL ISLANDS.

SARK, CHANNEL ISLANDS.

The Largest Hotel on the Island with a sea view, is nearest to the landing stage, and possesses excellent sleeping accommodation. Public Drawing and Smoking Rooms.

Large Dining Room (separate tables).

"The most bracing spot in the Channel Islands."

D. ROBIN, *Proprietor.*

N.B.—Steamers leave Guernsey daily for Sark after the arrival of Southampton and Weymouth Boats.

CHELTENHAM.

TATE'S PRIVATE HOTEL.

VISITORS RECEIVED BY THE DAY OR WEEK.

TERMS MODERATE.

Also Private Suites of Apartments under the personal management of the Proprietor.

CHESTER.

THE GROSVENOR HOTEL.

FIRST-CLASS.   Situated in the centre of the City, close to the CATHEDRAL and other objects of interest.

Large Coffee and Reading Rooms; Ladies' Drawing Room for the convenience of Ladies and Families; Smoking and Billiard Rooms.

Open and close Carriages, and Posting in all its Branches.

Omnibuses for the use of Visitors to the Hotel, and also the Hotel Porters attend the Trains. A Night Porter in attendance. Tariff to be had on application.

J. M. SIEGERS, *Manager.*

CHIRK HAND HOTEL.

Family and Commercial Hotel.

SIX minutes' walk from Chirk Station; one and a half mile from Chirk Castle, which is open to visitors on Mondays and Thursdays; situated on Offa's Dyke at base of Ceiriog Glen; surrounded by some of the most interesting scenery in North Wales.

POSTING IN EVERY DEPARTMENT.

Fishing Tickets for the River Ceiriog free for Visitors staying at the Hotel.

Cricket Ground within 200 yards.

MRS. E. GRIFFITH, *Proprietress.*

CHRISTCHURCH.

NEWLYN'S FAMILY & COMMERCIAL HOTEL.

CHARMING views of Priory Church, Norman Ruins, River Avon, and Gardens from the Balcony. Splendid Fishing free to Visitors staying at the Hotel. Billiards, Boating, etc. One and a half miles from sea.

Proprietor—ALBERT WHALEY.

COLWYN BAY, NORTH WALES.

POLLYCROCHAN HOTEL

(Late the Residence of Lady Erskine).

THIS First-Class Family Hotel is most beautifully situated in its own finely-wooded park in Colwyn Bay, commanding splendid land and sea views. It is within a few minutes' walk of the Beach, and ten minutes' of Colwyn Bay Station, and a short drive of Conway and Llandudno. A desirable Winter Residence, sheltered and also warmed.

Sea-Bathing, Tennis, Golf, Billiards, Posting.

J. PORTER, *Proprietor.*

PHILP'S
DUNBLANE HYDROPATHIC,
DUNBLANE, PERTHSHIRE.

SITUATED in one of the Healthiest and Loveliest parts of Scotland, forming a most excellent WINTER and SPRING RESIDENCE. *Climate* —Mild and equable, completely sheltered from north and east winds. The arrangements of the house are, beyond all question, unsurpassed in Britain. A most complete system of heating is adopted over the whole house. NEW RECREATION AND BILLIARD ROOMS; FULLY EQUIPPED GYMNASIUM; LAWN TENNIS COURTS; GOLF COURSE; MINERAL WELL. *Baths*—Turkish, Russian, Electric, Pine, &c.; Massage Treatment under Trained Attendants. The Sanitary arrangements are perfect. About an hour by rail from Glasgow and Edinburgh.

For Prospectus apply to the Manager.

T. W. DEWAR, M.D.,
Resident Physician.

EASTBOURNE-SOUTHBOROUGH HOUSE,

CARLISLE ROAD,

SUPERIOR Boarding Establishment, under personal supervision of proprietor and family, centrally situated near the Sea and Golf Links, and opposite Devonshire Park. Spacious Reception Rooms and Bedrooms, Smoking Room, Conservatory, large Garden for Lawn Tennis and other games, excellent Cuisine, terms moderate.

EDINBURGH.

DARLING'S HOTEL,

20 WATERLOO PLACE (Princes Street).

FIRST-CLASS TEMPERANCE HOTEL.

Under personal management of Miss DARLING.

EDINBURGH.

CONTINENTAL HOTEL,

MEUSE LANE.

Off South St. David Street, opposite Scott's Monument.

Unsurpassed for comfort and quietness.   Charges very moderate.
Tariff on application.

Breakfasts, Luncheons, Dinners, and Suppers *a la carte*
in the Restaurant.

G. RIETZ, *Proprietor and Manager.*

THE WINDSOR HOTEL, 100 Princes Street, Edinburgh.

(Opposite the Castle.)

THE WINDSOR HOTEL, 250 St. Vincent Street, Glasgow.

A. M. THIEM, Purveyor to Her Majesty's Lord High Commissioner.

Also to the Duke of Edinburgh, Salisbury, Rosebery, Tercentenary, and Balfour Banquets.

A. M. THIEM, PROPRIETOR.

FIRST-CLASS HOTELS FOR FAMILIES AND GENTLEMEN.

Greatly enlarged.　Exceedingly Comfortable and Prices Moderate.　Passenger Elevator.

Highly Recommended by Appleton's Guide-Books.

TELEPHONE No 3502.

WINDSOR HOTEL
GLASGOW

CONNECTED BY TELEPHONE

TELEPHONE No 273.

WINDSOR HOTEL
EDINBURGH

EDINBURGH.

THE
COCKBURN HOTEL,

Adjoining the Station and overlooking the Gardens.

NO INTOXICATING LIQUORS.

JOHN MACPHERSON, Proprietor.

Passenger Elevator.   Electric Light.

ROXBURGHE HOTEL,

CHARLOTTE SQUARE, EDINBURGH.

FIRST-CLASS FAMILY HOTEL.

In Connection with the above is CHRISTIE'S PRIVATE HOTEL.

J. CHRISTIE, *Proprietor.*

TO ALL INTERESTED IN THE SCOTTISH METROPOLIS.

*In Two Handsome Volumes, medium quarto, bound, price 25s.;
or royal quarto, on handmade paper, £3 : 3s.*

MEMORIALS OF EDINBURGH
IN THE OLDEN TIME.
NEW EDITION
By SIR DANIEL WILSON, LL.D., F.R.S.E.,
Late President of the University of Toronto, and formerly Acting-Secretary of the
Society of Antiquaries of Scotland.

Illustrated by 41 Plates and 100 Wood Engravings of Old Edinburgh
buildings from drawings by the Author, and a bird's-eye view of the City
as it appeared in 1647, by Gordon of Rothiemay. Forming an interesting
and authoritative record of the local antiquities, traditions, and historical
associations of the Scottish Metropolis.

"Produced in a manner that leaves nothing to be desired."—*Scotsman.*
'The bibliophile will value it as much for its material excellence as the antiquary
or its quaint lore."—*Glasgow Herald.*

LONDON: ADAM & CHARLES BLACK: SOHO SQUARE.

ENNISKILLEN AND LOUGH ERNE.

ROYAL HOTEL.

First-Class, recently rebuilt and enlarged, possesses every requisite for the comfort and convenience of visitors.

COMMERCIAL and Coffee Rooms. Billiard and Smoking Rooms. Ladies' Drawing Room. Private Sitting Rooms and Large, Airy Bedrooms. Hot, Cold, and Shower Baths. Good Cooking and Attendance. Gaze's and Great Northern Railway Co.'s "Hotel Coupons" accepted.

'Bus meets all trains.   *Posting.*
Telegraphic Address, "Royal," Enniskillen.

EXETER.

POPLE'S

NEW LONDON HOTEL.

Patronised by H.R.H. The Prince of Wales.

THIS FIRST-CLASS HOTEL is near the CATHEDRAL, and adjoining NORTHERNHAY PARK.

LARGE COVERED CONTINENTAL COURTYARD.

TABLE D'HOTE.   NIGHT PORTER.

HOTEL OMNIBUSES AND CABS MEET EVERY TRAIN.

POSTING ESTABLISHMENT.

Telegrams— "**Pople, Exeter.**"

Also Proprietor of the GLOBE HOTEL, NEWTON ABBOT, DEVON.

EXETER.

ROYAL CLARENCE HOTEL,

FACING GRAND OLD CATHEDRAL.

FIRST-CLASS FAMILY.   TABLE D'HOTE, 7 O'CLOCK.

Lighted with Electric Light.

Quiet and Comfort of Country Mansion. Moderate Tariff.

J. HEADON STANBURY, *Proprietor.*

Also GRAND HOTEL, PLYMOUTH.

The nearest and most convenient for any wishing to ascend the Ben.

Moderate Charges. Mrs. DOIG Proprietrix.

FORT-WILLIAM.

THE ALEXANDRA HOTEL,
PARADE, FORT-WILLIAM.

STEWART'S PRACTICAL ANGLER.

Tenth Thousand. 12mo. Price 3s. 6d.

The Art of Trout Fishing more particularly applied to Clear Water.

"Mr. Stewart's admirable Practical Angler."—KINGSLEY.

LONDON: ADAM & CHARLES BLACK, SOHO SQUARE.

GALWAY.

MACK'S ROYAL HOTEL.
(FAMILY AND COMMERCIAL.)

John Jameson's 7-Year-Old Whisky, guaranteed direct from the Distillery.
Henry Persse's 10-Year-Old Whisky, guaranteed direct from the Distillery.

GEORGE MACK, PROPRIETOR.

The Hotel Omnibus attends all Trains and Steamers free of charge.
Posting in all its Branches. Good Horses and Steady Drivers.

GIANT'S CAUSEWAY.

CAUSEWAY HOTEL AND ELECTRIC TRAMWAY.

THIS beautifully-situated Hotel is worked in connection with the GIANT'S CAUSEWAY ELECTRIC TRAMWAY. It is the most central spot for Tourists visiting the district, being close to the Giant's Causeway, and with Dunluce Castle, Dunseverick Castle, Ballintoy, and Carrick-a-Rede in the immediate neighbourhood.

The Hotel stands in its own grounds of 40 Acres, and has been greatly enlarged within the last few years to meet the growing popularity of the Establishment, and will be found replete with every comfort. The Hotel is lighted throughout with the Electric Light. There are Asphalte and Grass Lawn Tennis Courts, and Golf Links, about half a mile distant, free to visitors staying at the Hotel.

Guides, Boats, and Posting are attached to the Hotel, with fixed scale of charges.

Tram Cars leave Portrush Railway Station on the arrival of all trains, with through booking to the Causeway Hotel. Tourists are landed in the Hotel grounds without any trouble or change of Cars. There will be an increased service of Tram Cars on the Tramway during the summer months. The Antrim coast Tourists' Cars start from the Causeway Hotel, twice daily, for Ballycastle. Orders to view the Electric Generating Station at Walkmills, and trout-fishing in the River Bush, can be obtained at the Hotel.

Postal and Telegraph Address—The MANAGER, Causeway Hotel, Bushmills.

Note.—Always ask for through Railway Tickets to the Giant's Causeway.

CRANSTON'S
WAVERLEY TEMPERANCE HOTEL, GLASGOW,
172 SAUCHIEHALL STREET.

GLASGOW (*Note new address*) .	172 SAUCHIEHALL STREET.
EDINBURGH, "Old" . . .	43 PRINCES STREET.
EDINBURGH, "New" . . .	16 WATERLOO PLACE.
LONDON	37 KING STREET, CHEAPSIDE.

CAUTION.—As another Waverley Hotel has been opened in Glasgow under the name of "Old Waverley," with which we have no connection, parties going to Cranston's Waverley are particularly requested to see that they are taken to Sauchiehall Street.

Telegraphic address—"WAVERLEY HOTEL."   *Telephone No.* 128.

GLASGOW.

CITY COMMERCIAL RESTAURANT

(WADDELL'S).

CENTRAL AND COMMODIOUS.

Within Three Minutes' Walk of the Principal Railway Stations.

Proprietors—

CITY COMMERCIAL RESTAURANT CO., LIMITED.

60 UNION STREET, GLASGOW.

GLASGOW.

THE BATH HOTEL,
152 BATH STREET, GLASGOW.
The most comfortable First-class Hotel in Glasgow. Very Moderate Charges.
P. ROBERTSON, Proprietor.

GLASGOW.
ST. ENOCH STATION HOTEL.

Adjoins the
Glasgow Terminus of the
Glasgow and South-Western
Midland Railways.

CONVENIENTLY SITUATED.

Magnificent Public Rooms.   **Suites of Apartments.**
LARGE AND AIRY BEDROOMS.
PASSENGER ELEVATOR.   ELECTRIC LIGHT EVERYWHERE.
MODERATE TARIFF.
PHILIP BLADES, Manager.

FRAZER & GREEN'S
LAVENDER WATER

"DOUBLE DISTILLED."   "WORLD FAMED."

In Actinic Bottles, at 1s., 1s. 6d., 2s., 3s. 6d., 4s. 6d., 6s. 6d., and 8s. 6d.
Postage for 3 smaller sizes, 3d.; for larger sizes, 6d.

CHEMISTS TO THE QUEEN,
127 BUCHANAN STREET, GLASGOW.

THE HOTEL, GLENELG.

THIS beautifully-situated Hotel has been greatly added to and almost rebuilt, and is now one of the most comfortable Hotels in the North.
THE COFFEE ROOM is 40 ft. by 20 ft., and the BEDROOMS are VERY AIRY.
HOT, COLD, AND SHOWER BATHS. BILLIARD ROOM. TENNIS.
GENTLEMEN staying at the GLENELG HOTEL have the privilege of SALMON and SEA-TROUT FISHING FREE on the GLENELG RIVER; also SHOOTING, by the Week or Month, at a MODERATE CHARGE.
EVERY COMFORT FOR VISITORS, AND STRICT ATTENTION.
Magnificent Scenery, and easy access by Steamer from Oban daily.
Among places of interest near are the Pictish Towers of Glenbeg, Cup-Marked Stones, Glenbeg Waterfalls, Loch Duich, Loch Hourn, Glenshiel, Falls of Glomach, Shiel Hotel, &c.
Letters and Telegrams should be addressed, "THE HOTEL, GLENELG, STROMFERRY."
Telegraph Office—GLENELG.   **DONALD MACDONALD MACINTOSH,** Lessee.

(see p. 42)

GREENOCK.

TONTINE HOTEL.

ARDGOWAN SQUARE.

FIRST-CLASS Hotel, pleasantly and quietly situated, three minutes from Princes Pier and Station (Midland Railway), eight from Caledonian Railway, West Station. Perfect sanitary arrangements. Belfast Steamers arrive and leave from Princes Pier, also "Columba," "Lord of the Isles," "Culzean Castle," and Magnificent New Fleet of Glasgow and South-Western Railway Co.'s Steamers. Steamer for Helensburgh in connection with West Highland Railway.

GUERNSEY.

RICHMOND BOARDING-HOUSE,

CAMBRIDGE PARK.

THE principal Boarding-House in Guernsey, it has a splendid sea view from every room, facing south ; large Garden ; close to the Candie Library and public grounds ; ten minutes' walk to boats ; Terms, 5s. 6d. per day. Also from July 1st, 1897, GRANGE HOUSE, GRANGE ROAD, will be opened as a Boarding Establishment in conjunction with the above.

PROPRIETORS MR. & MRS. HART.

GUERNSEY.

OLD GOVERNMENT HOUSE HOTEL,

GUERNSEY.

Formerly the Official Residence of the Lieutenant-Governor of the Island.

THIS long-established and first-class Hotel for Families and Gentlemen is famed for its excellent *Cuisine*, its choice Wines, and the thorough comfort of all its arrangements, combined with the most moderate charges.

Standing in its own grounds, and situated in the higher and best part of the town of St. Peter-Port, it commands from its windows and lawn unrivalled views of the entire Channel Group—including Alderney on the north ; Jersey on the south ; Sark, Herm, and Jethou immediately opposite ; with the distant and historic coasts of Normandy beyond.

An extensive new wing has been added, comprising about forty additional apartments—including spacious and lofty Bedrooms, with southern aspect and magnificent sea views. Hot and Cold Baths. Smoking Rooms, and all the modern improvements. Tariff on application. Special arrangements during the Winter months.

The finest Dining Saloon in **the Channel Islands**, capable of accommodating two hundred guests. Table d'Hote. Separate Tables. **Splendid new Billiard Room, with two tables**, by Burroughes **and Watts.**

Private Carriages. Ici on parle Français. Hier man spricht Deutsch.

Five minutes' walk from the Landing Stages. A Porter from the Hotel attends the arrival of all Steamers. Rooms may be secured by letter or telegram.

Registered Telegraphic Address—"GOV. GUERNSEY."

JOHN GARDNER, Proprietor.

AN IDEAL POSITION.

ILFRACOMBE HOTEL.

THE PRINCIPAL AND ONLY HOTEL ON THE SEA SHORE.

THE FINEST PRIVATE MARINE ESPLANADE IN THE KINGDOM.

Unrivalled Sea Frontage and Open Surroundings.

Grounds 5 Acres.　250 Apartments.　Lawn Tennis.　Croquet Lawn.

Elegant Salle à Manger.　Drawing, Reading, Smoking, and Billiard Rooms, and Sumptuous Lounge Hall on the Ground Floor.　Moderate Tariff.

There is attached to the Hotel **one of the Largest Swimming Baths** in the United Kingdom (the temperature of which is regulated).　Also well-appointed Private Hot and Cold Sea and Fresh Water Baths, Douche, Shower, &c.

H. R. GROVER, *Manager,*
To whom all communications should be addressed.

THE ILFRACOMBE HOTEL CO., LTD.

INNELLAN.

On the beautiful Firth of Clyde, between Dunoon and Rothesay.

ROYAL HOTEL.

J. MAITLAND begs to announce that he has purchased the above large and commodious Hotel, which has lately undergone extensive alterations and additions, including one of the largest and most handsome Dining Rooms and Ladies' Sitting Rooms of any Hotel on the Firth of Clyde; also Parlours with Suites of Bedrooms on each flat. The Hotel is within three minutes' walk of the Pier, and being built upon an elevation, commands a Sea view of the surrounding country, including Bute, Arran, The Cumbraes, Ayrshire, Renfrewshire, and Dumbartonshire, making the situation one of the finest in Scotland. The grounds of the Hotel being laid out in walks, and interspersed with shrubs and flowers, are quiet and retired for Families. There are also beautiful drives in the vicinity. Steamers call at the Pier nearly every hour for the Highlands and all parts of the Coast. Tourists arriving at the Hotel the night before can have Breakfast at Table d'Hôte at 9 a.m., and be in time to join the *Columba* at 10 a.m. for the North, calling at Innellan on her return about 4 p.m. The *Cuisine* and Wines are of the finest quality.

Large Billiard Room attached. Hot, Cold, and Spray Baths.
Horses and Carriages kept for Hire.

FAMILIES BOARDED BY THE DAY OR WEEK.

INVERARAY.

ARGYLL ARMS HOTEL,

INVERARAY.

SITUATE near the head of Lochfyne, is one of the most beautiful Resorts for Tourists in the West Highlands. The Hotel is fitted up with every Comfort.

Excellent **Salmon, Sea** and Brown Trout Fishing **in the** Rivers Aray and Douglas **and the Dhu-loch—a** tidal water. There is also good **Sea-Fishing. Episcopal Church** close to Hotel. Golf Course within five **minutes' walk of Hotel.**

POSTING IN ALL ITS BRANCHES.

CHARGES MODERATE.

B. B. BANTOCK, Proprietor.

INVERARAY.

ST. CATHERINE'S HOTEL,

LOCH FYNE, FACING INVERARAY.

DONALD SUTHERLAND, *Proprietor.*

GOOD Shooting, Grouse, Black Game, &c., for Visitors; also Stream and Loch Fishing. Coaches in connection with Glasgow Steamers **start from and stop at** St. Catherine's. Posting. Carriages **on Hire.**

Moderate Charges.

INVERNESS.—THE CALEDONIAN HOTEL.

FACING the Railway Station, and within one minute's walk. Under new management. This well-known first-class Family Hotel is patronised by the Royal Family and most of the nobility of Europe. Having recently added fifty rooms, with numerous suites of Apartments for Families, and all handsomely re-furnished and re-decorated throughout, it is now the largest and best appointed Hotel in Inverness, and universally acknowledged one of the most comfortable in Scotland. Magnificent Ladies' Drawing Room overlooking the River Ness. Spacious Smoking and Billiard Rooms. In point of situation this Hotel is the only one overlooking the River Ness, the magnificent view from the windows being unsurpassed, and extending to upwards of fifty miles of the surrounding Strath and Mountain scenery of the great Glen of "Caledonia."

Every modern convenience and comfort, under the personal supervision of the Proprietor. The Sanitary arrangements are entirely renewed, and the house throughout is now in the highest state of efficiency. An omnibus attends the Canal Steamers. The Hotel Porters await the arrival of all Trains. Posting. Tariff very moderate. In connection with Station Hotel, Fort William. GEORGE SINCLAIR, *Proprietor.*

4

COUNTY KERRY.

SOUTHERN HOTELS, LIMITED.

HEALTH AND PLEASURE RESORTS.

SHOOTING, FISHING, GOLF, BOATING, BATHING, Etc., Etc.

SOUTHERN HOTEL, PARKNASILLA.

DELIGHTFULLY situated in own grounds (upwards of 100 acres), on an inlet of the sea. Magnificent and romantic scenery. An ideal holiday resort in Summer, and owing to its sheltered position and mild climate, a veritable Irish Riviera in Winter.

Coaches to Waterville and Kenmare daily, from May 1st.

A large new Hotel, one of the finest in the United Kingdom, is rapidly approaching completion here, and will be fitted with Turkish, and hot and cold sea-water Baths.

SOUTHERN HOTEL, WATERVILLE.

On the shore of Lough Currane, and within half a mile of the sea. Salmon and Trout Fishing commences here on February 1st, and the house is already well known to Anglers from all parts of Great Britain and Ireland. This Hotel has been enlarged, and every modern improvement introduced.

Coaches to Parknasilla and Kenmare, and also to Cahirciveen daily, from May 1st.

SOUTHERN HOTEL, CARAGH LAKE.

Within half a mile of Great Southern and Western Railway Station. Beautifully situated on the shore of Caragh Lake, and surrounded by unrivalled scenery. The Company has secured extensive and exclusive Fishing and Shooting rights, and good Golf Links for the use of its guests. This Hotel has also been enlarged and improved, and now contains spacious Coffee Room, Drawing Room, Billiard Room, Smoking Room, large and lofty Bedrooms, Private Sitting Rooms, etc.

SOUTHERN HOTEL, KENMARE.

This house has been quite recently built, and will be found replete with every modern comfort and convenience. It is just on the outskirts of the Town, and commands a grand view of the Kenmare Sound, and surrounding country.

Coaches run daily during the Tourist Season from this Hotel to Parknasilla, Waterville, and Cahirciveen, also to Glengarriff and Killarney. Passengers on either of these famous Coach Routes will find Kenmare a convenient and attractive resting place.

Full particulars of any of the above Hotels may be obtained on application to the General Manager,

EDGAR J. CLEAVER,
Parknasilla, Kenmare, County Kerry.

Illustrated pamphlet—"*The Lakes and Fjords of Kerry,*" post free.

LEICESTER.

STAG AND PHEASANT HOTEL.

FIRST-CLASS
FAMILY AND COMMERCIAL HOTEL.

E. HART, Proprietress.

LERWICK.

THE QUEEN'S HOTEL,
AT LERWICK, SHETLAND.

TOURISTS and Commercial Gentlemen will find this Hotel replete with every comfort and convenience. The Queen's, in Lerwick, is the largest and oldest established, and has the finest view overlooking the harbour. Has also SEA BATHING from the Hotel, and GOLF COURSE within five minutes' walk. The Proprietor has the management under his personal superintendence, and Visitors are assured of every comfort and attention.

All the Fishing on Hayfield Estate **is** preserved for Visitors **at the Hotel.**

TH. GOED, *Proprietor.*

LIMERICK.

ROYAL GEORGE HOTEL

FIRST-Class Family and Commercial, most Central in City; has undergone extensive alterations, newly refurnished—also ten newly furnished **Bedrooms added;** Hot and Cold Baths. Splendid Billiard Room. Sanitary arrangements perfect.

Cook's and Gaze's Coupons accepted. 'Bus meets **all Trains.**

P. HARTIGAN, *Proprietor.*

LIVERPOOL.

LAURENCE'S
COMMERCIAL & FAMILY TEMPERANCE HOTEL
CLAYTON SQUARE.

(*Within Three minutes' walk of Lime Street and Central Stations, and the Chief Objects of Interest in the Town*).

CONTAINS upwards of One Hundred Rooms, including Coffee Room, Private Sitting Rooms, Billiard and Smoke Rooms. Large and Well-Lighted Stock Rooms.

LIMERICK.
THE GLENTWORTH HOTEL.

THIS elegant and centrally situated Hotel has been prepared with great care and at considerable expense for the accommodation of ladies and gentlemen visiting Limerick, and possesses the freshness, neatness, and general comfort which distinguish the best English and Continental establishments.

The GLENTWORTH claims the support of the general public for the

SUPERIORITY OF ITS ARRANGEMENTS IN EVERY DEPARTMENT.

Including splendid Coffee Room, Commercial Room (Writing Room attached), Sitting Rooms, Bedrooms, Bath Rooms (hot and cold water), &c., &c. 21 new Bedrooms added to Hotel.

☞ Commercial gentlemen will find our STOCK ROOMS all that can be desired.

It is the nearest Hotel in the city to the Railway Station, Banks, Steamboat Offices, Telegraph and Post Office, and to all places of Amusement.   P. KENNA, Proprietor.

*** Omnibus attends the arrival of all trains and steamers.
Porter attends the night mails.*

LIVERPOOL.

LANCASHIRE AND YORKSHIRE RAILWAY

EXCHANGE STATION HOTEL

(Under the Management of the Company).

TELEGRAPHIC ADDRESS: STATION HOTEL, LIVERPOOL.   TELEPHONE: No. 1173.

In close proximity to the Town Hall, Landing Stage, Exchange, and Principal Centres of Business.

LIGHTED THROUGHOUT BY ELECTRICITY.

THE Hotel offers every accommodation for Visitors and Families at moderate charges. Rooms may be telegraphed for, free of charge, from any principal station on the Railway, on application to the Stationmaster or Telegraph Clerk. Further particulars can be had on application to THE MANAGER.

Refreshment Rooms at the following Stations are under the management of the Company :—

Accrington, Ashton, Bolton, Blackburn, Bradford, Fleetwood, Halifax, Liverpool, Manchester, Rochdale, Salford, Southport, Sowerby Bridge, Wakefield, and Wigan.

LIVERPOOL.

SHAFTESBURY
HOTEL.

MOUNT PLEASANT, LIVERPOOL.
About Three Minutes' walk from Central and Lime Street Stations, and Ten Minutes from Landing Stage. A Porter in uniform meets any train, on receipt of letter or wire, to bring luggage to Hotel FREE OF CHARGE.

GOOD STOCK ROOMS.

No ALCOHOLIC DRINKS SUPPLIED.

LLANDUDNO.

MARINE HOTEL.

First-Class Family Hotel, fronting the Parade and Sea.

CONTAINING spacious Dining, Drawing, and Reading Rooms. Smoking and Billiard Rooms. Private Suites of Apartments.

The Residence of Her Majesty the Queen of Roumania, Season 1890.

MODERATE TARIFF, AND TERMS EN PENSION.

Apply PROPRIETOR.

LOCH AWE.

PORTSONACHAN HOTEL.

THIS Hotel has superior advantages, being away from the noise and bustle incidental to railroad Hotels, and easy of access, only half an hour's journey from Lochawe Station (Callander and Oban Railway), where the Hotel steamer *Caledonia* makes connection with the principal trains during the season. Letters delivered twice, and despatched three times daily. **Postal, Telegraph, and Money Order** Office in Hotel buildings. **Presbyterian and Episcopalian** Churches within easy walking distance of Hotel. **Tennis court, beautiful drives, first-class boats, experienced boatmen.** Posting and Coaching. Charges moderate. Thomas Cameron, Proprietor, Originator of the Oban, Lochawe, and Glenaut circular tour. Telegraphic address,

CAMERON, PORTSONACHAN.

DRUMMOND ARMS HOTEL, ST. FILLANS, BY CRIEFF.

Post and Telegraph within three minutes' walk.

THIS Commodious Hotel, under New Management, beautifully situated at the foot of Lochearn, is well adapted for Families and Tourists. St. Fillans is one of the loveliest places to be met with anywhere. Boats for Fishing and Carriages for Hire. Caledonian Coaches pass daily during the summer months. Charges moderate.

JAMES CARMICHAEL, *Proprietor.*
Late Head Waiter, Loch Awe Hotel, Argyllshire.

LOCH EARN HEAD (PERTHSHIRE)

LOCH EARN HEAD HOTEL,

(Under Royal Patronage. Twice visited by the Queen.)

THIS Hotel, which has been long established, has excellent accommodation for Families and Tourists, with every comfort and quiet, lies high and dry, and charmingly sheltered at the foot of the Wild Glen Ogle (the Kyber Pass). It commands fine views of the surrounding Hills and Loch, the old Castle of Glenample, the scenery of the Legend of Montrose, in the neighbourhood of Ben Voirlich, Rob Roy's Grave, Loch Voil, Loch Doine, and Loch Lubnaig, with many fine drives and walks. Posting and Carriages. Boats for Fishing and Rowing free. A 'Bus to and from the Hotel for principal trains during Summer. **An Episcopal Church.**

EDWIN MAISEY, *Proprietor.*

LOCH LOMOND.

INVERSNAID HOTEL.

LAMBERT,

Goldsmiths, Jewellers, and Silversmiths

TO HER MAJESTY QUEEN VICTORIA.

LARGEST COLLECTION OF

Antique and Modern Diamond Work and Plate

IN THE WORLD.

Sacramental and Presentation Plate.

10, 11, 12 COVENTRY STREET,

PICCADILLY, LONDON, W.

MELROSE.

THE

WAVERLEY HYDROPATHIC.

ONE hour from Edinburgh, one and a half from Carlisle. Baths, Billiards, Bowling, Lawn Tennis, Trout Fishing in Tweed included. First-Class Table. Dinner, 7 P.M.

For Terms apply—MANAGER.

MELROSE.

THE ABBEY HOTEL, ABBEY GATE,

AND

GEORGE AND ABBOTSFORD HOTEL,

HIGH STREET, MELROSE.

THE only first-class Hotels in Melrose, both overlooking the ruins, and only 2 minutes' walk from the Railway Station. The Hotel 'Buses attend all Trains. First-Class Horses and Carriages for Abbotsford, Dryburgh, etc., can be had at both establishments.

G. HAMILTON, PROPRIETOR.

NAIRN.

ROYAL MARINE HOTEL,

NAIRN.

A First-Class Hotel for Families and Tourists, at Moderate Rates.

Hot and Cold Salt-Water Baths in the Hotel.

EXCELLENT GOLF COURSE.

DAVID SUTHERLAND, *Proprietor.*

NORTH BERWICK. N.B.

MARINE HOTEL

THE FINEST SEASIDE HOTEL IN SCOTLAND.

FAMOUS HEALTH AND GOLF RESORT - 35 MINUTES FROM EDINBURGH.

Unequalled for bracing seaside air, natural scenery, and as a golfing centre.

Extended Golf Links. Hydraulic Lift.

HIGH-CLASS HOTEL, thoroughly well appointed, and recently enlarged by an addition of forty rooms. All the Public Rooms overlook the Links and Firth of Forth. Numerous Private Apartments *en suite*, with bathrooms, lavatories, etc. Extensive system of Baths (heated), Salt-Water, Ozone, etc. Lawn Tennis Courts. Post and Telegraph Office in the Hotel.   W. NIEBECKER, *Manager.*

NORWICH.

ROYAL HOTEL, NORWICH.

THE principal Family and Commercial Hotel (facing the Market Place). The two businesses in separate blocks. Smoking Rooms, Ladies' Drawing Room, Stock Rooms, and every convenience. Tariff moderate. Electric Light. Night Porter.

The new premises will be open in the autumn opposite the G.P.O. and Agricultural Hall, and will be furnished and equipped with all modern appliances and improvements.

Registered Telegraphic Address—"PRIMUS, NORWICH."

C. BUTCHER, Manager.

OBAN.

THE HOTEL.

THE GREAT WESTERN.

Tariff on application.

Reduced Tariff and Special Terms for Boarders
up to 30th June.

The Golf Course of the Oban Golf Club is free to Visitors on very moderate terms.

An Omnibus attends the arrival and departure of Trains and Steamers.
Visitors conveyed to and from the Hotel free of Charge.

MRS. M. SUTHERLAND, *Proprietrix.*

OBAN.

VICTORIA HOTEL

FIRST-CLASS—TEMPERANCE.

IN close proximity to Railway Station, Landing Pier, and Post Office, overlooking the Bay with a Magnificent View of Mountain and Loch Scenery. *Special Feature, Low Charges.*—Bedrooms, 1s. 6d. and 2s. Teas and Breakfasts, 1s. 6d. and 2s. Dinners, *Table d'hôte* and *à la carte*, 2s. 9d. Baths—Hot and Cold.

Registered telegraphic address, "MACLACHLAN," Oban.

PENRITH.

THE GEORGE HOTEL.

FAMILY AND COMMERCIAL HOUSE AND POSTING ESTABLISHMENT.

FAMILIES, Tourists, Commercial Gentlemen, and Visitors are specially recommended to this Hotel for comfort and attention combined with strictly moderate charges. It is the largest and most central in town, and 'Buses meet all Trains. Night Porter in attendance. Cyclists' Headquarters by appointment. Wines and Cuisine of the highest order. Ullswater, to which Coaches run from the Hotel during the Season, Lowther Castle, Brougham Castle (ruins), Airey Force, and the Nunnery, etc., are within driving distance, and are well worth visiting. Orders by Letter or Telegram receive prompt attention.   FRED. ARMSTRONG, PROPRIETOR.

PENZANCE.

MOUNTS BAY HOTEL.

THIS First-Class Family Hotel is situated on the Esplanade, close to and facing the sea.

Ladies' Coffee and Drawing Rooms.

Private Sitting Rooms, with splendid Sea Views.   Hot and Cold Baths.

Table d'Hôte.   Horses and Carriages.

Omnibus and Hotel Porter meet all trains.

MODERATE TARIFF.   EN PENSION FOR WINTER MONTHS.

C. BALL, *Proprietor.*

PENZANCE.

WESTERN HOTEL.

THIS old-established Family and Commercial Hotel will be found replete with every comfort for Families, Tourists, and Commercial Gentleman. Centrally situated. Good Coffee and Commercial Rooms. Billiard and Smoke Rooms. Ladies' Drawing Room. Posting in all its branches. Omnibus meets all trains.   MITCHELL & CO., *Proprietors.*

ROTHESAY.

BUTE ARMS HOTEL.

THIS establishment is situated in front of the pier, where steamers arrive and depart almost every half-hour, and affords magnificent views of the Bay, Loch Striven, and the Kyles of Bute. Tourists by the *Columba*, *Iona*, *Lord of the Isles*, or other steamers will find the BUTE ARMS one of the most comfortable resting-places on the Western Coast of Scotland, and being under the direct superintendence of the Proprietor, visitors may depend on every attention. The Sanitary arrangements are entirely new throughout the house. Table d'Hôte, 6.30. Billiard Room. Parties boarded by the week or month. Charges strictly moderate.

ROBERT SMITH, *Proprietor.*

ST. ANDREWS.

BURNETT'S
ROYAL  HOTEL.

Enlarged and thoroughly renovated; occupies one of the finest positions in the City, overlooking Madras College and Black Friars Monastery; Superior Accommodation and Moderate Charges; Boarding terms according to requirements.

G. W. BURNETT, Proprietor.

SALISBURY.

THE WHITE HART HOTEL.

The Largest and Principal Hotel in the City.

AN old-established and well-known first-class Family Hotel, nearly opposite Salisbury Cathedral, and within a pleasant drive of Stonehenge. This Hotel is acknowledged to be one of the most comfortable in England. Table d'Hôte Meals at separate Tables two hours each meal daily.

A Ladies' Coffee Room, a Coffee Room for Gentlemen, and first-class Billiard and Smoking Rooms.

Carriages and Horses of every description for Stonehenge and other places of interest at fixed inclusive charges. Excellent Stabling. Loose Boxes, etc.

Posting-Master to Her Majesty.

Tariff on application to **H. T. BOWES,** *Manager.*

THE CROWN HOTEL,

ESPLANADE.

Manager: DOUGLAS GORDON.

THIS HIGH-CLASS HOTEL is situated in the centre of the Esplanade on the South Cliff, directly facing the sea. Acknowledged by all to be the finest position in Scarborough. Immediately opposite the Hotel is an entrance to the magnificent Spa. All rooms not facing the sea have a splendid view of the surrounding country. The Sanitary arrangements are perfect in every respect, the Hotel holding a certificate to this effect from the Sanitary authorities.

Electric Light in all Public Rooms, Bedrooms, and Sitting-Rooms.

There is a perfect system of Electric Bells to all rooms. The Public Dining Room has lately been enlarged and thorough ventilation ensured.

A HANDSOMELY FURNISHED POMPEIAN ENTRANCE LOUNGE,

seventy-five by forty-five feet, six new Bathrooms, and an Electric Passenger Lift have been added. Also a First-Class Billiard Room. Ladies' Toilet Rooms on each floor.

Since the season 1896 the Hotel has been refurnished and redecorated throughout by Messrs. Waring and Son of London.

Tariff on application to the Manager.

SOUTHPORT.

SMEDLEY HYDRO.

BIRKDALE PARK.

TERMS from 7s. 6d. per day, including Turkish, Russian, Plunge, and other Baths. Well adapted for Summer or Winter residence, for either Invalids or Visitors.

LAWN TENNIS, BILLIARDS, ETC.

For Prospectus, apply MANAGER.

SOUTHPORT.

PRINCE OF WALES HOTEL.

BEST Position. 120 Rooms. Handsomely Furnished. Billiard Room, 4 Tables.

Strictly Moderate Charges.

Special Week-end Terms.

TELEGRAMS: "Prince, Southport." TELEPHONE 15.

SOUTHSEA.

ROYAL PIER HOTEL,

SOUTHSEA, PORTSMOUTH.

Manageress:—Mrs. NICHOLLS.

QUEEN'S HOTEL,

SOUTHSEA, PORTSMOUTH.

Manageress:—Miss RICKARDS.

BOTH of these First-Class Hotels have been redecorated and refurnished. They are situated in the best part of Southsea, and are the most convenient for Naval, Military, and Official Gentlemen and Families.

The spacious Dining and Drawing Rooms, as well as the principal Bedrooms, immediately overlook the Common, the Channel, and the Isle of Wight.

Tariffs very moderate. Modified terms arranged for large parties or for long periods. Book to Portsmouth Town Station, from which the Hotels are only about five minutes' drive.

SPA HOTEL.

THE OLDEST-ESTABLISHED & LEADING HOTEL

HIGHEST SITUATION (400 feet above Sea-level).

THE SPORTING HOTEL OF
THE HIGHLANDS.

SALMON & TROUT FISHING FREE.
BOATING. GOLF. TENNIS.
CLOSE TO GOLF COURSE.

Extensive additions have just been completed.

CONTAINS Spacious Public Rooms, Private Apartments *en suite*, Recreation and Ball Rooms, Conservatories, and is secluded enough to ensure to visitors the Privacy and Quiet of an ordinary Country Residence.

Cycle Court with Professional attendants.

POSTING IN ALL ITS BRANCHES.

A. WALLACE, *Manager.*

THE
TROSSACHS HOTEL,
LOCH KATRINE.

R. BLAIR, Proprietor,

THIS First-Class Hotel is beautifully situated in the midst of the classic scenery of Scott's "Lady of the Lake," and is the ONLY HOTEL in the Trossachs.

Parties staying for not less than a week can be boarded on **SPECIAL TERMS**, excepting from 15th July to 15th Sept.

During the season Coaches run from Callander Railway Station to the Trossachs, in connection with all Trains, and in connection with all Steamers on Loch Katrine. These Coaches all stop at this Hotel, giving passengers time to Lunch.

Excellent Fishing in Lochs Katrine and Achray. Boats engaged at the Hotel, and at the Boathouse Loch Katrine Pier.

BILLIARDS. LAWN TENNIS.

Address **THE TROSSACHS HOTEL,**
Loch Katrine,
By CALLANDER, N.B.

R. BLAIR, *Proprietor.*

POST AND TELEGRAPH OFFICE IN HOTEL.

TROSSACHS.
STRONACHLACHAR HOTEL,
HEAD OF LOCH KATRINE.
DONALD FERGUSON, Proprietor.

THIS Hotel, the only one on the shores of Loch Katrine, is most beautifully situated in the heart of ROB ROY'S Country; GLENGYLE and the romantic GRAVEYARD of CLAN GREGOR, both described at page 77 of "Perthshire Guide," being in close proximity; and as a fishing station it is unsurpassed. The trout at this end of Loch Katrine average fully three-quarters of a pound each, and in favourable weather baskets of from two to three dozen and upwards are very often made. Excellent boats and experienced boatmen are kept for parties staying at the Hotel.

The Hotel is replete with every comfort, and is reached either by way of Callander and Trossachs and the Loch Katrine Steamer, or by the Loch Lomond Steamer and Coach from Inversnaid, there being a full service of Coaches and Steamers by both these routes during the season.

Post and Telegraph Office in Hotel.

BOARD BY WEEK OR MONTH.
Carriages and other Conveyances kept for Hire.

ADDRESS : STRONACHLACHAR, by Inversnaid.

TRURO.
RED LION HOTEL
(FAMILY AND COMMERCIAL).

ESTABLISHED 1671. Birthplace of Foote the Tragedian. Close to Cathedral. The principal Hotel in the City. Ladies' Coffee Room. Drawing Room, Smoke and Billiard Rooms.

Manager, Miss CARLYON.

TUNBRIDGE WELLS.
WELLINGTON HOTEL,
MOUNT EPHRAIM.

Under the distinguished patronage of His Grace the Duke of Wellington, K.G., the leading Nobility and Gentry, etc.

ELECTRIC LIGHT THROUGHOUT.

The HOTEL is 422 feet above sea level; south aspect; magnificent scenery; elegantly furnished; piano in every sitting-room; Cuisine, English and French wine connoisseur; Table d'Hôte, separate tables. Large dairy farm, supplies daily. Laundry. Under the management of Mr. and Mrs. H. W. Boston, late of Royal Sussex Hotel, St. Leonards-on-sea.

BELSFIELD HOTEL,

WINDERMERE.

"BELSFIELD HOTEL" has justified its claim to the premier position among the leading hotels of the neighbourhood. This palatial building—originally erected as a private mansion—stands within no fewer than eight acres of charmingly designed and well-wooded grounds that are remarkable as vantage-points for some of the most picturesque views. The interior has been superbly decorated, the ceilings and mural embellishments being really remarkable as works of art, while equal taste has been displayed in the details of the costly furniture. Indeed, such handsome surroundings are rarely to be met with at Hotels either in or out of London.

Private Omnibus attends all Trains, and also at the Steam Yacht Pier, Bowness Bay.

Four-in-hand Coaches leave the Hotel daily for all parts of the Lake District.

GOLF.   BILLIARDS.   FISHING.   TENNIS.

Lighted by Electricity.

Under the Personal Superintendence of the Proprietor,

TELEPHONE No. 123.

TELEGRAMS—
BELSFIELD, WINDERMERE.

A. D. M'LEOD

(Late Manager, Gairloch Hotel, Ross-shire).

NORTH DEVON.
LYNTON AND MINEHEAD.

The Well-appointed Fast Four-Horse Coaches

"LORNA DOONE" & "RED DEER"

Run for the Season, commencing on Easter
Monday, between Railway Station, Minehead, and
Royal Castle Hotel, Lynton. For particulars see G. W. Railway Time Tables
and Bills. **THOMAS BAKER, Proprietor.**

ROYAL CASTLE HOTEL, LYNTON, 1896.

SOUTH-WESTERN RAILWAY,

The Shortest, Quickest, and most direct route to the South-West and
West of England, EXETER, BARNSTAPLE, LYNTON, BIDEFORD,
("Westward Ho!") ILFRACOMBE, NORTH and SOUTH DEVON,
NORTH CORNWALL, BUDE *via* HOLSWORTHY, TAVISTOCK,
LAUNCESTON, WADEBRIDGE, BODMIN, PLYMOUTH, DEVONPORT, WEY-
MOUTH, SWANAGE, CORFE CASTLE, BOURNEMOUTH, SOUTHAMPTON,
PORTSMOUTH, STOKES BAY, and ISLE OF WIGHT.

FAST EXPRESSES AT ORDINARY FARES, AND FREQUENT FAST TRAINS.

The quickest and best Route to and from London and Portsmouth and the Isle of Wight.

Trains run alongside the Steamboats.

BOURNEMOUTH.—FAST EXPRESS TRAINS, performing the journey from and to
LONDON in two and a half hours. Special Cheap Return Tickets, 28s. 6d. First, 19s.
Second, and 12s. Third Class, are issued by all trains on Fridays, Saturdays, and Sundays, from Waterloo, Kensington, Chelsea, Vauxhall, Clapham Junction, Wimbledon, and
Surbiton Stations to Bournemouth. The 1st and 2nd Class Tickets are available to return
up to and including the Monday week following the day of issue, and the 3rd Class by
any train up to the Tuesday (day of issue included). PULLMAN CARS are run by the
9.30 a.m., 12.30, 2.15, and 4.55 p.m. trains from Waterloo, and by the 7.50, 9.15, and 11.0 a.m.,
and 1.55 p.m. trains from Bournemouth, W. (and the E. Station 10 mins. later) to London.

Cheap Tourist & Excursion Tickets are issued during the Season to all Parts.

Through Tickets in connection with the London and North-Western, Great Northern
and Midland Railways.

New and Improved Mail Steam-Ships, *via* Southampton, to and from the CHANNEL
ISLANDS, JERSEY, GUERNSEY. Also Fast Steam-Ships for HAVRE, ROUEN, and
PARIS, ST. MALO, CHERBOURG, GRANVILLE, and HONFLEUR. The Company's Steam-
Ships are not surpassed in Speed or Accommodation by any Channel Vessels. *Full
particulars may be obtained from* G. T. White, *Superintendent of the Line,* Waterloo
Station, S.E. **CHARLES SCOTTER,** *General Manager.*

WATERLOO STATION, LONDON, *March* 1897.

MIDLAND GREAT WESTERN RAILWAY.
CONNEMARA, ACHILL, AND WEST OF IRELAND

CIRCULAR TOURS

From Dublin to the Tourist, Angling and Shooting Resorts in the West of Ireland.

☞ Reduced Fares for Parties of Two to Four
Passengers.

₊ Extra Coupons issued for extended Tours
from Dublin, Broadstone Terminus, to the North
and South of Ireland.

TOURIST TICKETS

From the principal Towns in ENGLAND and
SCOTLAND for the Connemara Tour, or combined Tour, including Killarney.

Issued at the Offices of the Railway and Steam-
packet Companies and Tourist Agencies.

Public Cars run during the Season, from Clifden to Westport passing through Letterfrack for
Renvyle, Kylemore, and Leenane.

The M. G. W. R. Company's 6d. ILLUSTRATED HANDBOOK to the WEST OF IRELAND
Contains 16 full-paged toned Lithographs and numerous Woodcuts.

Application for Time Tables, Tourist Programmes, and information as to Fares, Routes, Hotels, &c.,
may be made at the Irish Tourist Office, 2 Charing Cross, London, or to the Company's Agents—Mr. J.
Hogy, 60 Castle Street, Liverpool, and Mr. J. F. Ritson, 178 Buchanan St., Glasgow, or to the undersigned. **JOSEPH TATLOW, Manager.**

Broadstone Station, Dublin.

FURNESS RAILWAY.

LAKE-LAND.—THE PARADISE OF TOURISTS.

Boating, Bathing, Fishing (Sea, River, and Lake), Golfing, Coaching, and Mountaineering.

THE FURNESS RAILWAY possesses the advantages of running through the finest and most picturesque scenery in the country, and affords at the same time a means of direct communication to some of the most beautiful and healthful pleasure resorts. Along the whole route a series of charming views present themselves in quick succession to the tourist.

TOURIST TICKETS available for two calendar months are issued from 1st May to 31st October from all the principal Railway Stations to Grange, Bowness, Coniston Lake, Cark, Ambleside, Ravenglass, Ulverston, Furness Abbey, Seascale, Windermere (Lake Side), and St. Bees, and holders of these tickets are allowed to break their journey at any intermediate Station on the Furness Railway between Carnforth and their destination.

CHEAP WEEK-END AND TEN DAYS' TICKETS are issued every Friday and Saturday from the principal manufacturing towns in Derbyshire, Lancashire, Yorkshire, and the Midland Counties to the Lake District and Furness Coast Stations (including Ulverston). **Weekly and Fortnightly Tickets from London** (Euston and St. Pancras) are issued every Saturday during July, August, and September to **Windermere and Coniston Lakes**, and the principal Coast Stations on the Furness Railway, available for return on the following Monday, Monday week, Saturday week, or Monday fortnight. These tickets are also issued from the chief stations on the Furness Railway to London for similar periods.

GRANGE combines with its natural beauties a salubrious climate, and is one of the best-known health resorts in the kingdom.

ARNSIDE, CARK, KENTS BANK, and **SILVERDALE** are delightful places of resort, in close proximity to the Sea and Windermere Lake. Cartmel Priory is within easy distance of Cark Station.

ULVERSTON, beautifully situated near the shores of Morecambe Bay, and a central point for the Lake District. **Two miles from the historical Conishead Priory, now a Hydropathic Establishment.**

WINDERMERE (LAKE SIDE), BOWNESS, AMBLESIDE, and **CONISTON** are the centres of the English Lake District.

FURNESS ABBEY. Visitors to the Lakes, Isle of Man, and Belfast should not fail to see the far-famed ruins of Furness Abbey. The Furness Abbey Hotel, under the management of Messrs. Spiers and Pond, from 1st July 1897, is one of the most comfortable hostelries in England.

SEASCALE and **ST. BEES** are seaside watering-places with a bracing climate. The sands are unsurpassed, and safe bathing may be had at all states of the tide. At Seascale there are extensive Golf Links.

CIRCULAR TOURS. During the summer months various Circular Tours by Rail, Steam Yacht, and Chars-a-banc, embracing the principal places of interest in the Lake District, can be made from Stations on the Furness Railway.

CHEAP DAY TICKETS by ordinary Trains at a single fare for the return journey issued daily from April to October, and **WEEK-END TICKETS,** at a fare and a sixth are issued every Friday, Saturday, and Sunday *all the year round,* available to return on the Sunday and following Monday or Tuesday, to and from all Pleasure Resorts and the principal Stations on the Furness Railway.

WEEKLY AND FAMILY TICKETS ON WINDERMERE AND CONISTON LAKES.

For full particulars of Circular Tours, Day and Week-end Tickets, Weekly Lake Tickets, etc., **see Bills and** Programmes **issued by the Company gratis.**

Time Tables, Tourist Programmes, List of Furnished Lodgings, &c., may be obtained at any of the Company's Stations, also from Mr. F. J. RAMSDEN, *Superintendent of the Line.*

BARROW ROUTE TO THE ISLE OF MAN AND BELFAST.

SWIFT STEAMERS, DAILY, From Barrow to Douglas (Isle of Man), from 1st June to 30th September, and **Direct Daily Service, BARROW TO BELFAST,** all the year round.

The New Fast Steamer "Duchess of Devonshire" (20 knots), will be ready for the Isle of Man season, and for the remainder of the year will run between Barrow and Belfast. Full particulars as to Time of Sailings, Fares, etc., can be obtained in application to Messrs. JAMES LITTLE & Co., Barrow-on-Furness or Belfast.

ALFRED ASLETT,
GENERAL MANAGER.

BARROW-ON-FURNESS, *March* 1897.

CAMBRIAN RAILWAYS.

TOURS IN WALES.

Bathing, Boating, Fishing (Sea, River, & Lake), Golfing, Coaching, Mountaineering.

TOURIST TICKETS available for two months, issued throughout the year, from London and all principal Stations in England, Scotland, and Ireland to **Aberystwyth, Borth, Machynlleth, Aberdovey, Towyn, Dolgelley, Barmouth, Harlech, Portmadoc, Criccieth, Pwllheli, Llanidloes, Rhayader, Builth Wells, and Brecon.**

CHEAP WEEK-END & TEN DAYS TICKETS are issued every Friday or Saturday **Throughout the Year**, from SHREWSBURY, BIRMINGHAM, WOLVERHAMPTON, STAFFORD, BURTON, DERBY, LEICESTER, PETERBORO, LEEDS, HUDDERSFIELD, STOCKPORT, OLDHAM, MANCHESTER, PRESTON, BLACKBURN, ROCHDALE, BRADFORD, WAKEFIELD, HALIFAX, BOLTON, WIGAN, WARRINGTON, CREWE, LIVERPOOL, STOKE, BIRKENHEAD, and other Stations to the CAMBRIAN WATERING-PLACES.

Every Saturday during June, July, August, and September, **Cheap Weekly** or **Fortnightly Tickets** will be issued **from London** to the Cambrian Coast and certain Inland stations, available to return on Monday, Monday week, or Monday fortnight, also on the **following** Saturday or Saturday Week by **one ordinary Train.** Tickets at same Fares are also issued during the same period on Every Monday **to London**, available to return on the following Saturday or Saturday week.

ABOUT 30 RAIL AND COACH EXCURSIONS DAILY

Are run from the Cambrian Railway, during the Summer Months, through the finest Scenery in the Principality.

Cycling and Walking Tours at cheap fares, through the Mountain, River, and Lake Districts.

For particulars see Rail and Coach Excursions' Programme, issued gratis.

EXPRESS TRAINS WITH 1st AND 3rd CLASS LAVATORY CARRIAGES LIGHTED WITH GAS
(LONDON to ABERYSTWYTH 6¾ hours ; BARMOUTH 7½ hours)

Are run daily during the Season in connection with Fast Trains on the London and North-Western and other Railways, between London, Liverpool, Manchester, Birmingham, Stafford, Shrewsbury, Hereford, Merthyr, Cardiff, Newport (Mon.), &c., and Aberystwyth, Barmouth, &c.

See the Cambrian Railway's new and beautiful album **" A SOUVENIR," Gems of picturesque scenery in Wild Wales. 55 SUPERB VIEWS. Price 6d.** At the principal Railway Bookstalls, the Company's Stations, and the undermentioned Offices, &c.

"PICTURESQUE WALES" (Illustrated).

The Official Guide-Book to the Cambrian Railways, edited by Mr. GODFREY TURNER, price 6d., can be obtained at the Bookstalls, and at the Company's Offices or Stations, also of Messrs. W. J. Adams and Sons, 59 Fleet Street, London, E.C.

FARM-HOUSE AND COUNTRY LODGINGS.

Attention is drawn to the illustrated pamphlet issued by the Company, **"WHERE TO STAY AND WHAT TO SEE!"** Price 1d. at the principal Railway Bookstalls and Company's Stations.

Time Tables, Tourist Programmes, Guide-Books, and full particulars of Trains, Fares, &c., may be obtained from Mr. W. H. GOUGH, Superintendent of the Line, Oswestry, at any of the Company's Stations, and at the Cambrian Office, Crue-Woode Buildings, 17 Back Goree, Liverpool, or on application to the undersigned. Also at the CAMBRIAN RAILWAY'S LONDON OFFICE, 41 GRACECHURCH STREET (opposite Monument Station), LONDON, E.C., and at the undermentioned Offices of Messrs. Henry Gaze & Sons, Ld., Excursion Tourist Agents—

London—142 Strand, 4 Northumberland Avenue, 18 Westbourne Grove, and Piccadilly Circus ; **Birmingham**—Stephenson Place, New Street Station ; **Manchester**—L. & N.-W. Booking Office, London Road ; **Liverpool**—25 Lime Street ; **Dublin**—16 Suffolk Street ; **Glasgow**—Central Station.

GENERAL OFFICES, OSWESTRY,   **C. S. DENNISS,**
April 1897   *General Manager.*

BELFAST & NORTHERN COUNTIES RAILWAY.

SUMMER EXCURSIONS IN THE NORTH OF IRELAND.

Antrim Coast Circular Tour.—The most varied and beautiful Tour in Ireland. Rail: Belfast to Larne, and Portrush to Belfast (92 miles). Coach: Larne to Giants' Causeway (55 miles) along the famous Coast Road, affording infinite variety of scene and interest. Electric Tramway: Giants' Causeway to Portrush (7 miles), 1st class, 21s.; 2nd class, 19s.; 3rd class, 17s.

Portrush and Giants' Causeway.—Excursion Tickets every day from Belfast. Fast trains between Belfast and Portrush, and Electric Tramway, Portrush and Giants' Causeway.

Glenariff.—The loveliest of the numerous and remarkable Glens for which the County Antrim is famed. Daily excursions from Belfast to Glenariff and back by Rail; also Circular Tour, including Glenariff, part of Antrim coast and Larne, at very low fares.

Donegal Highlands and Lakes Erne.—Circular Tour including Rail: Belfast to Portrush. Electric Tram: Portrush to Giants' Causeway and back. Rail: Portrush to Londonderry, thence to Donegal via Strabane and Stranorlar and Ballyshannon or Bundoran to Belfast, 1st class, 40s. 6d.; 2nd class, 30s. 6d.; 3rd class, 22s. 9d.

Many other Excursions of interest can be made from Belfast, for particulars of which apply to the undersigned.

THE NORTHERN COUNTIES RAILWAY HOTEL,
PORTRUSH (Giants' Causeway),

Under Railway Management, affords First-Class accommodation to Tourists visiting the Giants' Causeway, as well as Families and Gentlemen wishing to reside at the seaside. Grand Dining Room, Drawing, Reading, Smoke, and Billiard Rooms on the Ground Floor. Upwards of 120 Bedrooms. Hot and Cold Sea-water Bath Establishment. Lawn Tennis Courts. Best Golf Links in the Country. Hotel well situated and commands splendid view of Sea and Coast. 'Bus attends all trains. For further information apply to HOTEL MANAGER, PORTRUSH.

THE SHORTEST SEA PASSAGE BETWEEN GREAT BRITAIN AND IRELAND
IS via LARNE AND STRANRAER.

Daily (Sundays excepted) and daylight sailings by the new fast Mail Steamers, "PRINCESS MAY," "PRINCESS VICTORIA," etc.

Two Services (morning and evening) each way every Week-day from 1st June till 30th September.

Sea Passage . . . . 80 Minutes
Port to Port . . . . 2 Hours.

Trains run alongside Steamer at Stranraer and Larne. Through bookings from all the principal places in England and Scotland to the North of Ireland.

For full particulars apply to

EDWARD J. COTTON, General Manager,
B. & N. C. Railway, BELFAST.

"What sends picturesque tourists to the Rhine and Saxon Switzerland? Within five miles around the pretty inn of Glengarriff there is a country the magnificence of which no pen can give an idea."—THACKERAY.

CORK, BANDON, AND SOUTH COAST RAILWAY.

GLENGARRIFF and the LAKES of KILLARNEY

By the "Prince of Wales Route," via Dublin and Cork.

During the Tourist Season (May 1st to October 31st) Through RETURN CHEAP CIRCULAR TOUR TICKETS are issued at the principal Stations on the London and North Western and other chief English Railways, for Killarney *via* Glengarriff—the favourite and most expeditious Route.

On and after 1st May each year well-appointed Four-Horse Coaches run through the Tourist Season daily (Sundays excepted), between Bantry, Glengarriff, Kenmare, and Killarney, to meet Trains to and from Cork, stopping at Vickery's Hotel, Bantry, for Refreshments.

SOUTH OF IRELAND CIRCULAR TOUR.

CORK, BANTRY, GLENGARRIFF, KENMARE, AND THE LAKES OF KILLARNEY.

VIA DUBLIN AND CORK.

GLENGARRIFF.— "What appears chiefly to impress the mind in this lovely region is the deep conviction you feel that there is no dramatic effect in all you behold, no pleasing illusions of art ; that it is Nature you contemplate, such as she is, in all her wildness and all her beauty."

By this celebrated Route a direct and expeditious connection is given with the English and Dublin down and up day mails to and from Cork for Glengarriff and Killarney, *via* Bantry, as well as with the South of England, *via* New Milford or Bristol and Cork.

☞ *NOTE.—Passengers Booking through in Ireland or England should be certain to inquire for the cheap Tickets by the "Circular Tour" Route for Glengarriff and Killarney.*

GOOD ROADS FOR CYCLING.

For full particulars see Tourist Programmes and Pictorial Time Tables, sent free upon application to undersigned ; or apply to Messrs. COOK & SON ; GAZE & SONS, LTD. ; the Superintendent of the Line, Great Western Railway, Paddington ; or at the Company's London Office, 2 Charing Cross.

SALOON, LAVATORY, & SMOKING CARRIAGES BETWEEN CORK & BANTRY.

E. J. O'B. CROKER,
GENERAL MANAGER.

ALBERT QUAY TERMINUS, *April 1897.*

CORK AND MUSKERRY LIGHT RAILWAY.

Picturesque and Direct Route to the Famous Blarney Castle.

CORK TO BLARNEY IN 35 MINUTES.

(Tourist Tickets are issued by Messrs. THOS. COOK & SON and GAZE & SON.)

THE Terminus at Blarney is situated in the Castle Grounds, and the Trains run up to the Castle Gate. On WEEK-DAYS Trains leave WESTERN ROAD TERMINUS, CORK, at 8.15 and 10 a.m.; 12.15 noon; 2.40, 4.15, and 6.15 p.m. Returning from Blarney at 9 and 11 a.m.; 1.15, 3.25, 5, and 7 p.m. Return Fares —First Class, 1s. 2d.; Third Class, 10d. On SUNDAYS, *Reduced Fares*—Trains run every alternate hour from 10 a.m. till 8 p.m.

Visitors to Blarney Castle and Grounds can obtain Admission Tickets at Blarney Station on production of this Company's Ticket or Coupon at 3d. each. Holders of other Tickets charged 6d. The Railway passes through the most beautiful and charming country in the South of Ireland, and runs close to Dripsey Castle and Shandy Hall. There is also a station at St. Ann's Hill, two minutes' walk from the celebrated Hydropathic Establishment. For further information apply at Cook's Tourist Office, Academy Street, Cork; or to J. B. WILSON General Manager, Western Road Terminus, Cork.

GALWAY BAY STEAMBOAT CO., LIMITED.

THE cheapest, shortest, and most enjoyable route for tourists from England, Dublin, and the North of Ireland, to the beautiful scenery on the West Coast of Ireland, is by the Midland Great Western Railway, Dublin to Galway; and thence *per* new steamers "Duras," or "Citie of the Tribes," to the ISLANDS OF ARRAN AND KILKERRIN. Sailings every Tuesday, Thursday, and Saturday.

For Ballyvaughan in connection with the far-famed spa, Lisdoonvarna, sailings every Monday, Wednesday, and Friday during summer.

For further particulars apply to MANAGER, Midland Great Western Railway, Broadstone, Dublin; or to JAMES A. GRANT, Secretary, 13 Eyre Square, Galway.

ENGLAND AND NORTH OF IRELAND.

The best route is by the Direct Service of Express Steamers.

"MAGIC" (Twin Screw), "OPTIC," "COMIC" (Twin Screw), "CALORIC," "MYSTIC" (Twin Screw), &c.

Via LIVERPOOL and BELFAST.

Open Sea Passage about Six Hours.

The Steamers of the Belfast Steamship Company are lighted by Electricity, and are fitted with every modern improvement for the comfort of Passengers. The Cabins are amidships, the Saloon being on deck, with a spacious Promenade above.

From Liverpool (Prince's Landing Stage or Prince's Dock) for Belfast —Daily (Sundays excepted) at 10.30 p.m.

From Belfast (Donegal Quay) for Liverpool—Daily (Sundays excepted) at 8 p.m.; Saturdays at 10.30 p.m.

Omnibuses await the arrival of the Steamer at Liverpool, to convey Through Passengers and their Luggage to the Lime Street and Central Stations FREE of charge. Omnibuses also leave the Lime Street and Central Stations every evening, in time to convey all Through Passengers and their Luggage from all Districts to the Steamer FREE of charge.

Through bookings between all principal English Stations and Stations in the North of Ireland at fares as cheap as any other route.

For Fares, Rates, and all particulars apply to H. H. STEVENSON, 6 Brown Street, Manchester; BELFAST STEAMSHIP COMPANY, LIMITED, 5 Chapel Street, Liverpool; or to **The Head Office, Belfast Steamship Company,** Limited, Belfast.

Telegraphic Address—"Basalt. Belfast"; "Afloat, Liverpool."

FLEETWOOD TO BELFAST

AND THE

NORTH OF IRELAND.

EVERY EVENING (SUNDAYS EXCEPTED).

In connection with the Lancashire and Yorkshire and London and North-Western Railway Companies' Steamers, "**Duke of Lancaster**." "**Duke of York.**" "**Duke of Clarence.**"

LEAVE FLEETWOOD FOR BELFAST

Every Evening (Sundays excepted), at 11.35 p.m., or after arrival of trains from London, Birmingham, Hull, Newcastle, Bradford, Leeds, Liverpool, Manchester, Preston, and all parts of the Kingdom ; returning

FROM BELFAST TO FLEETWOOD

Every Evening (Sundays excepted), at 8.30 p.m., arriving in Fleetwood in time for early morning trains to the above places.

FARES.—(No Steward's Fee) SINGLE JOURNEY, Saloon, 12s. 6d. ; Steerage, 5s. ; RETURNS available for two months, Saloon, 21s. ; Steerage, 8s. 6d. Through Tickets (single and return) are also issued from all the principal Stations of the London and North-Western, Lancashire and Yorkshire, North-Eastern, Great Western, Great Northern, and Manchester, Sheffield, and Lincolnshire Railway Companies, to Belfast, and *vice versa*.

SPECIAL TOURISTS' TICKETS AVAILABLE FOR TWO MONTHS

Are issued during the Summer Season, *via* the Fleetwood Route, whereby Tourists may visit all places of interest in the North of Ireland and Dublin. For particulars, see the Lancashire and Yorkshire and London and North-Western Companies' Books of Tourists' Arrangements.

At Fleetwood the railway trains run alongside the steamers, and passengers' luggage is carried from the train at the quay on board FREE OF CHARGE.

Fleetwood is unrivalled as a steam packet station for the North of Ireland, and the unexampled regularity with which the Belfast Line of Steamers have made the passage between the two ports for more than forty years is probably without a parallel in steamboat service, and has made this Route the most popular, as it is certainly the most Expeditious and Desirable, for Passengers, Goods, and Merchandise, between the great centres of commerce in England and the North and North-West of Ireland.

FLEETWOOD AND LONDONDERRY

Screw Steamships "ELM" or "IVY."

From Fleetwood, every Saturday at or after 8.50 p.m. From Derry, every Friday at or after 5 p.m.

For full information apply to A. T. COTTON, 20 Donegal Quay, Belfast ; W. F. COPELAND, (L. & Y. Rly.), Irish Traffic Superintendent's Office, 122 Royal Avenue, Belfast ; C. W. LODGE (L. & N.-W. Rly.), 26 Royal Avenue, Belfast ; Capt. J. E. JACKSON, Marine Superintendent, Fleetwood ; S. WHITEHALL, District Superintendent, Fleetwood ; JOHN CARTER, Goods Department, Fleetwood ; WILLIAM PHILLIPS, Londonderry, or at any Lancashire and Yorkshire or London and North-Western Railway Station.

LONDON AND DUBLIN,

AND THE SOUTH OF ENGLAND.

The best route for Cornwall, Devon, Wilts, Sussex, Kent, Essex, Hants, and Surrey and for the Scilly Islands, the Isle of Wight, the Channel Islands and France.

The British and Irish Steam Packet Company's large and powerful Steam-Ships, fitted with electric light, and with superior passenger accommodation, and carrying goods, horses, carriages, &c. at moderate rates, leave LONDON and DUBLIN Twice a **Week** (unless prevented by unforeseen occurrences), calling both ways at

PORTSMOUTH, SOUTHAMPTON, PLYMOUTH AND FALMOUTH

SAILING DAYS

From **LONDON: Sundays** and **Wednesdays.**
From **DUBLIN: Wednesdays** and **Saturdays.**

Passengers from London can embark the evening before sailing day without extra charge, but must be on board not later than 10.0 P.M.

FARES FROM LONDON	1st CABIN.		2nd CABIN.		DECK.	
	Single.	Return.	Single.	Return.	Single.	Return.
	s. d.	s. d.	s. d.	s. d.	s. d.	s. d.
To Portsmouth	10 6	16 6	6 6	10 0	4 0	6 0
„ Southampton	11 0	17 0	7 0	10 6	4 6	6 6
„ Plymouth .	15 0	24 0	11 0	17 6	7 0	11 0
„ Falmouth .	20 0	32 0	15 0	24 0	10 0	15 0
„ Dublin .	25 0	38 6	17 6	27 0	11 0	17 0

Children from 3 to 12 years of age half fare. Return Tickets are available for two months, and passengers are allowed to break the journey at intermediate ports. Provisions are supplied on board at moderate rates. Private cabins can be reserved on payment of extra charge, on early application being made for same.

London Offices:—19 Leadenhall Street, E.C. JAMES HARTLEY & Co., Agents. Berth : North Quay, Eastern Basin, London Dock, near the Shadwell Stations, Great Eastern and Metropolitan Railways. Chief Offices, Dublin ; 3 North Wall. Telegraphic address ; Awe, Dublin. A. W. EGAN, Secretary.

SCOTLAND AND IRELAND.

ROYAL MAIL LINE.

QUICKEST, Cheapest, and Best Route between all parts of Scotland and the North of Ireland.

MAIL SERVICE twice every evening (Sundays excepted) to and from all parts of Ireland *via Belfast;* and all parts of Scotland, *via* Glasgow, *via* Greenock, and *via* Ardrossan.

DAYLIGHT SERVICE DURING SUMMER SEASON.

Glasgow to Belfast and back same day, by "Adder" from Ardrossan.

Also Steamers between—

Glasgow and **Manchester**, three times weekly.

Glasgow and **Liverpool** (calling at Greenock). Fast and commodious new steamers "Spaniel" and "Pointer." Cheap Excursion Fares. Five sailings in the fortnight. See newspaper advertisements.

Glasgow and **Londonderry** (calling at Greenock). Twice weekly.

For full details see Advertisements and Sailing Bills, or apply to

G. & J. BURNS,

Glasgow, Belfast. Londonderry, Manchester, and Liverpool.

British & Irish Steam Packet Co., Ltd.

GRAND HOLIDAY SEA TRIPS.

☞ (Magnificent Coast Scenery)

BETWEEN

LONDON AND DUBLIN

AND THE

SOUTH OF ENGLAND.

The best route for **Cornwall, Devon, Wilts, Sussex, Kent, Essex, Hants**, and **Surrey** and for the **Scilly Islands**, the **Isle of Wight**, the **Channel Islands** and **France**.

THE COMPANY'S LARGE AND POWERFUL STEAM-SHIPS

Fitted with electric light, and with superior accommodation for Passengers, leave **London** and **Dublin** twice a week, calling both ways at **Portsmouth, Southampton, Plymouth**, and **Falmouth**.

FLEET:

LADY ROBERTS (New Steamer) 1462 Tons.

LADY WOLSELEY	1450 Tons	LADY MARTIN	1352 Tons
LADY HUDSON-KINAHAN	1375 „	LADY OLIVE	1103 „

SAILING ⎫ From London—Sundays and Wednesdays.
DAYS ⎬ From Dublin—Wednesdays and Saturdays.

PASSENGER FARES (STEWARDS' FEES INCLUDED) BETWEEN	1st Cabin.		2nd Cabin.		Deck.	
	Single.	Return.	Single.	Return.	Single.	Return.
	s. d.	s. d.	s. d.	s. d.	s. d.	s. d.
LONDON and PORTSMOUTH .	10 6	16 6	6 6	10 0	4 0	6 0
„ SOUTHAMPTON .	11 0	17 0	7 0	10 6	4 6	6 6
„ PLYMOUTH .	15 0	24 0	11 0	17 6	7 0	11 0
„ FALMOUTH .	20 0	32 0	15 0	24 0	10 0	15 0
„ DUBLIN .	25 0	38 6	17 6	27 0	11 0	17 0
DUBLIN and FALMOUTH .	20 0	32 0	15 0	24 0	9 0	14 0
„ PLYMOUTH .	23 0	35 0	16 0	25 0	10 0	16 0
„ SOUTHAMPTON .	24 0	37 6	16 6	26 0	10 6	16 6
„ PORTSMOUTH .	24 0	37 6	16 6	26 0	10 6	16 6
FALMOUTH and PLYMOUTH .	5 0	8 0	4 0	6 6	3 0	4 6
„ SOUTHAMPTON .	18 0	28 0	14 0	22 0	9 0	14 0
„ PORTSMOUTH .	18 0	28 0	14 0	22 0	9 0	14 0
PLYMOUTH and SOUTHAMPTON .	13 0	20 0	10 0	16 0	6 0	9 6
„ PORTSMOUTH .	13 0	20 0	10 0	16 0	6 0	9 6

Children from 3 to 12 years old, half fare. RETURN TICKETS are available for two months, and Passengers are allowed to break the journey at intermediate ports. Provisions supplied on board at moderate rates.

Private Cabins can be reserved on payment of extra charge, on early application being made for same.

Tourists will find much interesting information in Longley's Holiday Guides, entitled *A Run to Dublin*, and *Four Channel Ports*, abundantly illustrated. Sent post free from any of the Company's Offices, or obtainable on board the Steamers.

Passengers from London can embark the evening before sailing day without extra charge, but must be on board not later than 10 P.M.

Special Cheap Excursion Tickets, 1st and 2nd Cabin, available for 14 days, are issued from Portsmouth, Southampton, Plymouth, and Falmouth to Dublin at a single fare and a quarter, from 1st May to end of September.

Full information as to Sailings, etc., can be obtained from JAMES HARTLEY & Co., 19 Leadenhall Street, London, E.C., and North Quay, Eastern Basin, London Docks, Shadwell, E. (where the vessels lie), or from any of the following Agents: R. CLARK & Son, or H. J. WARING & Co., Millbay Pier, Plymouth; W. & E. C. CARNE, Market Street, Falmouth; LE FEUVRE & SON, 8 Gloucester Square, Southampton; J. M. HARRIS, 10 Broad Street, Portsmouth; CAROLIN & EGAN, 30 Eden Quay, Dublin. **Chief Offices—3 North Wall, Dublin.** Telegraphic Addresses—"AWE," Dublin; "EMERALD," London.

A. W. EGAN, *Secretary*.

DELIGHTFUL STEAMER TRIPS on the THAMES.

SALOON STEAMERS run daily between **OXFORD, HENLEY,** and **KINGSTON,** from 17th May to end of September 1897.

DOWN TRIP.		UP TRIP.	
OXFORD TO HENLEY.	Daily (Sundays	KINGSTON TO HENLEY.	Daily (Sundays
HENLEY TO KINGSTON.	excepted).	HENLEY TO OXFORD.	excepted).

SPECIAL TRIP Windsor to Henley and back daily (Sundays excepted).

The through journey occupies two days each way, but passengers can join or leave the boat at any of the locks, or regular stopping places. Circular Tickets for Combined Railway and Steamer Trips are issued at most of the principal G.W.R. Stations, and at Waterloo Station L. & S.W.R. Time Table giving full particulars of arrangements, fares, etc., post free, 1d.

Rowing Boats of all kinds for Excursions down the River at Charges which include Cartage back to Oxford.

Full Particulars on application.

Steam Launches for Hire by the day or Week, and also for the Trip.

Boats of every description, Canoes, Punts, etc., built to Order.

A large selection, both New and Second-hand, kept in readiness for Sale or Hire.

Illustrated Price Lists may be had on application.

House Boats for Sale or Hire, and also built to Order.

SALTER BROTHERS,

Boat Builders,

FOLLY BRIDGE, OXFORD.

CARRON LINE.

SCOTLAND AND LONDON.

INCREASED AND ACCELERATED SERVICE.

Notice.—The new twin-screw steamer "Avon" is expected to be on the station in May. The service will then be increased and accelerated. For further particulars see daily papers.

Carron Company's splendid steamers "GRANGE," "FORTH," and "THAMES" (which have been specially built for the service, and are all lighted by electricity), or other steamers, are expected to sail, unless prevented by unforeseen circumstances,

From Grangemouth—Every Tuesday, Thursday, and Saturday. From Carron and London and Continental Steam Wharves. London—Every Monday, Wednesday, and Saturday. Average Passage 30 Hours. Trains run alongside the Steamers at Grangemouth. The only Route by which Passengers can obtain a Perfect View of the Forth Bridge—the Steamers of this Line sailing underneath.

Fares: Glasgow and London.

First Cabin, including 1st Class Rail		26s.	39s.
" " 3rd "		24s.	35s.
Second Cabin " 3rd "		17s. 6d.	26s. 6d.
Soldiers and Sailors on Deck, and 3rd Class Rail		12s.	..

Grangemouth and London.

First Cabin		22s.	84s.
Second Cabin		16s.	24s.
Soldiers and Sailors on Deck		10s.	..

Return Tickets available for Two Months.

Circular Tours, Glasgow to London returning by Clyde Shipping Co.'s Steamers ; also to Bristol, Dublin, Belfast, and Isle of Man, etc. Each steamer carries a Stewardess.

For Berths, Guide-books (free), and all information apply in LONDON at Carron and London and Continental Wharves, 87-93 Lower East Smithfield, E. ; City Office, 73 Great Tower Street ; in GLASGOW, at Carron Company's Offices, 125 Buchanan Street ; in Greenock, at City Buildings ; in EDINBURGH, to T. COOK & SON, 9 Princes Street, or J. & H. LINDSAY, 7 Waterloo Place ; and at Carron Company's Offices, GRANGEMOUTH.

THE LAIRD LINE.

Glasgow to Dublin—Every Tuesday, Thursday, and Saturday.	FARES—Cabin, Single, 12s. 6d.
Dublin to Glasgow—Every Tues., Thurs., and Sat.	Steerage, 5s. ; Return, 20s. and 8s.
Glasgow to Londonderry—Every Monday, Tuesday, Thursday, and Friday.	FARES—Cabin, Single, 12s. 6d. ; Steerage, 4s. ;
Londonderry to Glasgow—Every Tuesday, Wednesday, Friday, and Saturday.	Return, 26s.
Glasgow to Portrush.—See Monthly Sailing Bills.	
Portrush to Glasgow. " "	FARES.
Glasgow to Coleraine (with liberty to call at or off Portrush) Every Monday and Thursday.	Cabin, Single, 10s. ; Steerage, 3s. 6d. ;
Coleraine to Glasgow (with liberty to call at or off Portrush) Every Tuesday and Saturday.	Return, 15s. and 6s.

Glasgow to Sligo—Every Wednesday and Friday. See Monthly Sailing Bills.
Sligo to Glasgow—Every Tuesday and Saturday, at afternoon tide.
Glasgow to Ballina.—See Monthly Bills. | Glasgow to Westport.—See Monthly Bills.
Ballina to Glasgow. " " | Westport to Glasgow. " "

Fleetwood to Londonderry—Every Sat. at 8.45 aftern.	
Londonderry to Fleetwood—Every Friday at 5 aftern.	EXCURSION FARES!
Morecambe to Dublin—Every Mon., Wed., and Friday.	(One month)—Cabin, 15s. ;
Dublin to Morecambe—Every Tues., Thurs., and Sat.	Steerage, 6s.
Morecambe to Londonderry—Every Tues. and Sat.	
Londonderry to Morecambe—Every Mon. and Thurs.	

Liverpool to Larne, Portrush, or Coleraine, and Westport.—See Monthly Bills.
Westport, Coleraine, Portrush, or Larne to Liverpool. " "

For further particulars apply to ALEX. A. LAIRD & Co., 52 Robertson St., Glasgow ; Custom House Quay, Greenock ; 2 Upper Fountaine St., Leeds ; Quay, Ballina and Larne Harbour ; O. CARR, Morecambe Harbour ; M. LANGLANDS & SONS, Liverpool ; WELLS & HOLOMAN, Dublin ; ALEX. A. LAIRD & Co., Londonderry ; D. FALL & SON, or J. CALDWELL & SON, Portrush and Coleraine ; JAS. HARPER & Co., Sligo ; A. M. O'MALLEY, Westport.

LOCH-LOMOND.

"QUEEN OF SCOTTISH LAKES."

THE Dumbarton and Balloch Joint Line Committees' First-Class Saloon Steamers sail from Balloch Pier, calling frequently at all Loch-Lomond Piers, also in connection with **Trossachs Tours, Loch - Lomond and Loch - Long Tours, Trossachs and Aberfoyle Tours**, &c. &c.

The most direct and picturesque route to **Oban and Fort-William**, *via* Loch Lomond, Ardlui, and Crianlarich.

For Train and Steamboat hours see North British and Caledonian Railway Time Tables, or apply to both Companies' Stationmasters, and to WM. J. FRASER, 21 Hope Street, Glasgow.

WEEKLY CIRCULAR TOURS.

GLASGOW & THE OUTER HEBRIDES.

ONE Week's Pleasure Sailing by the splendid sea-going Steamer "Hebridean," sailing from Glasgow and Greenock, every MONDAY for Islay, Colonsay, Oban, Mull, Coll, Tiree, Skye, Uist, Barra, etc., affords the Tourist a splendid opportunity of viewing the magnificent scenery of the West of Skye and the Outer Hebrides.

Cabin for the Round 35s., Board included 65s.

ISLAND OF ST. KILDA— During the Season special trips are made to this far-famed Island, when passengers are given facilities for landing.

Cabin on St. Kilda Trips 50s., Board included 84s.

Time Bills, Maps of Route, Cabin Plans, and Berths secured at
JOHN M'CALLUM & CO., 10 Ann St., City, Glasgow.

GLASGOW AND THE HIGHLANDS.
WEEKLY CIRCULAR TOUR.

THE Favourite Steamer DUNARA CASTLE sails from Glasgow every Thursday at 2 P.M., and from Greenock, West Quay, at 7 P.M., for Colonsay, Iona, Bunessan, Tyree, Barra, Uist, Skye, and Harris, returning to Glasgow on Wednesdays. Affords to Tourists the opportunity of about a week's comfortable Sea Voyage, and at the same time a Panoramic View of the magnificent scenery of the Outer Hebrides.

CABIN FARE, £1 : 15s., INCLUDING MEALS, £3 : 5s.

Occasional Trips during **Season** to the Island of **St. Kilda**. Return Cabin Fare, including Meals, **£4 : 4s.**

Time Bills (with Maps) and Berths secured on application to
MARTIN ORME, 20 Robertson Street, Glasgow.

Berths may also be booked at the London Offices of the Clyde Shipping Company, 138 Leadenhall Street, E.C., and Carron Company, 87 Lower East Smithfield, E.C., and 73 Great Tower Street, E.C.

GENERAL STEAM NAVIGATION COMPANY.
55 GREAT TOWER STREET, E.C.

HAMBURG.—Greatly accelerated service. Express Route from Liverpool Street Station, Wednesdays and Saturdays at 8.35 p.m. The s.s. "Seamew," 3500 tons measurement capacity, 2600 horse-power, "Peregrine," 3000 tons, 3000 horse-power, both lighted with electricity, and having splendid passenger accommodation, have been placed on the route. Fares, 1st Class and Saloon, £1 17s. 6d.; 2nd Class and Fore Cabin, £1, 5s. 9d.; Return, £2, 16s. 3d. and £1, 18s. 9d.

From Irongate and St. Katharine's Wharf.

OSTEND, as per Time Table, 7s. 6d. or 6s.   Return, 10s. 6d. or 9s.

EDINBURGH, Weds. and Sats., 22s. or 16s. Return, 34s. or 24s. 6d.

BORDEAUX.—Leaving London on Saturdays and Bordeaux early Sunday mornings (passengers embarking in Bordeaux on Saturday evenings.

FARES—(no Steward's Fees): **Chief Cabin, £2, 10s.; Fore Cabin, £1, 15s.**   Return Tickets, (available for Two Months), **Chief Cabin, £4; Fore Cabin £3.** Children under 12 years half-price. Bicycles, at owners' risk 5s. each.

SPECIAL CHEAP EXCURSIONS to the PYRENEES and BACK

(Cook's Tours) Including food on board Steamer and Hotel Accommodation, carriage drives, etc.

18 Day Tour for THIRTEEN GUINEAS, 12 day do. 11 GUINEAS.

LEITH AND LONDON.

THE LONDON & EDINBURGH SHIPPING COMPANY'S First-Class Steamships, FINGAL (new steamer), IONA, MALVINA, MARMION (all lighted by Electricity), or other of the Company's Vessels, are intended to Sail (until further notice) from VICTORIA DOCK, LEITH, every WEDNESDAY, FRIDAY, and SATURDAY, and from HERMITAGE STEAM WHARF, WAPPING, E., every TUESDAY, WEDNESDAY, and SATURDAY.

FARES.—First Cabin, including Steward's Fee, 22s.; Second Cabin, 16s.; Deck (Soldiers and Sailors only), 10s.   Return Tickets, available for 12 months (including Steward's Fee both ways)—First Cabin, 34s.; Second Cabin, 24s. 6d.

Provisions, &c., may be had from the Steward on moderate terms.

Not responsible for Passengers' Luggage, unless booked and paid for.

CHEAP CIRCULAR **TOURS** round the Land's End in connection with Clyde Shipping Company's Steamers—Fare, 1st Cabin, 47s. 6d.; and by Bristol Channel, in connection with Messrs. Sloan & Co.'s Steamers—Fare, 1st Cabin, 35s. (Railway Fares extra.) By British and Irish Steam Packet Company's Steamer to Dublin. Steamer "Yarrow" to Silloth, and rail to Edinburgh. Fare, Saloon, and first-class rail, 52s. Saloon and third class rail, 47s.

Apply in London to LONDON & EDINBURGH SHIPPING COMPANY, Hermitage Steam Wharf, Wapping; ABERDEEN STEAM NAVIGATION COMPANY, 102 Queen Victoria Street, E.C.; M'DOUGALL & BONTHRON, 72 Mark Lane, E.C.; G. W. WHEATLEY & Co., 23 Regent Street; or to SEAWARD BROTHERS, LIMITED, Carting Agents, 7 Eastcheap, E.C. Edinburgh—COWAN & Co., 5 Princes Street. Glasgow—COWAN & Co., 23 St. Vincent Place. Greenock—D. MACDOUGALL, 1 Cross Shore Street; and to

THOMAS AITKEN, 8 & 9 COMMERCIAL STREET, LEITH.

1897.   **Telegraphic Addresses: Leith—'Aitken'; London—'Edina.'**

Commercial St. Office, Leith: Telephone No. 408.   Hermitage Wharf, London: Telephone No. 2394

ANCHOR LINE.

AMERICA, INDIA, and MEDITERRANEAN.

GLASGOW to NEW YORK,

Every THURSDAY.

S.S. CITY OF ROME, 8453 Tons.	S.S. FURNESSIA,	5495 Tons.
S.S. ANCHORIA, . . 4167 ,,	S.S. ETHIOPIA, . . 4004 ,,
S.S. CIRCASSIA, . . 4272 ,,	S.S. DEVONIA, . . 4270 ,,

NEW YORK TO GLASGOW,

Every SATURDAY.

To New York, Boston, or Philadelphia—Saloon Fares up to Twenty-One Guineas. Second Cabin and Steerage at Reduced Rates. Special Terms to Tourists and Parties.

The "CITY OF ROME," "FURNESSIA," and "ANCHORIA" are fitted throughout with Electric Light, and have excellent accommodation for all classes of passengers.

MEDITERRANEAN SERVICE.

GLASGOW for GIBRALTAR, GENOA, LEGHORN, NAPLES, MESSINA, PALERMO, and TRIESTE Fortnightly.

GLASGOW AND LIVERPOOL TO BOMBAY AND CALCUTTA,

Via SUEZ CANAL, FORTNIGHTLY.

Unsurpassed Accommodation for Saloon Passengers.

EGYPT and the HOLY LAND.

Fortnightly Sailings—PORT SAID, ISMAILIA, SUEZ, and CAIRO.

SALOON—Port Said, £12, Return, £21:12s.; Ismailia, £13, Return, £23:8s.; Suez, £14, Return, £25:4s.

To Cairo and Back, £26:5s.; or Returning from Cairo *via* Marseilles and Rail to London, £27:6s.; or Liverpool to Cairo and Back by Steamer to Marseilles only, £21.

MARSEILLES to LIVERPOOL and GLASGOW.

Steamers of the "ANCHOR" LINE leave MARSEILLES regularly for LIVERPOOL and GLASGOW.

Cabin Fare to Liverpool, £11; to Glasgow, £11 by direct Steamer.

Apply to HENDERSON BROTHERS, 17 Water Street, Liverpool; Equitable Buildings, 13 St. Ann Street, Manchester; 25 Albert Square, Dundee; 18 Leadenhall Street, E.C., London; 20 Foyle Street, Londonderry; Gibraltar; 7 Bowling Green, New York; and 47 Union Street, Glasgow.

LOCH TAY STEAMERS.

STEAMERS sail daily on Loch Tay from Killin Pier on arrival of principal trains from Edinburgh, Glasgow, Oban, Fort-William via Crianlarich, &c., and from Kenmore in connection with Highland Railway trains at Aberfeldy, thus maintaining regular through transit between both Railways.

Tickets for the grand Circular Tour of Loch Tay sold at all the principal Railway Stations in the kingdom.

For further information see Time Tables and Monthly Sailing Bills, or apply to

JOHN. P. STEWART, Manager,

Loch Tay Steam-Boat Company, Limited.

KENMORE, PERTHSHIRE.

LEITH to ABERDEEN, BUCKIE, LOSSIEMOUTH (for Elgin), BURGHEAD (for Forres), CROMARTY, INVERGORDON (for Strathpeffer), and INVERNESS.

S.S. **EARNHOLM** leaves **Leith** every Monday, and **Aberdeen** every Tuesday, for **Buckie, Lossiemouth, Cromarty, Invergordon,** and **Inverness**: leaves **Inverness** every Thursday for **Cromarty, Invergordon, Aberdeen,** and **Leith.** S.S. **JAMES HALL** leaves **Leith** every Thursday (and every Tuesday to **Aberdeen** only), and **Aberdeen** every Friday for **Burghead, Cromarty, Invergordon,** and **Inverness**: leaves **Inverness** every Monday for **Cromarty,** Invergordon, Aberdeen, and Leith. S.S. **EARNHOLM** or S.S. **JAMES HALL** leaves Aberdeen for Leith every Tuesday, Wednesday, and Friday. FARES MODERATE.

For further particulars apply to the Manager of The Aberdeen, Leith, and Moray Firth Steam Shipping Co., Limited, JAMES CROMBIE, Trinity Buildings, Aberdeen; or to M. LANGLANDS & SONS, 80 Constitution Street, Leith.

GRANTON TO FAROE ISLES & ICELAND.

THE Royal Danish Mail Steamers "Laura," "Thyra," and "Botnia" will sail as under during 1897:—

LEITH TO FAROE AND ICELAND.—25th April, 20th May, 5th June, 22nd June, 13th July, 22nd July, 2nd August, 21st August, 15th September, 25th September, 13th November.

ICELAND TO FAROE AND LEITH.—13th May, 13th June, 20th June, 13th July, 30th July, 14th August, 15th August, 2nd September, 11th October, 20th October, 30th November.

For Freight or Passage apply to GEO. V. TURNBULL & CO., Leith,

Agents for the United Steamship Co. of Copenhagen.

BAGGAGE FORWARDED TO AND FROM ALL PARTS OF CONTINENT !!

DAILY DISPATCHES by "Goods" and "Express" Services, at cheap fixed *through rates* per 112 lb., *saving trouble and expense.*

Full instructions, adhesive labels, tariffs of rates, and lists of Correspondents, sent post free.

PITT & SCOTT, Foreign Carriers,

25 CANNON STREET, E.C., and 25 REGENT STREET, S.W., LONDON.

7 South John Street, LIVERPOOL.; 7 Rue Scribe, PARIS; 39 Broadway, NEW YORK.

N.B.—Secure Storage, 1/ per Trunk per month. PASSAGE TICKETS for all Steamship Lines.

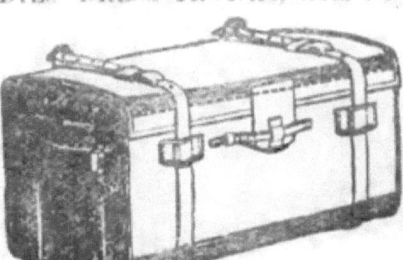

WATERPROOF REQUISITES.

Telegrams :
"SHETLANDS," EDINBURGH

Shetland Goods

John White & Co.,
10 Frederick Street,
Edinburgh.

Illustrated Price List free.

"CLUB ALE" and "CLUB KOLA" New Specialities.

CANTRELL & COCHRANE were awarded a GOLD
MEDAL for ALL their products at Liverpool
Exhibition, 1886.

CANTRELL & COCHRANE are the only Manufacturers who were awarded a MEDAL for their products
at Paris Exhibition 1889, GOLD MEDAL at Kingston
Jamaica Exhibition 1891, making a grand total of

THIRTY-TWO GOLD AND PRIZE MEDALS AWARDED.

LONDON DEPOTS—

Wyndham Place, and Crawford Street, W.

GLASGOW DEPOT—53 Surrey Street.

Works: BELFAST AND DUBLIN.

MEDICAL REPORTS.

"This is one of the purest Waters which has ever come under my notice or of which I have seen any record."

FRANCIS SUTTON, F.C.S., F.I.C.

"For gouty people the Cwm Spring Water is specially suited, owing to its peculiar freedom from lime and other dissolved mineral matters."

W. N. THURSFIELD, M.D., C.S., &c.

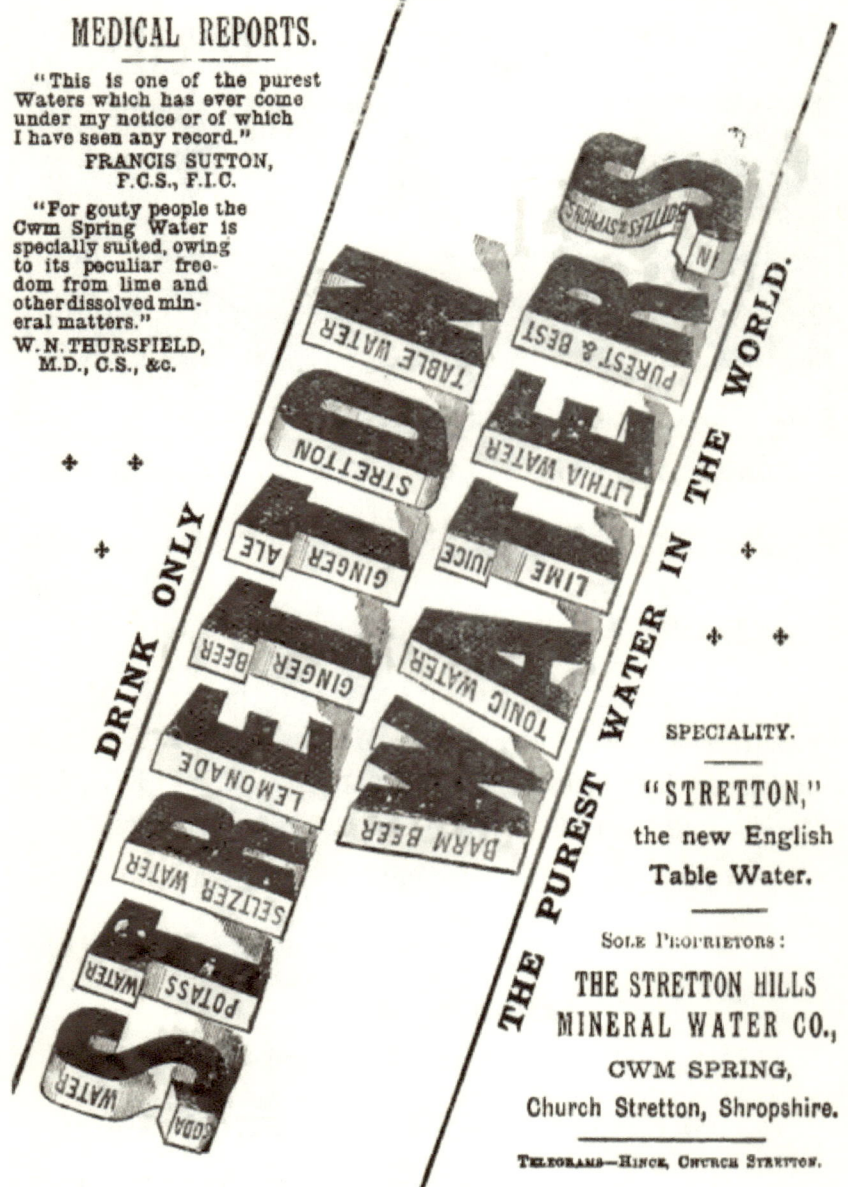

DRINK ONLY STRETTON WATERS

THE PUREST WATER IN THE WORLD.

SPECIALITY.

"STRETTON,"
the new English
Table Water.

Sole Proprietors:

**THE STRETTON HILLS
MINERAL WATER CO.,**

CWM SPRING,

Church Stretton, Shropshire.

TELEGRAMS—HINCK, CHURCH STRETTON.

MAPS FOR TOURISTS AND TRAVELLERS.
ENGLAND—JOHNSTON'S MODERN MAP OF ENGLAND AND WALES.

In Four Sheets. Size of each Sheet 35 by 29¼ inches, scale 7 miles to 1 inch. Shows all Towns, Railways (with Stations marked), Roads, Rivers, Canals, etc. Price of each Sheet, folded in cloth case, 2s.; mounted on cloth and in cloth case, price 3s. 6d. The four Sheets mounted as one Map on rollers and varnished, 21s.

ENGLAND—JOHNSTON'S POPULAR MAP OF ENGLAND AND WALES.

Size 36 by 25 inches, scale 14 miles to 1 inch. Shows all Railways, Towns, Villages, Country Seats, and the Principal Roads; also a Plan of the Environs of London. Total number of Names given is over 12,000. Price, folded in cloth case, 1s.; mounted on cloth and in cloth case, 2s.

SCOTLAND—JOHNSTON'S POPULAR MAP OF SCOTLAND.

Size 36 by 25 inches, scale 10 miles to 1 inch. Showing New County Boundaries, Railways, Towns, Villages, and Principal Roads. Over 10,000 Names given. Price, folded in cloth case, 1s.; mounted on cloth and folded in cloth case, 2s.

SCOTLAND—JOHNSTON'S NEW "THREE MILES TO INCH" MAP.

Seven Sheets already Published. Please apply for Index Map with full details and prices.

IRELAND—JOHNSTON'S ROYAL ATLAS MAP OF IRELAND.

Size 22 by 25 inches, scale 12½ miles to 1 inch. Mounted to fold in cloth case, with complete Index, price 4s. 6d.

(Maps Selected from the "Royal Atlas," giving the most recent information.)
Mounted on Canvas, and bound in a Pocket-case.

					s.	d.
Africa, South	1 Sheet, with index of	2,793 Names,	4	6
America, U.S.	4 ,,	,,	16,062	,.	15	0
America, South	2 ,,	,,	6,558	,,	8	0
Australia	1 ,,	,,	4,817	,,	4	6
Australia, South, etc.	1 ,,	,,	4,416	,,	4	6
Austro-Hungary	2 ,,	,,	6,816	,,	8	0
Belgium and the Netherlands	1 ,,	,,	4,226	,,	4	6
Canada, Central and East	2 ,,	,.	4,537	,,	8	0
Canada, West	1 ,.	,,	2,877	,.	4	6
China and Japan	1 ,,	,,	3,218	,,	4	6
France	1 ,.	,.	4,643	..	4	6
Germany, N.	1 ..	..	3,560	,,	4	6
Germany, S.W.	1 ,,	,,	5,628	,,	4	6
India	2 ,,	,,	8,335	,,	8	0
Italy	2 ,,	,,	6,187	,,	8	0
Mediterranean Shores	1 ,,	,,	2,318	,,	4	6
New Zealand and New Guinea	1 ,,	,,	2,146	..	4	6
Palestine	1 ,,	,,	2,502	,,	4	6
Spain and Portugal	1 ,,	,,	4,040	,,	4	6
Sweden and Norway	1 .:	,,	2,259	,.	4	6
Switzerland	1 ,,	,,	4,572	,	4	6

Complete Catalogue of Maps, Atlases, Globes, Wall Illustrations, Post free to any address.

W. & A. K. JOHNSTON,
GEOGRAPHERS TO THE QUEEN,
EDINA WORKS, EASTER ROAD, EDINBURGH; AND
5 WHITE HART STREET, WARWICK LANE, LONDON, E.C.

Dr. J. COLLIS BROWNE'S
CHLORODYNE

ORIGINAL AND XIX CENTURY

IS THE GREAT SPECIFIC FOR CHOLERA,

COUGHS,
COLDS,
ASTHMA,
BRONCHITIS.

DR. J. COLLIS BROWNE'S CHLO-
RODYNE.—Dr. J. C. BROWNE
(late Army Medical Staff) DISCOVERED
a REMEDY to denote which he coined
the word CHLORODYNE. Dr. Browne
is the SOLE INVENTOR, and, as the
composition of Chlorodyne cannot pos-
sibly be discovered by Analysis (organic
substances defying elimination), and
since the formula has never been published, it is evident that any statement
to the effect that a compound is identi-
cal with Dr. Browne's Chlorodyne *must
be false.*

This Caution is necessary, as many
persons deceive purchasers by false
representations.

DR. J. COLLIS BROWNE'S CHLO-
RODYNE.—Vice-Chancellor Sir W.
PAGE WOOD stated publicly in Court
that Dr. J. COLLIS BROWNE was
UNDOUBTEDLY the INVENTOR of
CHLORODYNE, that the whole story
of the defendant Freeman was deliber-
ately untrue, and he regretted to say
it had been sworn to.—See *The Times*,
July 13th, 1864.

DIARRHŒA, DYSENTERY. GENE-
RAL BOARD of HEALTH, Lon-
don, REPORTS that it ACTS as a
CHARM, one dose generally sufficient.
Dr. GIBBON, Army Medical Staff,
Calcutta, states: "2 DOSES COM-
PLETELY CURED ME of DIAR-
RHŒA."

DR. J. COLLIS BROWNE'S CHLO-
RODYNE is the TRUE PALLIA-
TIVE in
NEURALGIA, GOUT, CANCER,
TOOTHACHE, RHEUMATISM.

DR. J. COLLIS BROWNE'S CHLO-
RODYNE is a liquid medicine
which assuages PAIN of EVERY KIND,
affords a calm, refreshing sleep WITH-
OUT HEADACHE, and INVIGOR-
ATES the nervous system when exhausted.

DR. J. COLLIS BROWNE'S CHLO-
RODYNE rapidly cuts short all
attacks of
EPILEPSY, SPASMS, COLIC, PAL-
PITATION, HYSTERIA.

IMPORTANT CAUTION.—The IM-
MENSE SALE of this REMEDY
has given rise to many UNSCRUPU-
LOUS IMITATIONS. Be careful to
observe Trade Mark. Of all Chemists.
1s. 1½d., 2s. 9d., and 4s. 6d.

SOLE MANUFACTURER,
J. T. DAVENPORT,
33 Great Russell Street, W.C.

Commercial Union Assurance Company, Limited.

FIRE—LIFE—MARINE.

Capital fully Subscribed £2,500,000

Life Fund in Special Trust for Life Policyholders £1,763,291

TOTAL ASSETS EXCEED FOUR MILLIONS.

Total Annual Income £1,600,000

HEAD OFFICE:—24, 25, & 26 CORNHILL, LONDON, E.C.

WEST END OFFICE:—8 PALL MALL, LONDON, S.W.

NEW BRIDGE STREET OFFICE:—20 NEW BRIDGE STREET, LONDON, E.C.

HOME BRANCHES:—Manchester, Liverpool, Newcastle-on-Tyne, Leeds, Nottingham, Birmingham, Leicester, Norwich, Bristol, Exeter, Bradford, Gloucester, Dublin, Edinburgh, and Glasgow.

DIRECTORS.

W. REIERSON ARBUTHNOT, Esq.
ROBERT BARCLAY, Esq., of Barclay & Co., Ltd.
W. MIDDLETON CAMPBELL, Esq., of Hogg, Curtis, Campbell, & Co.
JEREMIAH COLMAN, Esq., of J. & J. Colman.
The Right Hon. L. H. COURTNEY, M.P.
WILLIAM C. DAWES (J. B. Westray & Co.).
Sir JAMES F. GARRICK, Q.C., K.C.M.G.
FREDERICK W. HARRIS, Esq., of Harris & Dixon.
F. LARKWORTHY, Esq.
CHARLES J. LEAF, Esq.
JOHN H. LEY, Esq.

The Right Hon. A. J. MUNDELLA, M.P.
Sir HENRY W. NORMAN, G.C.B.
Sir HENRY W. PEEK, Bart.
Sir HENRY WYLIE NORMAN, G.C.B.
P. P. RODOCANACHI, Esq., of P. P. Rodocanachi & Co.
THOMAS RUDD, Esq., Rudd & Co.
Sir ANDREW R. SCOBLE, K.C.S.I., Q.C., M.P.
P. G. SECHIARI, Esq., of Sechiari Bros. & Co.
ALEXANDER B. SIM, Esq., of Churchill & Sim.
JOHN TROTTER, Esq., of John Trotter & Co.
HENRY TROWER, Esq., of Trower & Sons.

Secretary—HENRY MANN.

PROSPECTUSES and all information needful for effecting Assurances may be obtained at any of the Company's Offices or Agencies throughout the World.

FIRE DEPARTMENT.

Manager—E. ROGER OWEN. *Assistant Manager*—GEO. C. MORANT.

Undoubted Security guaranteed by the fully subscribed Capital and large invested funds and income.

Moderate Rates of Premium, Special terms for long period insurances. Rates quoted and Surveys made free of charge.

Claims liberally and promptly settled.

LIFE DEPARTMENT.

Actuary—T. E. YOUNG, B.A.

The Life Funds invested in the names of Special Trustees. The Assured wholly free from liability.

Four-Fifths of the Entire Life Profits belong to Policyholders.

Interim Bonuses are paid.

The Expenses of Management limited by Deed of Settlement.

Liberal Surrender Values guaranteed; and Claims paid immediately on proof of death and title.

Married Women's Property Act (1882)—Policies are issued to husbands for the benefit of their wives and children, thus creating, without trouble, expense, stamp duty, or legal assistance, a Family Settlement which creditors cannot touch.

MARINE DEPARTMENT.

Underwriter—J. CARR SAUNDERS.

Rates for Marine Risks on application.

EDINBURGH BRANCH . . 37 Hanover Street.

GLASGOW BRANCH . . . 19 St. Vincent Place.

SCOTTISH UNION AND NATIONAL
INSURANCE COMPANY.

LONDON: 3 KING WILLIAM STREET, E.C.
GLASGOW: 150 WEST GEORGE STREET.

HEAD OFFICE: 35 ST. ANDREW SQUARE, EDINBURGH.

Secretary: J. K. MACDONALD.   *Actuary:* COLIN M'CUAIG, F.F.A.
General Manager: A. DUNCAN.

EARLY BONUS SCHEME (E.B.)

The following among other special advantages apply to ordinary Policies issued under this Scheme. Besides being payable immediately on proof of death and title, they are, *at the end of Three years from their date,*

Entitled to rank for Bonus Additions;
Indisputable on the ground of Errors or Omissions;
World-Wide without Extra Charge; and
Liable only to Reduction in Amount on Non-payment of the Premiums.

At the Division of Profits for the Five years ending 31st December 1894, Ordinary Life Policies under this Scheme received a **Bonus Addition of £1:10s. per cent.** for each year since they were entitled to rank.

SPECIAL BONUS SCHEME (D.B.)

Under this Scheme PROFIT POLICIES are issued at Rates, which do not exceed, and in many cases fall short of the Non-Profit Rates of other Offices.

They share in the profits when the Premiums received, accumulated at 4 per cent. compound interest, amount to the sum assured.

Policies issued at these very economical Rates practically receive a Large Bonus at the outset.

At age 30, £1200 with right to Profits can be insured for the same Premium as would be charged for £1000 under the usual Profit Schemes of most Offices.

Policies of this class which for the first time became entitled to rank for Bonus, received Additions at the rate of £10 per cent. besides a further progressive addition of £1 per cent per annum, and Policies which participated at last division received a further addition of £2:10s. per cent, and to those which then received a contingent addition a Bonus at the rate of 10s. per cent in respect of each year which elapsed since the date of their commencing to rank was added.

FIRE INSURANCE.

Almost all descriptions of Property insured on the most favourable conditions.

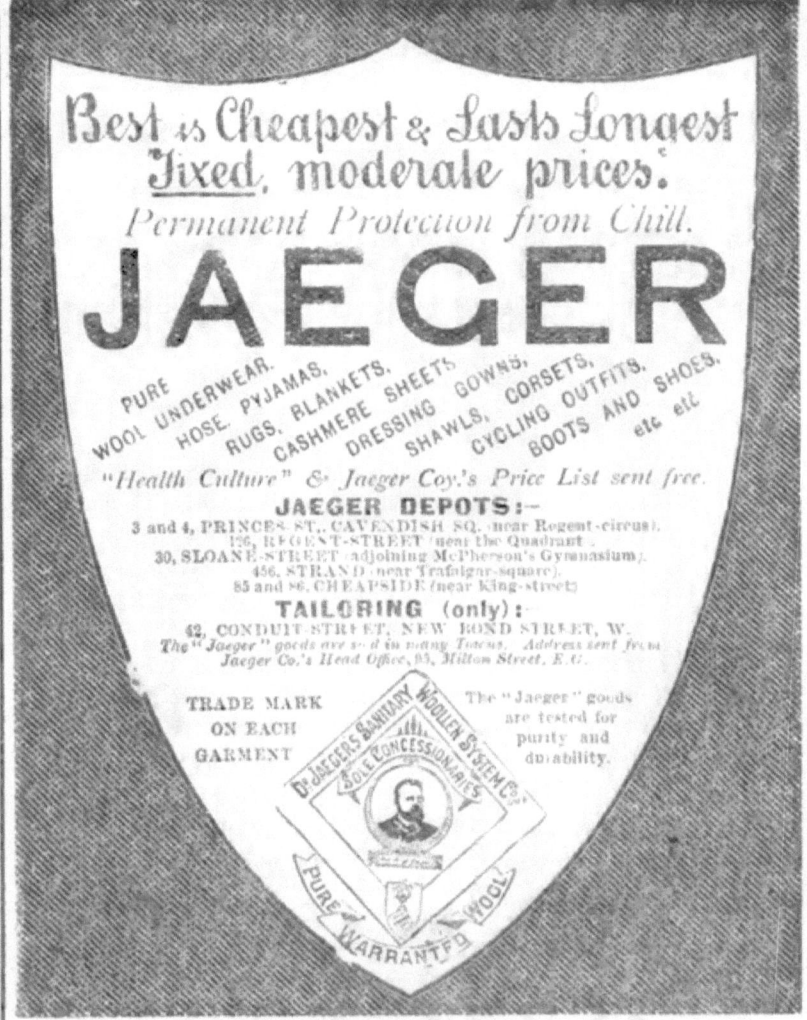

THE WAVERLEY NOVELS.

AUTHOR'S EDITIONS.

COMPLETE SETS at the following prices :

1. Price £1 : 1s. **Four Volume Edition**, Royal 8vo, half French morocco.

2. Price £1 : 4s. **Five Volume Edition**, Royal 8vo, half Cape morocco.

3. Price £1 : 17s. **Pocket Edition**, Illustrated with 125 Wood Engravings, in 25 vols., 12mo, cloth. The same in limp Cape morocco, price £3 : 3s.

4. Price £2 : 8s. **Twelve Volume Edition**, reprinted from the Plates of the Centenary Edition. Illustrated with Steel Frontispieces and Woodcuts. 12 vols., crown 8vo, cloth.

5. Price £2 : 10s. **Two Shilling Edition**, reprinted from the Plates of the Centenary Edition. Illustrated with Frontispieces and Vignettes. 25 vols., crown 8vo, cloth.

6. Price £3 : 3s. **Half-Crown Edition**, printed from the Plates of the Centenary Edition. Illustrated with Steel Frontispieces and Vignettes. 25 vols., crown 8vo, cloth, gilt top. The same may be had in half ruby Persian calf, or in half blue morocco.

7. Price £4 : 4s. **Centenary Edition**, with Additional Notes. Illustrated with 158 Steel Plates, in 25 vols., crown 8vo, cloth. The same may be had in half calf.

8. Price £6. **Roxburghe Edition**, Illustrated with 1600 Woodcuts and 96 Steel Plates, in 48 vols., fcap. 8vo, cloth, paper label ; or in half French morocco, price £8 : 8s.

9. Price £6 : 5s. **Dryburgh Edition**. Illustrated with 250 page Illustrations by eminent Artists. 25 vols., large crown 8vo, cloth. The same may be had in half calf or half morocco.

LONDON : ADAM & CHARLES BLACK, SOHO SQUARE.

BLACK'S GUIDE-BOOKS

Bath and Cheltenham, 1s
Belfast and the North of Ireland, 1s (cloth 1s 6d)
Brighton, 1s
Buxton, 1s
Canterbury and Rochester, 1s
Channel Islands, 1s (cloth, with extra maps, 2s 6d)
Clyde, 1s.
Cornwall and Scilly Islands, 2s 6d
Derbyshire (Buxton, Matlock, Chatsworth), 2s 6d
Devonshire (Torquay, Plymouth, Exeter), 2s 6d
Dorsetshire (Swanage, Weymouth), 2s 6d
Dublin and the East of Ireland, 1s (cloth 1s 6d)
Edinburgh, 1s
English Lakes (Flintoft's & Foster's Illustrations), 3s 6d
    Do.   Cheap Edition, 1s
Galway and West of Ireland, 1s (cloth 1s 6d)